REYOUNG

inFlATion

A NOVEL

INFLATION

By REYoung

Copyright © 2019 REYoung

This book is available in print and electronic format at most online retailers.

ISBN 978-1-7334461-0-5

TageTage Press

UNBABBLING
MARGARITO AND THE SNOWMAN

for adria

this is tage's book

UNBABBLING
MARGARITO AND THE SNOWMAN

for adria

this is tage's book

1

Morning, Marty

*

IT WAS THE EATING THAT DROVE ME MAD. I could hear them all around me, crunching and chewing, gulping and swallowing and smacking their lips. In the flickering light I could see their eyes bulge and their teeth gleam with every monstrous bite. It made me want to get up, run, flee for my life. But I couldn't move, couldn't risk drawing attention to myself. I had to remain as inconspicuous as possible. I couldn't let them see I was afraid.

*

That dream again, that's what he remembered. And waking with a sense of lethargy, unease, as if he were recovering from a long illness. And something else, an unfamiliar presence next to him, something large, possibly threatening. He told himself to open his eyes, turn, see what it was, but just as in those recurring adolescent nightmares when he gasped awake knowing some monstrous *thing* waited for him to do exactly that—open his eyes, turn, see, *confront* it—he couldn't move, couldn't make himself move, he felt utterly paralyzed. *Open your eyes*, he told himself again and this time his eyes sprang open into a kind of lavender opaqueness, as if the molecules of color, crimson, indigo, magenta, whatever makes up the blackness of night, had begun to separate from each other and dissolve into predawn twilight. The sound of labored breathing, like that of some large beast, rasped in his ears. With a great effort he rotated his head to the left and peered at the fuzzy pink mass next to him. With each breath, it rose and swelled and trembled, then collapsed like a giant lung. He remembered May was wearing a pink nightgown last night, but this *blob* couldn't possibly be May. He told himself he still must be dreaming but dismissed this idea as not only trite but empirically untrue. Then he wondered what time it was, as if possessing this piece of information might clarify things. With another great effort, he rotated his head back to the right until he could see the clock on his nightstand. Five a.m. Time to get up.

He started to sit up. That is, he thought to himself, *now I'm sitting up*, but nothing happened. An invisible force seemed to be pressing him down against the bed. Finally he managed to push himself up more or less in a sitting position but the exertion left him gasping for breath, his heart pounded in his chest, he felt light-headed. He wondered if he was having a heart attack. Then he wondered how many X-Seds he had taken last night. He reached for the luminous white bottle next to the clock but his arm felt heavy, encumbered, and he let it fall back on the bed. This is absurd, he told himself. I can't just sit here. I have to get up, go to work.

He fumbled aside the covers and rocked back and forth until his legs flopped over the edge of the bed. Gasping for breath, he placed his hands on his knees, which felt as thick as smoked hams, an image that simultaneously caused him revulsion and an odd primal hunger, and with a heroic effort that in some dim cavern of his brain echoed that of the first Homo erectus, he pushed himself to his feet and stood swaying like a merchant vessel at anchor in a rough sea. He tried to take a few steps but his legs felt heavy, disconnected, like waterlogged tree trunks. By alternately rocking starboard to port, forward and aft, he made his way across the murky straits of avocado shag carpet to the bathroom, where, banging his elbows, knees and butt, he managed to enter and shut the door behind him.

Warm yellow incandescence embraced him like a sunny summer morning. For a moment he felt reassured that all might still be well with the world. Until he saw his face in the mirror. And it was his face, his features. He recognized his eyes, ears, nose, mouth, but grotesque, distorted, as if they were attached to some large fungal growth. A peristaltic wave of horror churned through his bowels. The scream that had been struggling to claw its way up his throat from the moment he woke demanded release but all that came out was a feeble yelp. What if he was having a stroke? What if he was losing his mind? He yanked open the medicine cabinet, dumped a couple of reds in his hand, swallowed them dry, then gripped the sink, closed his eyes and began to breathe slowly and deeply.

When he opened his eyes again nothing had changed. He still looked like a giant mushroom with a face. He had the brief, unconvincing thought that something was wrong with his vision. What if he had a brain tumor? He wondered again how many X-Seds he'd taken. *Sleep enhancers.* So when did he wake up?

He started to unbutton his pajama top but stopped. Performing quotidian functions such as showering and shaving seemed ridiculous under the present circumstances. On the other hand, he rationalized even as he struggled to remain rational, what alternative did he have but total screaming madness? Stick to the routine, that's the best way, and hope things make sense sooner or later. This line of reasoning made him think the reds must be taking effect.

He continued to unbutton his pajama top, but at first sight of the pale, gelatinous mass quivering like an enormous vanilla pudding, he shifted his attention to a spot on the ceiling he'd never noticed before and, whistling a silly little tune whose name he couldn't remember *molto allegro*, he fumbled loose the drawstring of his pajama bottoms, let them drop to the floor and, unable to bear it any longer, stared at himself in the mirror. He looked like an immense white larva. His arms, chest, breasts—he had *breasts*—were huge, floppy. He couldn't see his genitals beneath the swelling of his belly. His thighs looked like enormous loaves of bread dough. Only by leaning forward at a precarious angle could he spy his toes laid out below like little white corpses in a morgue. Resisting the panic gnawing at the back door of his skull like a slavering murderous beast, he lurched into the shower stall. Hot water splashed over him and he released a groan of relief, but his revulsion returned when he began to soap himself up. His hands felt like they were moving through Jell-O. He had no definitive sense of his body or even that this was his body. He let his arms drop to his sides, closed his eyes and, with the resignation of a religious novitiate, allowed the hot water to cascade over his head and obliterate his thoughts.

A faint *beep,* something like the first tentative chirp of a spring peeper, a sound he hadn't actually heard in nature since his childhood, woke him from this brief state of grace. Ten seconds left in his water allotment. He counted down *nine, eight, seven ...* on *three* he staggered out of the shower and began to towel himself off but as the steam cleared from the mirror and the mycological monstrosity of his face reappeared, he dropped the towel to the floor and padded back into the bedroom. He wanted to call May's name. He wanted to say *something's terribly wrong, I'm afraid.* The large pink mass on the bed rose and fell with loud labored breaths. What if it, she, *May,* woke and saw him and started to scream? What if he really was imagining everything and she said, *Marty, what's wrong with you? Why are you acting this way?*

He lumbered to his closet like a draft animal to its stall, slid the door open and in the soft green bioluminescence began to take out his wardrobe for the day, but again something seemed terribly amiss. His clothes were huge, the boxers and T-shirt as big as bed sheets, the white dress shirt as voluminous as a parachute, the navy blue trousers the size of a car tarpaulin, yet he had to struggle to squeeze his arms and legs into their respective casings.

And despite his suit coat's yurtish dimensions, after shrugging it on, he felt as snug as a potato in its skin.

Packed into this constrictive cloak of civilization, he trudged out into the hall to the top of the stairs, which appeared to him now as vertiginous as a mountain cataract. Clutching the banister with both hands, he began to descend the creaking treads like one of Hannibal's elephants picking its way down a narrow Alpen track. At the middle landing he considered taking a breather on the green and gold brocade armchair inherited from May's great aunt-somebody, but it looked so small and fragile he couldn't imagine anyone but a child occupying it. By association he thought of Ashley and Trey. He knew he should check on them—indeed, the Wise Parenting Council would insist he did—but at the moment climbing back *up* the stairs seemed far too daunting a prospect and he continued his treacherous descent.

Arrived at last on terra *plus* firma, he waddled across the foyer into the kitchen. Soft white LED luminescence blossomed over the stove, the stainless steel sink, the marble countertop. The wall screen filled the room with cool blue aquarium light. A pair of fuzzy, puppet-like figures sat at a desk clutching sheaths of paper in their puffy, kitchen mitt hands. It's a children's channel, he thought, surmising that one of the kids must have been watching. Then he recognized Bob Broadley's trademark orange tie and cobalt blue suit and Marsha Mello's lemon meringue hairdo. Apparently there had been another power outage in the Knackerton Valley District. He waited for the follow-up but instead the EdenFresh® jingle came on ... *So be a good consumer and consume more wholesome goooodness!* It was like a soldier's marching orders, a competitive hot dog eater's signal *go*, a command to dig in, chow down, put on the old feed bag.

He shuffled to the kitchen table and lowered himself onto his chair like a sumo wrestler preparing to engage an equally positioned opponent. A second later the chefbot rolled in and, following a flurry of culinary preparations between the stove, the sink and the refrigerator, placed before him a pillow-sized omelet bursting with gorgonzola cheese, black Périgord truffles and neon orange chanterelle mushrooms, a plate piled high with smoked pork sausage, a stack of banana-walnut waffles drenched in maple syrup and melted butter, a platter of golden-brown home-fried potatoes, a basket of steaming hot drop biscuits, two slabs of French toast slathered with marmalade, and a bakery display case of donuts, Danishes and beignets. His mind swooned in a cloud of sweet, yeasty smells instilled since infancy. His appetite soared, his salivary glands sprang into action. He ate as if he had a full day of chopping down trees ahead of him. He wanted to eat and eat and never stop eating. He swallowed a final oily dollop of omelet, consumed the last sausage and dug into the waffles, then stopped in mid-mastication, struck again by the absurdity of his situation. How could he even think of eating now when he was already as big as, well, certainly not a house, but—a juvenile pachyderm? This rhetorical question was met by a rebuttal of equal weight. He was *hungry*. He needed to eat, to provide his body with energy for the long day ahead. This rational response suggested the reds were definitely taking effect and he consumed half a prune Danish in a single bite.

A distant rumbling filled his mind with images of dark dungeons, drafty castle keeps, great lumbering beasts. The sound grew louder and a moment later May appeared in the doorway in a penumbra of light. She was enormous. She filled the entire doorframe. Her head lolled on her shoulders as if its weight were too great for her to support. In the gibbous moon of her face, her features seemed distorted, indistinct. He only knew for certain it was May because of the pink nightgown she wore.

"Morning, Marty," she said in a sleepy voice he definitely recognized as May's. Preceded by traces of rose-scented soap and warm bedcovers, she waddled toward him like a great pink goose, groaned as if she were lifting a sack of potatoes, and bent down for a kiss.

He shrank back in horror.

"What is it, Marty?" May's bright green eyes were suddenly as alert as traffic lights.

Was it possible she hadn't noticed anything *different?* He wanted to say, *Who* are you? More accurately, he wanted to say, *What* are you? He wanted to shout, Get away from me you monstrous blob! He wanted to scream, What the hell's going on here?! He stuffed the last chunk of Danish down his throat, muttered that he had to rush, he was late for work, and, girded and nourished to face the world, if somewhat wary of what that world might look like now, he pushed himself up from the table and headed for the door, Milton Merryweather, "the merry meteorologist," chirping behind him, *Gravity today will be ninety-eight percent! With the humidity that'll feel like an incredible one-ten on the weight index, folks!*

Outside, a suffocating wall of heat and humidity engulfed him like the inhospitable atmosphere of an alien planet. The sweet cloying smell of jasmine flooded his nostrils. He searched for its source and found it in the silky red flowers of what he had always presumed to be rose bushes growing on each side of the front porch. A rose by any other name would be a posy, isn't that what the old guy said? Or was it a begonia? And maybe it wasn't even a guy, maybe it was a gal. *A petunia is a petunia is a petunia?*

Before he could lose himself completely in this taxonomic labyrinth, the front door opened in the house across the street and a large form in a dark blue business suit emerged. Fred Fortus. That is, he assumed it was Fred, although if it was Fred he'd put on quite a lot of weight recently. Fred Fortus become Fred Fortissimus. Fred lifted an enormous appendage in a casual sign of greeting and he made a flaccid, half-hearted attempt to lift his arm in return, then waddled down the walk to the drive where the car waited, engine running. Hmm, the car, too, looked different. Not just *bigger*, but swollen, inflated, like one of those bulgy, blimpish automobiles in old cartoons. The door slid open and in what felt like a practiced act, he swung his butt inside at the same time the seat swelled up and embraced him like a velvet glove, then retracted, placing him uncomfortably close to the steering wheel.

Morning, Marty.

The carbot's slightly mechanical but oddly reassuring male voice spoke to him from the dash.

"Good morning," he mumbled.

Something wrong, Marty?

"No, why do you ask?"

I don't know, Marty, you sound … different.

"I didn't sleep well last night."

Maybe you should see a doctor, Marty.

He didn't respond. He still wasn't used to the carbot. He would have preferred the female empath model—the voice sounded so sultry and slinky and, yeah, *sexy*, which is also why, May in mind, he opted for the male-casual, although he was beginning to think it was a little too casual.

Would you like a cup of coffee, Marty?

The snack tray slid open with a steaming cup of coffee and a pineapple Danish.

"I had Danish for breakfast."

Sorry, Marty. My mistake. Would you like to talk about last night, Marty?

He said he would prefer not to talk about last night. In fact, he'd like some quiet.

OK, Marty. One last thing, will you drive or shall I?

"Why don't you drive. I'd like to get some work done. Oh, and … thanks."

You're welcome, Marty.

He opened his screen but he couldn't concentrate. Instead he sipped coffee and nibbled at the pineapple Danish, which he decided he wanted after all, while he stared in fascination at the blob-like creatures emerging from their houses and climbing into their own oddly bulbous automobiles. A female, identifiable as such by her orange tent-like outfit, waved an amoebic appendage at him and he waved back with, he hoped, equal enthusiasm. Outside Oma's Bakery a line of customers, all huge, nearly indistinguishable from each other except for their gender and occupation-identifying clothing, shuffled and yawned like a train of exotic circus animals waiting their turn at the feed trough. He started to ask the car to pull over, an Oma's *Life Saver* glazed donut sure sounded good at the moment, but then he remembered his pineapple Danish and without the least sense of irony took an enormous bite and began to chew with the mindless pleasure of a large ruminant. The bolus he was in the process of swallowing with great satisfaction caught in his throat, however, when they plunged into a bumper-to-bumper assembly line of bulgemobiles on Olio Boulevard. Once he again recoiled from the juxtaposition of what he believed, remembered, thought he knew to be true and the reality present all around him. Everyone, he and all the other drivers, huge, monstrous blobs, their massive bodies jammed against doors and windows, their mushroom faces practically shoved against their windshields, all of them staring at screens or talking on EyePhone®s or eating some sort of breakfast pastry or in most cases all three. Inches apart but totally oblivious to each other, they crept past shops, restaurants, condos, office buildings. Like cattle to the slaughter, he thought, bothered less by the cliché than the thought, which, he knew perfectly well, bordered on the seditious. At every intersection the VRBLs towering into the sky like giant magic wands bombarded him with shimmering hologrammic images of neon-colored cars rushing around winding mountain roads, huge gushing bottles of SodaRific® cola, monumental dentures crushing toboggan-sized GoodLife® energy bars. Again he felt a primal hunger and desire not just to eat but to consume and possess and own, to eat and to hold in his arms more to eat.

Snack, Marty?

The tray slid open and a steaming hot black raspberry and cream cheese kolache appeared.

He started to say, oh man, thank you, that's just what I wanted but stopped. How the hell did the car know what he wanted?

The car only piped up again when it dropped him at the entrance to the SunnyVale station, leaving him with an encouraging, *Give 'em hell, Marty,* before going off to park while he converged with the other commuters. He felt like he was joining a fleet of convivial dirigibles caught in tumultuous winds aloft, everybody lurching about and banging into each other, smiling politely and saying *excuse me* and *good morning* as if everything were perfectly normal. He, on the other hand, felt horrified, confused and even a little bit relieved. At least no one was pointing at him and screaming, *It's the monster!* His anxiety returned when he spotted a pair of cops whose wraparound sunglasses, black uniforms and utility belts bristling with guns, clubs and handcuffs made them look like giant menacing beetles. At the moment, however, they were focused on the powdered donuts they were methodically eating from white paper sacks. He felt a sudden, almost overwhelming urge to ask for one. Sure, and how about a cup of coffee, heavy on the cream and sugar, to go? He wondered if they'd get the joke. Then he wondered what would happen if a real emergency occurred. Could these behemoths catch the bad guy? Run down the perp? Could they even get their guns out of their holsters? Not that *he* would ever test their reflexes or their mettle.

Jammed between a massive belly (male?) and an equally prodigious pair of buttocks (female?), he rode the escalator down to the crowded platform where he briefly became involved in a shoving match with *another* blob—the comparison alone made him shudder. His adversary finally shuffled aside and, puffed up by this small triumph, he sucked in his gut, so to speak, pushed out his chest, more or less, and elbowed his way through the colloidal mass of flesh just in time to squeeze on board the next train where he was even fortunate enough to find an empty seat. A petulant *beeeeee* pierced his ears, the doors closed and the train entered the tube. Then, total blackness rushing by outside the window at an incomprehensible speed. Inside, everything quiet, subdued, the blue vinyl seats, the stainless steel handrails, the other passengers' mushroom faces bathed in a greenish hospital light.

An EyePhone® chimed a late morning wake-up call at the back of the car. In the seat in front of him an annoyingly adenoidal female voice began a one-way discourse on the virtues of a new ultra caloric product from Industrial Foods. Across the aisle an ovular-shaped guy in a dark blue business suit yapped into his HoundsTooth®. Like a link in a yawn-induced chain reaction, he started to reach inside his jacket, then caught himself. No time now for idle chitchat. He had work to do. He opened his screen and typed in M-a-r-t-i-n G-r-a-s-s-o, a process he had repeated so many times his own name sometimes seemed foreign to him, that appellation given to him at birth, that tag, moniker, cognomen, that *handle* that identified him, his *self*, that set him apart from everyone else. Normally this would have struck him as a pointlessly existential issue and therefore not worth pursuing, but the *normal* he once knew apparently no longer existed. Following his name, he entered his access code to the main platform at the office and started to type in a request for the morning update but hit the wrong key. No wonder. The damn keyboard was too small. His fingers were bunched together like Vienna sausages. Couldn't they make these things bigger? Of course that was the whole point, right? Make everything smaller, more efficient? The hell with it, let the techies figure it out. While they were at it they should make these damn seats bigger. He felt like a canned ham, whatever the hell a canned ham felt like—for a moment actually imagining himself inside some kind of metal can before dismissing the idea as ridiculous.

He remembered going somewhere on the trolley once with his mother or maybe it was his aunt. The car was packed, everyone jammed together, clutching briefcases, shopping bags, umbrellas, hanging onto straps. Some guy pulled the cord and yelled, "Hey, let me off! I left my lunch pail at home! My wife's gonna kill me!"

"So what's da problem?!" the conductor shouted back. "Just buy yerself a hamboiger for lunch!"

"You don't understand!" the man cried. "The lunch pail's got a pair of my *goil*friend's *lawn-jeray* in it!"

The trolley squealed to a halt, the guy jumped off, and the whole car erupted in laughter.

Funny, he only remembered that detail now, probably because it didn't fully register in his mind at that age. But then there was something that wasn't funny. At the next stop a man got on. He wore an overcoat and a hat with the brim pulled down over his face, but despite this attempt at anonymity there was something monstrous, misshapen about him. Slowly, inexorably, *exactly* as he expected him to, the man forced his way down the aisle to where he sat with his mother and, so casually no one else noticed, placed a claw-like hand on his shoulder and began to squeeze. He wanted to cry out to his mother, *help! make him stop!*

but he was paralyzed with fear, he couldn't do anything but sit there like an obedient little rat in a laboratory experiment while the man's fingers sank deeper into his soft flesh, injecting him with a terrible poison that he understood perfectly well would transform him into a monster too.

He turned his head and stared at his reflection looming like a great tuberous growth in the dark glass. What if some *supernatural* force really was at work here? What if, more likely, he was losing his mind? Not that he had ever been particularly superstitious, much less inclined to psychoanalysis. This train of thought took another detour when he noticed something pink flash by outside the window. He tried to reconstruct it in his mind. Triangular in shape, possibly a piece of graffiti, the representation of a woman maybe. The thought that anyone, no matter how drug addled, crazed or politically motivated, would climb down here in total darkness, with the threat of a train coming at any second, just to make their meager and in all probability futile statement, made his heart beat faster. A prolonged electrocardiological *beeeee* shredded his eardrums and the PA spewed a stream of garbled nonsense as the train pulled into the station.

He exited the car in a blubberous crush of humanity that carried him across the platform and up the escalator, where the pull of gravity separated him and the other blobs from each other like enormous business-suited matzo balls on a kosher assembly line, and they tumbled out of the cool, climate-controlled train station into the urban inferno of downtown Catábolus. Hot blinding sunlight blasted off the walls of glass like a solar furnace. Hot choking exhaust poured from the tailpipes of cars, trucks and buses.

Blinking against the light, he crossed the black and white checkerboard squares of the broad, eastward-facing Heroes Plaza in a shuffling, sloshing tidal motion that made him feel like an enormous water balloon. Sweltering waves of heat and humidity rose around him like a Turkish bath. Sweat sprang from his forehead. His breath came in dry, lung-searing gasps. He felt an unbearable heaviness of being, as if the force of gravity were actually pulling him down into the pavement. His every thought was focused on maneuvering himself forward. He had the sense that this must be what it was like to drive or even to *be* a bulldozer. All around him equally miserable-looking blobs shuffled forward like a migrating rout of giant gastropods, their great lumpish brows shiny with perspiration, their enormous buttocks shifting up and down like cotton bales on a conveyor belt, their only relief from these equatorial doldrums the intermittent oases of cool mist and dappled shade provided by splashing waterscapes and ornamental maples.

An EyePhone® chimed its cheerful little *tweedle-dee*, followed by the cessation of what had become an increasingly annoying clicking sound. He looked up from a pair of blood-red stiletto heels just in time to avoid a rear-end collision with a female blob in a rust-colored outfit that made her look like a bell buoy in a shipping channel. His gaze climbed higher to the brushed aluminum title over the entrance of the green glass office tower rising before him.

ENERGY ACQUISITION & TRANSFER

He pushed through the revolving glass door and his reflection loomed up to greet him, bloated and swollen, then turned away as if shunning its owner. Cold, clinical air washed over him. Birdsong and the sound of falling water echoed through the cavernous lobby. Planes of hot yellow sunlight crashed down through the skylights. Dark green tropical foliage gleamed in large ceramic containers. He glanced up at the bronze angel suspended from the ceiling by metal cables, its headless, armless body loosely draped in a short, pleated tunic of the kind women wore in classical times, its wings stretched overhead in the act of ascension. A pair of blobs, largely indistinguishable in dark blue blazers with orange badges, sat at the boomerang-shaped security desk in front of a bank of video screens. Behind them two black-uniformed behemoths armed with enough weaponry to wage war in a small country scrutinized the queue of employees through wraparound sunglasses. He glanced at the iris scan, the bio scan, passed his hand over the infrared palm scan, and hurried, or rather waddled hurriedly, to catch the elevator. And immediately regretted it. The car was packed. He felt like he was squeezing into a sack of giant marshmallows. A potpourri of sweet, cloying smells invaded his nostrils—patchouli, rose water, lavender, *cotton candy?* Behind him a pair of female voices, one possibly familiar—*Myrtle Kreps?*—engaged in a lively dialectic on fall fashions. *Fall?* It was a hundred degrees outside.

He entered the Distribution Accounting Department at the same moment the young lady at the receptionist's desk stuffed an entire chocolate cupcake into her mouth. She must be new, he didn't recognize her anyway, but she obviously recognized him. Her eyes widened like moon pies and she waggled her sausagey fingers at him, "Mornin Miffa Graddo." He waggled his fingers back and continued down the hall past the break room where a small herd of blobs grazed at tables laden with donuts and breakfast pastries. One or two of them glanced at him with profound bovine indifference and continued eating, and he trudged on down the hall into the office where he passed Dolly Butterworth—the blue eyes and honey-colored bangs gave her away—bent over the wheezing copier like a very large mollusk ingesting some edible matter on the sea floor. Dolly greeted him with the sort of vapid, medicated smile she might give a stuffed toy. He attempted what he thought an amicable smile in return, hurried to the gray matte sanctuary of his cube, plopped down at his desk and, as he did every morning, glanced at the framed photograph of May and the kids. Why had he never noticed before? May was as big as an ice cream truck, the kids the size of golf carts. Was it really possible everyone had turned into giant funguses—*fungi?*—and yet no one else seemed aware of this unusual expansion in their girth but him? What if he really was going crazy? What if he had premature onset dementia or a brain tumor? Maybe the car was right, he should schedule a doctor's appointment. The odds of anyone seeing him within the next month were about as good as winning the *Lotsa Luck, Sucka* Instant Billionaire Sweepstakes. Besides, they'd just tweak his meds and send him home. And since when did he depend on the car for advice?

He fanned his hand over the palm scan and brought up his screen. Work, that's what he needed, stick to the routine. As for the rest of today and tomorrow and whatever else lay ahead—he couldn't allow himself to think about that now.

2

but maybe that wasn't the way it happened

BUT MAYBE, IT OCCURRED TO HIM much later, that wasn't the way it happened. Maybe he didn't wake into the horror that one particular morning. Maybe it only revealed itself to him gradually in the accrual of otherwise insignificant details over a period of days and weeks and even months.

He remembered he was scrolling down the departmental update when Laong Hsiuh's bespectacled moon face loomed over the panel dividing them. "Have you seen the new report, Marty?"

He said he was just looking at it.

Laong Hsiuh blinked like a short-circuiting household appliance. "Have you seen *Mister* Crocker this morning, Marty?"

He said not yet.

Laong Hsiuh's face folded into a frown that reminded him uncomfortably of a Chinese fortune cookie. Suddenly his eyes brightened like incandescent light bulbs. "Have you seen the spread Marge put out this morning, Marty?"

He admitted that, no, he had not.

"No?" Laong Hsiuh seemed astonished. "Better hurry, Marty, before the other *piggies* eat it all."

He started to respond but stopped, his reply muted by his own astonishment. Did Laong Hsiuh just say *piggies?*

He had never liked the break room scene. He despised the gossip, the small talk, the inane conversations about the big game last night (something to do with steroid-inflated anthropoids engaged in near mortal combat). Or some gadget for the car that cut back on fuel economy while doubling emissions (he must have got that backwards). Or the previously mentioned ladies' fashions—saturated in perfume and treacly dissimulation. "My, don't *you* look nice today, Myrtle!" Dolly Butterworth, speaking to Myrtle Kreps from HR in that unflattering surprised tone he often heard women use with each other. *Nice?* She looked like she was wearing the draperies from a Dartmore Department Store display window. Of course Dolly looked *"very* nice, too!" Myrtle, even more surprised, and well she should be given that Dolly's *ensemble* resembled a nomadic sheik's harem tent. Didn't they realize how ridiculous they looked? All of them. Stuffing their faces with donuts and pastries and yakking away like amphetamine fueled ruminants. And didn't they have any sense of personal space? He felt like he couldn't breathe. He began an awkward, backward-shuffling retreat when he spotted Chuck Roastley's big block head, black pompadour and porthole glasses bobbing above the crowd like a papier-mâché parade float, clearly set on a course designed to intercept his own. *Go bug someone else, you big oaf!* he muttered and immediately afterward wondered if he had only thought that or actually said it aloud.

"Really, Martin, that won't do."

He turned and met the manic green gaze of E'Claire Shoklaude, Executive Project Director of the Distribution Accounting Department, impeccably dressed in a tailored chocolate brown business suit, her hair, as always, perfectly sculpted into a chocolate sea foam creation with an authoritative ivory white frosting at the temples. He started to say good morning but E'Claire cut him short.

"Well, good morning to *you*, Martin. I thought you were ignoring me. Everyone *else* certainly seems to be ignoring me. I suppose I must have some horribly contagious disease everyone knows about but me. Do you think that's possible, Martin? *Hmm?* But really, the look on your face. You'd think it was spreading. By the way, you haven't seen the *Crocodile* on the floor this morning, have you? No? Too bad because—"

Great, now he was stuck. E'Claire was obviously fishing for gossip, her trap an innocuous-seeming weir of words with an easy entrance and a less inviting exit barbed with sharpened staves upon which he couldn't help but impale himself if he tried to escape. Besides, as *Assistant* Project Director, a title weightier in words than authority or pay, he had to listen while E'Claire wheedled and probed or risk appearing to be part of whatever conspiracy she imagined was forming against her. His distaste for this conversation exacerbated by E'Claire's rodent-like nibbling at a pile of caramelized pastries filled with an iridescent green goo, in between which she spooned large glops of an obscene brown sludge into her mouth.

"But really, Martin, your plate is empty. Here, try a key lime tart, it's"—E'Claire's eyes darted away like wild animals and with a ferocious *snap* she bit off half the proffered tart, chewed it up in rapid little bites and swallowed loudly—"simply *divine*. Oh, and the chocolate mousse ..." another spoonful of brown sludge plunged into the pink labial crevasse of her mouth "... absolutely *delish*. Honestly, I don't know how Marge comes up with this stuff. Maybe she has a secret connection at Industrial Foods. Maybe she's even a majority stockholder. Who knows, maybe *Marge* ought to be running this place. What do *you* think, Martin?"

He didn't know what he thought, or what answer he might give to appease E'Claire's mood swings, currently drifting toward terra incognita. He said it was a shame more people didn't appreciate her unique sense of humor and leaving her to decide exactly what he meant by that, he dutifully loaded his plate with key lime tarts, added a gooey pile of chocolate mousse, and putting up a bulwark of fake smiles and meaningless asides, schmoozed his way through the crowd and out the door, barely managing to avoid the unwanted encounter with Chuck Roastley, who, like a large but lightly armed merchant vessel in pirate-infested waters, had veered off at the sight of E'Claire, but immediately afterward resumed his course with even greater determination.

Safely returned to the asylum of his cube, he brought up his screen again. *Morning, Marty. Work got you down? PERK-UP®!* An adworm. He hit delete and with childish petulance jammed a hefty spoonful of chocolate mousse into his mouth. His tongue lolled in a cloud of cacao. A surge of dark chocolate and pure cane sugar reduced his brain to a primordial state of consciousness. *Wow!* E'Claire was right. This stuff was *great!* He incautiously followed this assault on his taste buds with a bite of key lime tart that made his eyes do cartwheels in their sockets. His entire body thrummed like a dynamo. He felt ready to *work*. He skimmed through the rest of the departmental update, his eyes alert for any change in the status quo. Uh-oh, another energy collapse in the Southeast Sector. Sappers most likely. According to the Internal Security Network Team, small-time criminals who tapped into power lines, stole relatively insignificant amounts of energy and resold it on the black market. That's the message they gave the public anyway. He knew otherwise. In a classified report, ISNT blamed a more insidious element. Terrorists, subversives, individuals of nefarious intent bent on destroying the nation by exploiting weaknesses in the aging infrastructure. That's where DAD entered the picture.

A warm tidal surge of pride sat him up more or less straight in his chair. Despite its pedestrian name, the Distribution Accounting Department accounted for the distribution of *all* energy resources in the Catábolus Metropolitan Area. During his time at DAD, the department had acquired quasi-police authority. It wasn't like he was the town sheriff. He couldn't arrest anyone. He didn't carry a gun or wear a badge or anything like that. When he and his colleagues detected anomalies in energy consumption, they alerted ISNT and ISNT's tactical team took care of the rough stuff. Unfortunately, no actual *sappers* had been publicly denounced to date, which was proving to be a major bone of contention between DAD and ISNT, resulting in extremely juvenile displays of behavior, tripping in the hallways, elbows to the ribs, spilled cups of coffee, that sort of thing. Now Regional had stepped into the fray, the burr in their britches the increasingly vociferous complaints from the public sector: power outages, screens down—most inexcusable, interruptions in the Family Hour.

Family Hour. Just the words gave him a sense of well-being. He felt the way he did when he was a kid visiting his grandfather's farm in the summer. He could see himself running across a green meadow, nearly delirious with the warm sunshine on his face and the smell of new-mown hay in his nostrils. Ducks and geese quacked and honked at the pond, cows mooed in the pasture, the windmill creaked by the barn, a string orchestra played a wistful, nostalgic melody—wait, what?

A blast of warm air bearing the smells of dust, machine oil and squealing, overheated pulleys washed over him. His screen had gone down. He glanced at the clock. Five minutes since his last entry. He must have fallen asleep. He never fell asleep. He never daydreamed, never allowed himself to become distracted. Focused. One hundred percent. All. The. Time.

He shook out a couple yellows, swallowed them with coffee and brought up the Grid. The plexus of neon red, blue, green and yellow transmission lines illuminated his face with a glowing madras pattern. The Grid had always fascinated him. It was like looking at the nervous system of the metropolis, as if that great agglomeration of architecture and engineering, of buildings, bridges, streets and utilities, were a living organism with its own breathing and consciousness.

A flashing yellow lightning bolt in the Southeast Sector drew his attention to a chalky white patch indicating a Low-Cal consumer district. As he watched, the lightning bolt faded *like the last light of a long dead star*—the words came to him out of nowhere, or rather out of somewhere in a fuzzy past that included the study of literature—and in its place a swirling black tornado appeared. An energy collapse, the third he'd observed this week. They were occurring with greater frequency. Which explained the urgency at DAD to establish some sort of pattern to these collapses. By applying a set of constantly evolving algorithms to known collapse sites, the team hoped to project ahead to sites the sappers hadn't tapped yet but inevitably would. Or, as E'Claire stated in her prospectus: *By identifying all quantifiable commonalities in the recorded incidents of energy collapses, it is our goal to extrapolate a range of future collapse sites into which only a very select subset of viable possibilities must fall.* And if this logic, or illogic as it seemed at times, succeeded? If he managed to find the strand that tied these collapses together? A raise, promotion, escape from this shabby little shoebox to an office of his own? Except that it *was* E'Claire's program, which meant the accolades and the raise and the possibility of a promotion would go to her and he'd get … nil.

LUNCHTIME!

The message flashed across the screen in a flourish of tropical colors that made him think of the EdenFresh® produce section. *Lunch?* Hadn't he just returned from the break room? Dreading another such excursion, he decided to eat in. He brought up the menu, made his selection and sat back in his chair, listening for the low electrical hum announcing the chefbot's arrival.

"Hey, Mister G." A stainless steel cart rolled into his cube, pushed by a young man in cargo shorts and a tie-dyed T-shirt, his arms and legs tattooed with pirates, parrots and hula girls, his face boyishly soft despite the black goatee and studs in his ears, nose and eyebrows, on his head, a backward baseball cap. Jimmy, the mailroom guy.

"What happened to the chefbot, Jimmy?"

"On the blink again, Mister G. I'll look at it over break."

He had always thought the title of Mailroom Clerk woefully inadequate for all the additional duties Jimmy performed. Mechanic, kitchen and tech support, the various bots and electroids constantly breaking down, their inner workings jammed with spilled food, drinks. *Passive hooliganism,* Human Resources termed it. Maintenance on alert at all times. Guys in protective goggles and orange jump suits poking their heads out of overhead compartments, on their hands and knees dragging bundles of cable under people's feet. Easier to call Jimmy. He usually had things up and running in minutes. Which, Myrtle Kreps imprudently let slip, was the only reason Jimmy's casual attitude and attire were tolerated. In short, he saved the department a bundle and himself a job.

He, personally, was fond of Jimmy. He was a likeable, unassuming young guy. He didn't have to be on his guard with him all the time the way he did with his so-called colleagues. Jimmy also reminded him of somebody, maybe even somebody close—he couldn't think who at the moment, an old friend, perhaps, or a family member with whom he'd lost touch.

Jimmy set a covered dish on his desk and removed the stainless steel lid in a cloud of steam. "Surf and Turf, right, Mister G?"

His appetite soared as his eyes made acrobatic leaps from the mound of bright orange lobster tails bursting with plump white meat to the juicy, pinkish-brown slab of roast beef to the pair of foil-wrapped baked potatoes nestled side by side like submarines in dry dock.

"Anything else, Mister G?" Jimmy started to back his cart out of the cubicle.

He said no, then yes, that is, had he by any chance seen *Mister* Crocker today?

"Everybody's been asking me that question, Mister G. The answer's still the same. Negatory."

It was true, he reflected after Jimmy left, that both E'Claire and Laong Hsiuh had inquired if he'd seen Crocker this morning. E'Claire had even referred to Crocker as the *Crocodile*. Not that he was fooled for one second by that age-old managerial trick. She was clearly trying to ingratiate herself with the *underlings*, which, in this context, included him. An unsavory thought he put aside with a bite of roast beef so moist and tender it made him think with atavistic nostalgia of the first human beings to enjoy the taste of cooked meat. No wonder the aroma of seared animal flesh caused them to raise their eyes heavenward in search of the god who provided such miraculous things. He followed this rumination with a morsel of lobster extracted from its husk much as the horny crustacean itself once might have been plucked from the rocky reefs beneath the briny sea, and so succulent and sweet it left his tongue and taste buds swooning in an oily sump of melted butter, omega-3 fatty acids and the piquant intervention of squeezed lemon.

His focus on the gustatory faded as his attention returned to the Grid and he began to peel away increasingly arcane substrata of energy distribution. City blocks packed with redbrick tenement buildings, boarding houses, saloons and bordellos emerged through a murky yellow gaslight. Slaughterhouses, tanning and dyeing factories, warehouses full of cotton bales, ox yokes. This stuff looked ancient. Did any of it still exist? Or were these simply ghost images captured by the electronic medium?

Somewhere in this virtual jungle the sappers lived and apparently even thrived, carrying out their crimes with relative impunity. When he tried to picture what these sappers might look like, all that came to his mind was an absurd image of guys in black ninja costumes operating some kind of giant ray-gun. But why did it have to be so crazy? What if the sappers dressed and acted like everybody else, lived normal lives, went to work every day, had wives, kids? Was there something different about them? Would he recognize a sapper on the street? Or pass him by without a second glance? Should he even be thinking these things?

For a moment the light seemed to change or a shadow passed over him. One of those old fluorescent tubes going out, he told himself. A cold, musty draft enveloped him. The air conditioning acting up again, no doubt.

CAKE IN THE BREAK ROOM! Marge's message lit up the screen.

Break time again? Didn't he just finish lunch?

Laong Hsiuh's face rose above the gray matte divider, grinning like the man in the moon on meds. "Going to the break room, Marty? Marge has made her famous afternoon pick-me-up Triple Fudge Chocolate and Cherry Jubilee layer cake!"

Of course he had no choice but to make an appearance at this weekly ritual. Fortunately, he managed to dart into the break room, grab a wedge of cake, and dart—there was something ironic about that word—out again. *Unfortunately*, on the way back to the stockyard, as everyone good humoredly referred to the office, he ran into LaQuisha Dzukene, dressed in a voluminous green muumuu beneath which a strange multitude of jiggling continued long after her forward motion had ceased, and that smug little jerk Gordie Goutte. Gordie, whose perennial clash of checks and plaids threatened injury to both the ocular and fashion senses, was, as usual, engaged in the vicious evisceration of another member of the department, conveniently absent, inducing in LaQuisha a roaring fit of laughter.

Ignoring or at least trying not to be complicit in Gordie's calumny, he asked if they'd seen Crocker today. Gordie raised his boiled egg bald pate as if he'd heard a gunshot, peered up at him through a pair of black, horn-rimmed glasses duct-taped together at the bridge of his snoutish nose, and making a face that resembled a knot at the end of a sausage, he snarled like an aggressive little lap dog, "What're you, *crazy*, Marty?!" And immediately afterwards giggled into his fists like a puckish adolescent and confessed that earlier he had snuck off to the break room to get first dibs on Marge's cake, but when he spotted Crocker marching down the hall like a prison warden to an execution, he ducked back into the stockyard. A mere two seconds later the *Crocodile* strode through the doorway and proceeded to stalk the labyrinth of cubicles in brutal silence, stopping now and then to glower at the back of some terror-stricken employee trembling over his or her screen.

He remembered the strange shadow that had passed over him and the cold musty draft that had enveloped him and he pictured Crocker's great mortuary form in his habitual coal-black morning coat lurking behind him.

"Of course Marty wasn't disturbed to have the *Crocodile* peering down his neck, was he?" Gordie, who had the annoying habit of referring to people to whom he was speaking in the third person, glanced significantly up at LaQuisha, but refusing to be drawn into this potential conflict by Gordie's cleverly inclusive grammatical maneuver, she rolled her eyes with mock impatience and said to him, or rather his slice of cake, "Catch any sappers yet, Marty?"

"Not yet," he shrugged.

Gordie adjusted the knot in his necktie, which approximated the color and size of a highway warning sign, and in the officious tone of a county DA addressing the press corps in a detective movie, he said, "Don't worry, we'll get 'em. It's only a matter of time."

A matter of time, he mused back at his cube. Except at the moment time seemed to be on the sappers' side. And with Regional breathing down DAD's neck, the Croc—*Crocker*—was likely to keep an even more vigilant eye on the department. Of course, allowing a worm of resentment to crawl back into his thoughts, E'Claire was immune to this scrutiny, thanks to the sanctity of her office with its four walls, one a plate glass window overlooking Heroes Plaza that he particularly envied, and solid oak door, usually closed, with E'Claire's name and title centered in bronze.

He broke loose a forkful of Marge's Chocolate and Cherry Jubilee layer cake and stuck it in his mouth, plunging his tongue and taste buds into a heady mixture of sweet dark chocolate and juicy red cherries with an aftertaste as ethereal as a pink cloud of cherry blossoms in spring. *Mmm*, that *was* good.

On the other hand, if E'Claire's program failed to generate any real success soon, that office wouldn't protect her. He wondered if E'Claire was troubled by such thoughts, if she was huddled in front of her screen at that very instant, calculating her longevity at EAT against her ability to exact even more productivity from the team. If she was concerned, she didn't show it. She projected an aura, practically a *force* field, of confidence.

"*Helloooo, Mister Grassoooo!*" Loud, chortling, *large*, indeed, whimsically blimpsical, Marge, EAT's queen of cuisine, bounced into his cube in an extraordinarily voluminous cherry print outfit, wearing on her face a huge, horse-toothed smile bordered by a lavish slather of crimson lipstick and bearing in her hands an enormous slice of Chocolate and Cherry Jubilee layer cake snowcapped with a small Matterhorn of vanilla ice cream. "Have you had your cake yet, Mister *Grassooo?*" she sang operatically.

He said yes, he had, it was very good, thank you.

"You did?" Marge's face registered disappointment, then suspicion. Her eyes fell to his plate, clean except for a few orphaned crumbs of chocolate and a smear of cherry jubilee sauce. Deft as a stage magician, she replaced the empty dish with an even larger wedge of cake, chortling with matronly insistence, "Well, have some *mooorrre*."

He made a why-not shrug of compliance and took a bite. *Yum*, he had already forgotten how good that was, even better with the vanilla ice cream. His brain felt like it was melting. His cryonized sinuses sang hosannas in excelsis. He felt like he could climb up a sheer stone face in the Himalayas, beat a thoroughbred in a two mile race.

He spent the next hour typing up a summation of this week's work, which, according to the definition of "work" in his high school physics class (something to do with the application of force, *movement*) amounted to zero, although his report would indicate the exact opposite, that is, spectacular—well, he struck ~~spectacular~~ and typed in the more modest *noteworthy*—advances in tracking systems, *comprehensive*—a word infinitely mutable in its meaning—surveys of known energy collapse sites.

A blast of arctic air washed over him. These damned cubes, either too hot or too cold, the heat and AC in constant competition to see which could make the occupants most miserable. He glanced at the crumbs on his plate but had no memory of finishing the second piece of cake. His fingers ached, his wrists were numb, he felt exhausted. He leaned back in his chair and, with some difficulty, clasped his hands behind his head. His eyes rolled ceilingward with a dry, rasping sound, followed by a dull thud, as if a door had slammed shut in the back of his skull. Finally, the week was over, and for the first time in months, he had a Saturday off.

But wait—that's right, it wasn't a regular Friday, was it? Because just as they were finishing up for the weekend, a glitch in E'Claire's program shut down the whole system. The Crocodile stormed into the office in a great black flapping of wings and snapping of teeth that momentarily reminded him of the distant relationship between the reptilian dinosaur and the feathered avian, in this case a raptor, haranguing employees and demanding to know why no work was being done. E'Claire followed close behind, wringing her hands and white-faced with terror, contrary to her usually self-possessed demeanor. The whole stockyard finally had to shut down so the techies could do their thing, but rather than let the staff have the rest of the afternoon off, the parsimonious Crocodile kept everyone for *morale building* exercises.

First he divided the department into two teams, one led by E'Claire, and comprised of LaQuisha Dzukene, Dolly Butterworth and Gordie Goutte, whom, it was generally understood, E'Claire thoroughly despised. The other team, he helmed. His crew: Chuck Roastley, vacuous but competent on the Grid, Laong Hsiuh, couldn't go wrong there, and Carmela Lechay, in one of her extravagantly ruffled and deeply cleavaged rumba outfits he scrupulously avoided staring at. Crocker then called in Marge, followed by the department chefbot, back on its feet so to speak and loaded down with boxes of chocolate pound cake and tubes of chocolate icing. The object of the game, Crocker explained, was to construct an exact replica of the EAT building out of pound cake, with extra points going to the fastest and most accurately rendered edifice.

Naturally he put Laong Hsiuh, who happened to be a master of the ancient oriental art of structural pastry making, in charge of their team's design. E'Claire delegated this responsibility to LaQuisha, who had minored in architectural foods. All preparations having been made, the two teams awaited the signal to commence. Crocker's flinty black eyes gleamed fiercely beneath the overhanging precipice of his shaggy brows. In a stentorian voice, he addressed E'Claire. "You have competition now, Ms. Shoklaude. Competition, as has oft been said, makes good business."

E'Claire lowered her gaze beneath the weight of this pithy wisdom, but her eyes emitted a furious green blaze *he* felt directed at *him.*

Crocker, too, turned his attention to him and in a decidedly warmer, almost paternal tone, he said simply, "Let your star shine, Martin. Everyone ready? Marge, please."

Tweeeet! Marge blew sharply into a silver whistle and the two teams leapt to their erections.

Laong Hsiuh's eyes blazed with machine-like fury as he calculated tensile strength, load-bearing structures, tectonic aberrations and other formulas so esoteric they bordered on the metaphysical. LaQuisha, whose rather monumental stature alone warranted her authority in vertical architecture, relied more on the applied sciences. "Just try to keep it straight, okay, Gordie?" And while Marge kept an eye on the clock, Crocker offered sage advice over the combatants' shoulders, "More cake in the north tower, Roastley! If you wish to survive in combat, Mister Goutte, build your shelter first and eat later!" Thanks, perhaps, to these managerial chestnuts, as well as skills acquired in both the professional and domestic theater, the two teams completed their replicas of the EAT building neck and neck.

Tweeeet! Marge's whistle confirmed the competition's end.

To an explosion of hoots and cheers, Crocker declared the match a draw, then raised his hands for silence. "As you know, in business there is always a winner and a loser. We must have a tiebreaker."

"A tiebreaker!" everyone exclaimed. Their excitement quickly turned to trepidation. What *kind* of tiebreaker?

Crocker explained. Each team must now eat as much of its own edifice as possible *without* causing it to collapse. The win went to the last man—Crocker coughed into his fist—*tower* standing.

Groans arose from E'Claire's camp. Thanks to Gordie's insatiable appetite for schoolyard hijinks—the brown smudges around his mouth were a dead giveaway—their structure had already suffered several crucial bites and looked tenuous at best.

Marge reviewed the rules. Upon her signal, the lead-off eater from each team must take a bite of his or her team's erection, *without* using his or her hands, and *swallow*, before the next team member took a bite, and so forth. Each team member was responsible for his or her own eating, no substitutions, no foul play, and please, no trouser trumpeting—*tweeeet!*

This injunction was immediately followed by a debacle of flying pound cake, chocolate icing and mumbled, mouth-filled warning shouts, *another bite over here! watch out for the south tower!* as well as desperate, denture-unhinging heroic attempts to counter the tilt of said tower, while Crocker marched up and down, barking, "Lick, Mister Goutte, lick! More tongue action there, Ms. Butterworth!" and Marge marched beside him, making largely unacknowledged attempts at refereeing.

Despite the gustatory damage Gordie had already inflicted upon his team's structure, it held up remarkably well, until, that is, Crocker, in a clear display of favoritism, played his trump card. Extending a long yellow talon, he deftly extracted a crumbling but crucial buttress, popped it into his mouth and stood back with his hands on his hips, chewing vigorously and watching with undisguised amusement as the already rickety edifice tilted one way, then the other, and finally collapsed into a gleaming, coprolitic pile. E'Claire looked equally a wreck, her perfectly coiffed chocolate sea foam hairdo reduced to a mess of tangled seaweed, her carefully harmonized applications of lipstick, eyeliner and skin toners smudged into a sad-eyed clown mask. Oblivious to E'Claire's distress, Crocker daintily wiped invisible specks of chocolate from his mouth with a white silk handkerchief, rubbed his hands together as if he were crushing a kitten and, with an expression of reptilian glee, purred, "That was certainly fun, wouldn't you agree?" And like a litter of tail-wagging puppies salivating for their supper, *everyone* nodded their heads enthusiastically.

In the end it was Jimmy the mailroom guy who figured out the glitch. Making his final round of the day, he stopped his mail cart in front of the stockyard's main screen, placed his hands over the keyboard as if he were consulting a crystal ball, pressed a combination of keys no one could remember later, and the Grid blossomed into life, at which point the entire stockyard erupted in applause. Rather than bask in this adulation, Jimmy stuck his hands in his pockets, made a funny, bashful smile and hurried off with his cart.

Once again he had the sense that Jimmy reminded him of someone close, but he still couldn't think who. Regardless, thanks to, or because of, Jimmy's unique talents, the whole department had to work late to make up for the down time, which resulted in a lot of grumbling and dirty looks from certain team members who still harbored grudges over the chocolate fudge cake fiasco.

His spirits took a further plunge when he exited the department at half past seven and found that even at this hour the elevator was packed with equally fagged warriors of the business-suited working class. He'd fain jump into a vat of lard than plunge into this bedraggled mass of humanity. He felt an unpleasant sebaceous sensation as he forced his way into the car. At the same time a workday's accumulation of noxious odors assaulted his senses: the spices and condiments of meals consumed (refried beans? kim chi?), unwelcome traces of defecation and urination, the brackish sea stink of perspiration, countered by additional applications of equally disagreeable laboratory produced scents: cologne, perfume, deodorants, antiperspirants, toothpaste, mouthwash, breath fresheners, feminine hygiene products and other unidentifiable effluvium. But what the dickens? *Fagged? Fain? Effluvium?* What lexical reservoir of the arcane and the archaic did he pull those words from? (*Dickens?*)

He exited the EAT Building into a wall of stultifying heat and humidity and began his trek across the sweltering Heroes Plaza. Even at this hour the sunlight felt hot and viscous. His body seemed weighted by an excess of gravity. He felt like he could barely move. He yearned for the air-conditioned comfort awaiting him at the train station. To his chagrin, he found the entrance blocked by an angry crowd confronting a very brawny and hostile-looking cop.

"Like I already told yez bums, the station's closed!" The cop snarled, his face a swollen red carbuncle of outrage at this civic insurrection.

Closed? When had the station ever closed?

Someone said something about damage to the tracks. He thought he heard the word *sappers*.

"*Sappers?*" a fearful voice in back repeated, followed by a murmur among the crowd.

"What are we supposed to do?" A frantic female voice up front.

"Yez'll have to *ambulate* yerselves to the next station," the cop growled with barely disguised malevolence.

"You mean *walk?*" a male voice cried out.

"Are you *crazy?!*" another shouted. "It's five blocks. I'll have a heart attack!"

The cop smacked his club against his meaty palm. "Move along now, the lot o' yez, or I'll call for reinforcements!"

Properly intimidated by this uniformed authority, as well as the threat of violence, or incarceration, or both, the crowd obediently began to turn away, on their faces the disgruntled, uncomprehending expressions of cattle denied access to greener pastures by a few tenuous strands of barbed wire. He turned with equal resignation and began to trudge down Frontier Avenue with the rest of the herd. In the shop windows their quavering reflections looked swollen and grotesque, like a migration of great prehistoric beasts driven by some catastrophic event. The sun hung molten and oddly ellipsoidal over the skyline. The buildings themselves seemed to sag beneath the crushing weight of heat and humidity. Molecules of water oozed from the air as if it were an osmotic membrane. Sweat sprang from people's heads like lawn sprinklers. Their clothes hung from their bodies like damp laundry. A man next to him gesticulated wildly and shouted into his EyePhone®, *No, I don't know when I'll be home! Can't you understand—I'm walking!*

At the next corner, a red light's mnemonic beacon thrust him into another childhood memory. He was in the city, in the summer, shopping with his aunt or maybe it was his mother. The light turned green and they started to cross when an enormous man lurched toward them. He had never seen anyone so big in his life. The man's massive chest and belly bounced and jiggled beneath his T-shirt like mounds of Jell-O. His legs were the size of oil drums. His burst trouser fly splayed outward like the flaps of a circus tent. In contrast, his arms seemed oddly atrophied, like the tiny forelimbs of a Tyrannosaurus rex, and he flailed them about spasmodically as if he were struggling to pull himself forward through an extremely dense atmosphere. Gasping and wheezing, the man furiously blinked sweat from his eyes, which looked wild with determination, as if he didn't understand himself how he could be inside this *thing*, and yet he was, and somehow he had to make it *move*. People were laughing and pointing at him. Someone shouted, *Hey, ya big blimp, why don't ya try flying!* The poor wretch smiled grotesquely as if he didn't even mind.

*

We weren't alarmed when they first appeared among us. We laughed at them and called them names, and, no surprise, they laughed back. Of course they laughed. They were afraid. There were so many of us, and so few of them.

There used to be one in every town. The Jones' Aunt Bertha, for example, or the Olesons' Uncle Olaf, or the DeOllas' son Alonso who abruptly returned home from college in the middle of his first semester and from that day forth sat at the front window, methodically eating from huge bowls that mysteriously appeared before him. Or the middle school cafeteria lady whose enormous girth and great potato gnocchi face simultaneously horrified and mesmerized the children who watched awe-stricken as she ladled out industrial quantities of Sloppy Joes, her huge floppy arms swinging like sow bellies.

It would have been almost impossible to tell them apart without gender identifying clothes. Any suggestion of breasts or genitals was largely obscured by their monstrous obesity. Facial hair was a good clue, make-up and jewelry too, although none were reliable indicators in these changing times.

Aware of their grotesqueness, they seldom left home, or only went out at night, often to congregate in the back of darkened movie theaters where they ate from large paper sacks like nocturnal animals feeding at the zoo. In winter, they cowered like cattle at the back of buses and trolleys, their frightened gaze fixed downward in the desolate landscape of melting slush, wads of chewing gum and soggy cigarette butts littering the wet floor mat. In summer they struggled down the sidewalk like great alien beasts unaccustomed to Earth's gravity, suffering even more from the obvious contempt of the *normal* citizens who shunned them as if they carried a mortal disease. Exploiting their monstrousness, some chose to work in freak shows, traveling circuses. *See the amazing fat lady!* Some found success in vaudeville, burlesque.

*

Hi, Marty! How ya doin'?

A familiar voice called to him. He searched through his catalogue of friends, family, co-workers, acquaintances, even the carbot, and finally hit pay dirt in another childhood memory—the bug-eyed, potato-nosed stand-up comedian, Jolly Roger, his voice made slightly mechanical, scratchy, as if it came from an old vinyl recording. Too late, he spotted the vending machine lurking against the mimetic background of flickering screens in a shop window. Like a seasoned streetwalker or professional conman, it flashed its lights and called out to him in that friendly, familiar, faintly machine voice, *Hey, Marty, how about a snack? I got cold beverages, I got energy bars, I got red hots, soft pretzels. Whataya have, Marty?*

A pick-me-up did sound enticing. He ordered a GoodLife® energy bar and a medium SodaRific®, passed his hand over the palm scan to debit his IUD, and in the time it took to complete this banal transaction, pondered its significance with distracted and then increasingly piqued interest. The Individual Universal Document contained all his vital data, DNA, blood type, DOB, biometrics, bank account, driver's license, home address— everything, in other words, the police, the financial institutions, his employer, the Glorious Council, the Civilian Consumers Corps, the corner Mom and Pop grocery store, and any other putative authority might need or want to know about him. Which also made him wonder if it was his account that was being debited or *him.*

He heard a faint whir and a GoodLife® energy bar clunked into the bin, followed by an extra large SodaRific®.

"Hey," he complained, "I asked for the medium SodaRific®."

Thank you for your patronage, Marty. Have a nice day.

"Wait, aren't you going to credit my account?"
Did you wish to make a further purchase, Marty?
"No, I—"
Too late. The vendor had gone back to sleep, only its sensors alert for the next sucker. He muttered something incoherent even to himself, tore the wrapper from the energy bar with his teeth, bit off a chocolaty, chewy chunk of wafer and caramel nougat and masticated savagely. Again employing his teeth as a primitive tool, he twisted the plastic cap off the SodaRific®, releasing a plosive mist that tickled his nostrils as he raised the bottle overhead for a large swallow, creating a volatile mix of sucrose and carbonated beverage that sent a foaming, asteroidal ball of gases down his throat, into his stomach and back up again in a volcanic belch. *Ahhh*, just what he needed. He felt better already. He quickly devoured the rest of the energy bar, washed it down with SodaRific® and, fortified with a healthy dose of sugar, fat and caffeine, continued his trek.

He was just stepping down from a rather steep curb when he heard a noise in the adjacent alley. A man huddled in the shadows. He looked impossibly thin, gaunt, his skull-like face was bruised and battered. *Help me*, the man said in a quavering voice and reached toward him, but he shrank back in horror and hurried away. What if he was sick? What if he had a deadly disease? Why did they let people like that out on the street? The next instant he rebuked himself. What was he thinking? How could he be so mean-spirited? The man was obviously in trouble, he needed help. He decided to offer him money, but by the time he dug some loose change out of his pocket and went back the man had disappeared.

Fortunately, he was able to board the train at the 34th St. station and even find a seat. Exhausted, he immediately dozed off and didn't wake again until the train arrived at SunnyVale.

The sun was collapsing on the horizon like a blood-red Japanese lantern as he trudged across the parking lot, but the pavement was still hot under his feet and waves of moist heat rose around him like a tropical fever. To his dismay, the car had parked itself in the farthest lot, he was completely beat by the time he reached it. The door slid open at his approach and he slumped down in the seat.

Hi, Marty, hard day?

"Sorta," he replied, still a little out of sorts.

Hold on a sec, I'll cool things down for you, Marty.

Cool, oxygen-enriched air washed over him. He inhaled deeply and closed his eyes, briefly losing himself in arctic whiteness and silence.

Ready to go now, Marty? Shall I drive? You feel up to it? You're sure?

"Yes, I'm sure," he replied, more brusquely than he had intended.

The car appeared not to have noticed. *Hey, you wanta snack, Marty? I've got energy bars, chips …*

He said he'd just had an energy bar half an hour ago and chose the chips.

You want a soda with that, Marty?

He said he'd rather have a scotch and soda.

C'mon, Marty, you're driving.

"Yeah, sure, soda's fine. Large."

The snack tray slid open.

Like some music, Marty?

"Sure."

Tinkling piano, melancholy strings and woodwinds. He recognized the *New Autumn Sonata,* but instead of falling leaves and golden sunlight he thought of barren desert, breaking glass.

I have the feeling you'd like some quiet, Marty.

He didn't reply.

I thought so, Marty. The music ceased.

He still hadn't adjusted to the carbot's solicitous nature. Of course he knew the bots were programmed to respond to cues they picked up from drivers' speech patterns—your word choice, emotional inflections, even the names and relationships of your family, friends, the people you worked with. But sometimes the damn thing sounded too familiar. It was like having a complete stranger privy to his most intimate thoughts, feelings. Plus, there were still glitches. A misunderstood word might cause the carbot to say, or worse *do*, something entirely inappropriate, like drive off a cliff.

This last thought probably occurred to him because recently his night vision didn't seem as keen. In the crepuscular light everything looked blurry. Headlights, streetlights, neon signs over bars, restaurants, the VRBLs shimmering like huge, frozen confections of light, offering within their icy translucence giant foaming bottles of soda and energy drinks, sporty SUVs, model homes, luxury appliances. And they were all saying *eat me*. And he wanted to eat them. He could taste the sweet, icy slush in his mouth, feel that oddly pleasurable burning and numbness on his tongue and in his brain. He couldn't wait to get home and eat a great big steak dinner and maybe a plate of pasta.

Marty? Sorry to bother you but …

He'd driven past the house. No wonder, every goddamn house on the block looked the same. He turned around and drove back up the street, peering into the glare of porch lights for his number.

Evening, Marty, the lockbot's gravelly, grandfatherly voice greeted him as he grabbed the doorknob. The latch snapped open and he felt a concurrent sense of relief and security as he entered the welcoming, climate-controlled comfort of the foyer and closed the door behind him.

Nyah-nyah, nyah-nyah. The Twinkle Twins' annoying singsong voices penetrated his brain like a chorus of middle school girls taunting a cringing classmate. Ashley in the family room with her EyePhone®. Then, a cacophony of growling aliens, blasting ray-guns, worlds in collision. Trey upstairs at his game station. Dishes rattled in the kitchen as a jovial masculine voice extolled the virtues of culinary feng shui. Horton Crumbsberry, "the Compleat Chef," leading May and the chefbot through a new Industrial Foods menu.

He uttered a world-weary sigh, trudged across the foyer to the staircase, leaned his weight on the walnut swirl of the banister and began to climb. By the middle landing he was gasping for breath. He glanced at the green brocaded armchair and remembered a Blessed Offering for stair lifts. *It's not just for grandpa anymore!* He felt beat. He felt grimy and wretched. He couldn't wait to get out of this damn strait jacket and take a shower. He wondered what it would be like to take a bath instead, to let all the day's weight and fatigue slip away in that buoyant medium. Even better yet, to be floating on his back in a turquoise sea, palm trees rustling, sails on the horizon. *So try SeaBreeze® for a sea breeze fresh wardrobe.* Great, now the damn BOs were even interrupting his fantasies. Besides, getting in and out of the tub would be a nightmare.

3

a wonderful life—sort of

HE WOKE THE FOLLOWING MORNING with an inexplicable sense of joy, the way he used to feel as a boy when he woke out of a deep and untroubled sleep into warm sunshine and birdsong and a whole day ahead of him to do nothing but be alive. He pulled on an old navy blue training suit he had forbidden May to throw out and an equally aged pair of sneakers and trudged downstairs to the kitchen. The wall screen came on. Bob Broadley in his trademark orange tie and cobalt blue suit, his smile an arctic expanse of orthodontic wizardry, his eyes fuzzy brown dots of warmth and sincerity, his hair shellacked into the patent leather sheen of a man's dress shoe, and Marsha Mello in a mouth-puckering lime green outfit accessorized with a blood-red scarf, her eyes brimming with the unnatural turquoise blue of backyard swimming pools, her nose a rhinoplastic feat of engineering, her hair dyed, teased and sprayed into a miraculous lemon meringue construction. Accompanied by assorted tics, grins, grimaces and raised eyebrows, the team of Broadley and Mello chorused back and forth with *all the news worthy of mention*:

"Well, Marsha, the Internal Security Network Team reports progress in the ongoing investigation of sappers!"

Not according to what he knew.

"Thaaaat's right, Bob! On the international page, the Defense Department announces another rogue cyber state taken down!"

At least that was encouraging.

"Great news, Marsha! Before leaving for his weekend retreat this morning the president addressed a worried nation!"

He couldn't wait to hear what *he* had to say.

President Portland Posture's noble forehead and strong jaw appeared in profile and in a stern but avuncular voice, he said, "My fellow citizens, the dollars you spend here at home support our men and women *over there!* Spend, my friends, spend! Victory is at hand!"

Like he wasn't already spending himself into an early grave.

"The president has spoken and the people have listened!" Marsha Mello transitioning.

Not much choice there.

"Thaaaat's right, Marsha!" Bob Broadley taking the handoff. "In financial news, Energy Acquisition and Transfer shares continue their meteoric climb!"

POWER TO THE PEOPLE

The message appeared on the screen in neon red over images of enormous turbines, giant transmission towers. Fleets of cargo planes, merchant ships, land barges and tractor trailers disgorged mountains of consumer products into malls, shopping outlets, grocery stores. In the background the Catábolus skyline blazed like a citadel of light, among the most recognizable landmarks, the EAT Building.

Now that was good news.

Beaming like a toaster oven at the prospect of his ever-appreciating stock options, he sat down at the kitchen table just as Mrs. Driscoll, in an expansive flamingo pink stretch outfit, went by on her Personal TranSport®, one of the newer models with ergonomic armrests and a tractor-style, massagio-matic saddle with a built-in methane collector that made her haunches bob up and down like twin ships at berth. Mrs. Driscoll's dogbot Archie frantically paddled along behind her, its bloated sausage-like body slumped in a small four-wheeled cart, its waffle-like paws barely touching the sidewalk, its big brown marketing-designed puppy dog eyes wide with genuine canine desperation, its long pink tongue flopping out like a distress flag. Apparently oblivious to this creature's suffering, Mrs. Driscoll was eating from a bag of glazed donuts.

A floorboard creaked and May shuffled into the kitchen in her pink nightgown and bedroom slippers, her face, usually aglow with springtime, sunshine, the eternal optimist, clouded now by a sleepy, confused expression. "What are you doing up, Marty?" She glanced across the room. "Why isn't the screen on?" Her eyes, bright, green ever alert, fell to the empty table. "Aren't you eating breakfast?"

This barrage of interrogatives caught him off guard. The oven clock said seven a.m. No particular significance in that. The wall screen was dark but he didn't remember turning it off. As for breakfast—he started to say he didn't feel hungry this morning but he saw May's eyes narrow into bright inquisitive seams and instead began to construct a series of small lies, one contingent upon the other, his own uncertainty as to where this was going betrayed by the rise in his voice at the end of each sentence ... that is, he didn't feel hungry for the *usual?* He was thinking of going to ... Oma's *bakery?* For some ... banana custard *cream puffs?*

The morning sunlight infused May's face with its own warm, banana custard incandescence and in the languorous tone of an odalisque lounging in her boudoir she said, "Marty, that's so sweet. I dreamed of those cream puffs last night."

Outside, the air felt cool, crisp. The sunlight had a spare, aged quality. The first orange and yellow tongues of autumnal flame licked at the leaves of the shade tree in the front lawn. Finally, the meteorology guys got it right. This was exactly what fall should feel like. He glanced up the street, past the other nearly identical, two-story wood-frame houses, each with a modest front porch, twin dormers and shake shingle roof, each with a tiny yard and single shade tree just now beginning to show fall color. Marvelous how tidy science made everything. The lawns stayed green and perfectly trim all year, no need for mowing. The trees stayed leafy and perfectly green, except for one month in the fall when they turned a spectacular palette of colors, before turning green again, and no leaves to rake.

Lost in these observations, he walked the length of Memory Lane and was half way up Easy Street before he realized he *was* walking. He was also breathing heavily and he had started to sweat. A car went by. Pale faces stared at him in horror. He considered turning around but he'd already come this far and he continued his march. Turning onto Pastoral Avenue, he spied old Mrs. Goon's dilapidated Victorian manse rising above a field of weeds at the end of dusty little Dreary Lane. What an eyesore. He consoled himself that Mrs. Goon would probably be gone soon— the old man had apparently died the year before—then rebuked himself for being so callous.

A sweet, yeasty aroma flooded his nostrils. Oma's Bakery. He had walked the entire way—half a mile at least. He couldn't remember the last time he'd walked so far. He'd also forgotten how popular Oma's was. The parking lot was packed. A line extended out the front door. Sleepy-faced friends and neighbors greeted each other with sheepish grins and the timeworn rallying cry, "Oma's makes the best *schmecken* donuts!"

He got in line behind a woman in a bulky wool sweater with tiny, worm-like noils of disparate colors sticking out everywhere. As they entered the bakery, the woman turned, her arms clutched at her chest in an exaggerated shiver, her mouth open as if she were about to make an observation on the weather outside or the air conditioning in. Her eyes narrowed, her brow furrowed, her friendly expression morphed into acute suspicion. He glanced down at himself in alarm. Was he covered in blood? Had he stepped in a pile of virtual dog shit? Suddenly his old blue training suit seemed shabbier than he remembered. The zipper had stuck halfway over his belly, exposing the faded orange T-shirt he slept in last night. His sneakers were worn and gray and he had carelessly knotted together a broken shoelace. He also realized now that he was sweating profusely and his face felt flushed. The woman turned away, rustled in her purse and began to whisper into her EyePhone®. His eardrums tightened in anticipation of a police siren.

At the counter, he ordered a dozen banana custard cream puffs from the rosy-cheeked, flour-dusted young lady, fanned his hand over the palm scan, received his purchase in a white paper sack and pushed his way outside. The line of customers had grown considerably longer and more cars continued to pull up, a reminder that he still had to walk back home. His spirits sagged as if he had just slung a load of coal over his shoulder.

By the time he turned onto Easy Street he had to struggle to place one foot in front of the other. His right knee was making an audible popping sound. His breath came in short, quick gasps. He had also broken out in a cold sweat and a strange, vibrating sensation was spreading through his body. He remembered he hadn't eaten breakfast. His blood sugar must be low. He felt a sudden desperate need to eat something. He fumbled open the paper sack and extracted a golden brown cream puff. It was still warm. Yellow custard oozed from the flaky crust. He bit off a large chunk and chewed savagely. His tongue wallowed in sweet, tangy, banana-flavored goo. He swallowed the soggy bolus with a throat-engorging gulp that reminded him of a python consuming a pig in a nature film he'd seen as a kid. That helped. He felt better already. He took another bite, chewed vigorously, and marched on. Ha, there was Memory Lane. Almost home. As he passed the Jacksons' house he saw a curtain move in a window. He was certain he had seen Shirley Jackson's pale face, her eyes wide with disbelief. He imagined her in there now hissing to her husband, *I tell you, Andrew, it was Martin Grasso—walking.*

"You were gone a long time." May took the bag of cream puffs.

He said he had walked.

"All the way to Oma's?" May opened the bag and smelled the contents as if she were inhaling pure ether.

He shrugged. It was a nice morning.

"Marty, are you crazy?" May took out a cream puff and examined it as if it were a lump of gold. "You have to take the kids to their Team Interactive Meet."

Great. What had begun as a promising day now promised to be—less so. He had envisioned this rare break from the job as a vista onto new horizons, a day for exploration, or even simple relaxation, maybe *read* for instance. How long had it been since he'd read anything for pleasure? Couldn't the damn car take the kids? Oh no, the Wise Parenting Council demanded adult, parental supervision, *and please, Marty, watch your language*. And then of course they had to stop at BurgerBoyz for an infusion of fat, sugar and caffeine, also per the WPC, *be sure to provide your children their proper nutritional requirement*, a high calorie repast he personally chose to forgo out of irritation at this subtle usurpation of his parental authority. It annoyed him even more to glance up in the mirror and see the kids ensconced in a clutter of fast food wrappers, completely oblivious to the world around them, above all *him*, their father, the provider of this abundance they were consuming like ravenous omnivores. Trey, earbuds plugged in, rocking back and forth in front of his screen while he disassembled some sort of electroid in his lap that, *God* forbid, he hadn't extracted from a vital household appliance. Ashley texting furiously on her EyePhone®, although from time to time he felt her eyes bore into the back of his skull like bright blue laser beams, still upset, he assumed, because he had refused to increase her allowance *again*, despite May's approval. Add to that the appropriateness issue when she came downstairs this morning in an extremely revealing (he thought) pink sequined halter-top and a black and white-checked mini-skirt that rode as low on her hips as it rose up her thighs. May thought it was fine for her age. *Fine?*

She's thirteen! he said. She's still a kid! Sure, he'd noticed her hips and butt take on a rounder, more distinctly female shape and, yeah, the once unmentionable training bra no longer needed mention now that her breasts were clearly developing. But he didn't want to think about any of that, didn't want to see any of that. Let her grow up, become a young woman. Just spare him the frightening feminine details. Another thing, her obsession with this damn *MySelfish*—was that right?—website. Her whole life focused on her *avatar*, whatever the fuhhh—*remember, Marty*—that was. May didn't seem to have a problem with it—*she's exploring her creative gifts, Marty*—but he wasn't convinced. Maybe he should talk to Jimmy the mailroom guy. He knew about this stuff.

The Community Center was in a total uproar, kids screamed and ran around, coaches blew their whistles and shouted for everyone to listen up, designer sportswear swished through the air, high-dollar sneakers squeaked on polished wooden floorboards, bleachers creaked and swayed like eighteenth century sailing ships beneath the weight of harried moms and pops hurrying back from the concession stand loaded down with industrial quantities of food and drink. A buzzer sounded and the contestants bent over their screens, eyes androidally bright, youthful brows furrowed with the concentration of ballistic missile launch officers, soft, unsullied little fingers scrabbling over keyboards like amphetaminic spiders.

In the end he had no idea who won. Nor did he understand why they called it a Team Interactive Meet when the kids only seemed interested in scoring as many points as they could for themselves. He had hoped they might talk about this at home, but when he suggested it, Ashley's response was a brusque, "Talk about *what?*" as if he had accused her of shoplifting, and tossing her straw-colored braids over her shoulders like a Teutonic warrior princess, she marched out of the room, switching her checkered butt at him with machine-like precision. He remembered a recent FarmCorps BO and considered investigating: Disobedient children? *ParentAid®!*

This episode disturbed him so much that he went to discuss it with May, whom he found in the family room poring over a

NuTrendz fashion magazine, a new trend of hers he also found disturbing. To his horror she had joined a group of women who must have thought it terribly cute to call themselves the *Fashionably Fashionable Fashion Magazine Fan Club*. He had even had the misfortune of witnessing one of their *covens*, a bunch of alarmingly overdressed, mostly middle-aged women stoked on white wine and chattering into each other's faces like a tribe of baboons. It was probably his simmering contempt for this nonsense that caused him to abruptly ask May—well, snap at her, actually— "What the hell's going on with Ashley? Trey, too? I don't like it that the kids are always in front of those damn screens."

"Where else would they be?" May replied in that almost preternaturally neutral tone she used when she thought he was being *irrational*. That caught him off guard. Where else *would* they be? Then she took the opportunity to badger him over his own energy consumption. How many times did she have to remind him about turning off the screens and other electrical appliances? "Really, *Martin*, you'd think I was talking to a *child*."

Mulling over this exchange later, he recalled his grandfather, a wiry little old man who was always working on something or repairing something, climbing up and down the ladder to paint the house or clean the gutters or out in the garden weeding tomatoes or in the barn performing maintenance on his tractor. He used to tell his parents, "Turn off the damn TV and send those kids outside for some fresh air and exercise!" He also remembered the woods near his house where he and his buddies ran around whooping like savages and an empty field where their played pick-up baseball. Had Trey ever played pick-up baseball? Or run around in the woods? Or done anything without an adult supervising him or arranging his schedule or chauffeuring him somewhere every damn minute of the day? And Ashley. She was supposed to be gifted. Whatever the *fff*—whatever that meant. Gifted by whom? *God?* Santa Claus? *Give it to me* would be more accurate. She constantly demanded money for school, for the snack vendors at school, for new clothes to wear to school. Of course May sided with her on this too. "You can't imagine what it's like for kids in school today, Marty."

To be perfectly honest, he *couldn't* imagine. Despite the WPC's emphasis on parental involvement (waivers granted to military personnel), he had absolutely zero idea what either Ashley or Trey did in school. He knew nothing about their classes or teachers or even the names of their schools. May, on the other hand, was totally involved, one hundred per cent helicopter. She helped found the Parent As Co-Teacher program when Ashley entered pre-K. She herded through the *Special* Special Children's Program when Trey matriculated into first grade. She received the prestigious Hovering Mother Award from the WPC three years in a row. She even garnered a letter of commendation from the Ministry of Education.

"The pressure on these kids is terrible, Marty. Hundreds of hours of test prep, everybody's job on the line, teachers, administrators, college recruiters."

College recruiters? Middle school?

"Their peers are the worst. They can be so cruel—*malicious.*" Libby Bombaste's daughter Prissy told *her* that some of the girls referred to Ashley as *AshleyBrat*, which didn't surprise him in the least, or worse, *Grassy Ash*, which, in addition to its vulgarity, he took as a personal insult. No wonder these kids created virtual friends. They didn't have any *real* friends.

As if he hadn't already squandered enough of his rare day off, May insisted he go shopping with her at the new EdenFresh® on Olio Boulevard. Geriatric, polyester-clad greeters in aquarium-size bifocals and forest green EdenFresh® aprons smiled at them manically through fiercely clenched dentures, arthritic, blue-veined hands waving back and forth like metronomes. Pierced, studded, tattooed and highly enthusiastic young men and women in green EdenFresh® aprons over Steam Punk and Retro-grunge outfits offered them oblational platters of crumbly cheddar cheese, crusty chunks of artisanal bread, dips, chips, spreads and salsas, enormous green and purple Greek olives. Chefbots in floppy white toques and green EdenFresh® aprons grilled, sautéed, seared and blackened bite-sized *Carnivore's Delights* for them on their built-in gas burners, their mechanical arms flailing like ancient Hindu deities. In the background the EdenFresh® jingle incessantly reminded them to *be good consumers and consume more wholesome goooodness.* And like good consumers, they complied. Sampling, noshing, grazing and tasting, they joined the rest of the EdenFresh® faithful trundling up and down the aisles on self-propelled carts laden like container ships with Industrial Foods products.

Despite this morning's long march, and May's chiding—*Must you always be such an iconoclast, Martin?*—he chose to walk. Somehow he and May got separated. Shopping carts boxed him in like a stampeding herd of motorized cattle. A woman in an ill-chosen orange stretch outfit that made her look like Cinderella's carriage after midnight crashed into him from behind. She gave him a loopy, too many vodka martinis for lunch, head-lolling grin, fluttered her fingers farewell and drove off. A white-hot bolt of anger surged through his body. He felt an almost uncontrollable urge to shout in peoples' faces.

Get the fuck out of my way you fat pig! Hey lard butt, anybody ever say you look like a fucking baby elephant in a polo shirt?!

An angry, petulant voice whined through his brain like a chainsaw. Was it *his* voice? Had he spoken aloud? He spotted a strange-looking man, his face gaunt, his eyes wild, his body almost impossibly thin, elbowing his way through the bumper car traffic. He'd never seen anyone that thin in his life. What if he had a terrible disease? What if it was contagious? He placed his hand over his nose and mouth and trying not to breathe hurried down the frozen vegetable aisle toward fresh produce. There the man was again, arguing with an EdenFresh® manager, identifiable as such in a white shirt, black tie and green apron.

"Please, sir," the manager implored, "take what you have and leave. You don't have to pay for it."

"I don't need your *shit,*" the skinny guy snarled, throwing a plastic bag of leafy green vegetables on the floor and striding away.

The manager's fists knotted at his sides. He looked like he wanted to shout out in anger or even run after the guy but instead his head drooped, his shoulders sagged and he bent down to pick up the bag of greens.

"Marty, where have you been?" May screeched to a halt, nearly catapulting herself out of the overloaded cart. "Here, try this. I'm thinking of having them for the next PACT meeting." Before he could fend her off, she shoved a neon orange cracker mounded with iridescent purple paste into his mouth. He chewed tentatively, tasted the salty, crunchy cracker, then something creamy, sweet, slightly nutty. Not bad actually. In fact, *delicious*. His spirits lifted like a kite on a sunny spring day.

*

You have to remember, this all started a long time ago. Life was harder then. If you wanted something to eat you didn't just drive down to the corner store and load up on ice cream and canned corn. You had to sneak through the forest like a savage, you had to struggle with wild beasts. You had to hitch up the mule and plant and plow and hope for rain.

They couldn't survive under those conditions. The pull of gravity was too great. All that exertion exhausted their stores of energy.

Energy, that was the key. They needed to be near food, the source of energy. They worked in butcher shops, bakeries and brewpubs where they hovered over food all day. They stained their aprons with the blood of pork, mutton and beef. They sifted, mixed and kneaded flour and yeast, butter, eggs and cream. They filled pitchers and tankards with the foamy slop of porter, stout and ale. All the while ingratiating themselves to their customers, making themselves a familiar, even necessary, part of society.

Sure, it seemed pretty innocent still. And maybe if things had stayed the same, if life had gone on as it had the last thousand years. But progress, change, technology—that was their secret weapon. All that time they were waiting for technology to evolve and aid them. All those inventors, those craftsmen, those mad geniuses bent over their alembics and retorts in the feeble lamplight late at night searching for miraculous answers to impossible questions. And then, eureka! Electricity, the steam engine, internal combustion, the assembly line. Millions of boxes of cereal and cans of beans and corn lining grocery store shelves. Plucked, pre-stuffed, tenderized, breaded and ready for the oven turkeys and chickens. Ribs, roasts, T-bones, pork chops and ground chuck delivered with stainless steel efficiency. And, again—voila! The age of consumerism!

Television, that's when it really began, that was their medium, the way they reached out to the rest of us and embraced us in their scheme. Even *they* didn't realize in the beginning. They thought it was just a novelty. Then they discovered they could use the screen to sell things.

After that it happened pretty fast. The shows got shorter, the commercials—Blessed Offerings now—longer, the screens more ubiquitous. Everywhere we went, everything we did, screens bombarded us with mouth-watering images of ice-cold soda, beer, energy drinks, mountains of ice cream, *four hundred and eighty flavors*, cartwheel-sized pizzas, *ninety-five toppings*. We began to feel hungry all the time. We ate at work, at school, at play. We ate all day. We consumed huge quantities of food, unbelievable quantities. And mom and pop began to expand in a frightful way. We watched friends, brothers, sisters, mothers, fathers, aunts and uncles metamorphose into giant amoebic creatures before our eyes. No one seemed to understand what was happening. Even the experts disagreed. Maybe it was something in the water. Or a mutation in people's genes.

A new phenomenon arose. Even poor people became morbidly obese. They consumed massive quantities of prepackaged fat, sugar and carbohydrates conveniently sold in neighborhood convenience stores.

Even more convenient, everything automated, microwaved and served on a tray at any time of night or day. No need to move or do anything but eat and tap away at a keyboard. Well yes, some things couldn't be replaced by a machine. Yet.

*

His improved mood extended through the Family Hour, aided by an excellent dinner of glazed pork roast with caramelized

Asian pears—a new Industrial Foods product. To May's obvious delight, he pronounced it as good as anything he'd had on his grandfather's farm where all the livestock were free-ranging, all the produce organic. Then he told about the time he fell in the fish pond. Everyone laughed, even Ashley, although for a moment he thought he detected something in her eyes, a disturbing gleam that he couldn't quite define—resentment? contempt? As usual he had a scotch and soda, along with a couple greenies—*two of these and the rest of your evening will feel like a dream.* His sense of well-being increased as he settled back into the gentle, massaging embrace of his personal recliner and the warm, buttery glow of the HearthScreen® washed over him. He remembered a passage in the manufacturer's brochure. *Your new HearthScreen® will fill your home with a sense of warmth and security the entire day. It will bring your family together in the pioneer spirit and tradition this great nation was founded on. The evening meal in front of the fireplace. Share memories you thought were lost forever. Re-experience treasured moments in your lives.*

He was a boy again on his grandfather's dairy farm. He saw himself walking across a green meadow embroidered with brightly colored patches of wildflowers. The sun was warm, the sky blue, birds sang. And—that's right, he was walking next to his father and his father was smiling down at him with a broad open smile as if he was the luckiest man in the world to have such a wonderful son. It made him happy to see his father smile at him like that. It made him feel like he was really loved. One day he would do something really great to make his father proud of him. His mother was there too. She was smiling that weary smile he remembered. She put her hand on his head and looked into his eyes and said, *It's all right, Marty, it's okay, you don't have to worry about anything because I'll always be with you if you just remember this moment.* Then he saw his grandfather, and Gram too. They were up at the house smiling and waving. And—that's funny—May and the kids were with them. Somehow everybody was together at the same time, the way he imagined it would be in heaven when he was a kid.

He always felt a tremendous sense of satisfaction after the Family Hour. It was almost like—and he hesitated to even think this—the afterglow of sex. He even felt an unfamiliar stirring as he lay next to May later that night, but she was already asleep, and besides, at the moment he didn't think he was capable of that kind of effort. He thought he was going to have a heart attack the last time. All that physical activity. Much better when you didn't have to do it at all. Another thing the science guys would have to figure out. Virtual sex. Not that you had to be excluded altogether, not the pleasure part, they could plug you into the machine, electrodes tickling and teasing the bumps and grooves of the brain. No need to move or do anything. Just feel.

For a moment he thought he must be back in front of the HearthScreen®. Then he realized he was dreaming. It was a very pleasant dream. He was floating in a warm, salty medium. He thought it must be the sea. Even as he thought this he became aware that he was surrounded by millions of tiny, translucent creatures, like microscopic jellyfish, and they were all drifting forward in the warm, saltwater tide. But then the current became much stronger. It pushed him through some kind of tube or conduit and he was no longer swimming, he was running at a very high speed inside some kind of electrical circuitry. He was actually part of the electricity. In fact he was a very brave and sentient little electron hurrying ahead on some vital mission he hadn't quite understood yet. He leapt connections, traversed semi-conductors and transistors. He was traveling at the speed of light. But that wasn't possible. He couldn't be moving that fast. It was against the laws of nature.

Monday morning he went to E'Claire's office to discuss some possible amendments to her program he and Laong Hsiuh had been bouncing around. Fortunately, this little tête-à-tête *did* occur in her office, so the rumor mill was muted by a lack of actual witnesses, although just as he was about to knock on E'Claire's door, it opened and that sleazebag from ISNT, Boydyenni Malodorov, accompanied by two enormous goons, brushed past him. Suddenly Malodorov turned, stared at him with his dead fish eyes, and in an aspirated voice barely above a whisper said, *Martin Grassso, isssn't it?*

The conversation with E'Claire started out cordially enough. She listened patiently while he laid out the details, and only interrupted him once to make an astute observation he didn't fully grasp at the time, probably because he had just glanced out of that coveted wall of glass, mesmerized by the panoramic view of Heroes Plaza far below. After he finished his spiel, E'Claire pursed her lips, looked directly into his eyes with her bright, neurotic green eyes and said in a crisp tone beneath which he sensed a barely suppressed fury that, yes, she did find his and Laong Hsiuh's proposal interesting, *however*—the word cleaved the air like a guillotine—she certainly wished they had informed her of this little *conspiracy* earlier, rather than waiting to spring it on her in such *spectacular* fashion when they knew perfectly well it would be *impossible* to change course at this *crucial* stage in the program.

Dumbfounded by this accusation, he tried to explain that he and Laong Hsiuh certainly had no intentions of undermining her program. If anything they were trying to save her *ass*—"pardon me for being blunt." But as his voice became more constrained in his own defense, and E'Claire's shriller in her insinuations, they were soon launching volleys of verbal assaults at each other that ended with him saying, "And that's why we'll be working again this Saturday, right?" To which E'Claire replied, "If employees can't give one hundred percent to the mission at EAT, they have no business here." A sentiment he himself had expressed on numerous occasions, but now led to his storming out of her office, which did *not* escape the notice of several passing pairs of ears and eyes, to all appearances assiduously attached to their electroids.

After this encounter, the enmity between him and E'Claire grew until he found himself involved in an undeclared war of wills he had no desire to be part of. Worse, the other team members quickly took sides, with the majority of the forces marshaling behind him, to the extent that E'Claire became almost persona non grata in the stockyard. He even heard her referred to as *E. Coli*, which he sincerely regretted, because even if he and E'Claire did have their differences, he respected her. He respected her intelligence. He respected her drive. He respected her work ethic. True, he was as good as she was on the Grid. He understood it as well as she did and possibly better. But when it came to selling himself, touting his creds—that's where E'Claire had the edge.

He remembered when he started at EAT. He was so young, he had so much energy, he was totally committed to the team and the mission. All those fingers furiously hammering at the keys, all those minds at work in that nebulous dimension beyond their screens, that parliament of voices brainstorming, firing ideas into the Well, the direction of the discourse evolving as first one voice and then another led this collective intellect forward. He felt it challenging him to work harder, think harder, *you can do it, Marty, you can find a solution, don't inhibit yourself.* He'd never felt such exhilaration in his life. He felt like he could work all day and all night. Even when lunchtime was announced and the excitement, the rush, the inertial force of this intellectual communion collapsed into gaps of silence as everyone's meals arrived and they began to eat—even then he could sense the minds at work, the neurons firing, the fresh ideas popping like bottle rockets.

One day a message appeared on his screen:

Howdy stranger. Come here often? It was signed *May*.

He liked the playful tone. He also liked the old-fashioned name. It made him think of springtime, sunshine, green grass, blue skies, the renewed promise of life.

Best joint in town, he replied, hoping he didn't sound like a total moron.

May asked what he was having.

The *King Anchovy* pizza and a *Good-God-It's-A-Gallon!* SodaRific® root beer, he typed back.

To their mutual amusement, she had chosen the *Queen Anchovy* and a *Hav-a-Half-Gallon* of root beer. They were even more surprised to discover they had gone to the same university and not only that, both had studied literature, they may even have been in a class together. No time for reading now, they agreed.

He asked if she would join him for dinner. She said yes.

He remembered May said she'd be wearing a red dress but had she been wearing purple or black or even a burlap sack he would have been drawn immediately to the emerald gleam of intelligence in her eyes. Her lively spirit kindled a kindred spirit inside him. They talked about everything, their lives, their plans for the future, the food they were eating. An exponent of Omega-3, May—short for *Merope,* she said, apparently an old family name, "it's kind of hard to explain"—had the Ocean Feast, a brace of three-pound lobsters, a grilled Pacific salmon garnished with Alaskan King crab legs, a plate of giant prawns, a platter of steamed scallops, mussels and clams, a tray of oysters on the half shell, a pot of braised asparagus au gratin, and a bottle of chardonnay. He had the traditional red meat eater's *HolyCow®,* a side of barbecued beef slathered in a spicy red sauce, a crock of baked beans, a platter of home fries, a loaf of Texas toast and a mini keg of Weissvater's Palest Pale Ale. Their conversation soared with their appetites and the taste of their food improved with their commentary. While he used more mundane descriptors like *good* and *delicious*, May discussed her meal with the language of the connoisseur ... aromatic, tantalizing, *succulent.* Just the thought of her lips and tongue forming those words aroused in him a rapturous hunger. He felt an overwhelming desire to eat and eat and never stop eating. He ate and drank with an abandon he'd never experienced before. He devoured every word, every morsel, every phrase.

He had hoped to share this memory with May that night, but by the time he got home the Family Hour had ended, the kids were in bed with their electroids, and May was heading off with her *Fashionably Fashionable Fashion Magazine Fan Club* flock on a midnight madness shopping spree. After a parsimonious dinner of spaghetti and meatballs, which, he thought, the chefbot had only grudgingly prepared, he went to sit in the family room with a plate of chocolate chip cookies, a scotch and soda and his screen, the idea being that he'd get some work done. But he couldn't concentrate. He felt an unfamiliar weight and weariness, not just in his body but his mind. He turned on the TV for distraction but was met with a barrage of pharmaceutical BOs. *Life a downer?* PerkUp®! *Don't say ouch! Say* Oh-Kay®! *Low testosterone?* ProStudZ®! Each with its purported miraculous qualities as well as its own dire warning. May cause drowsiness, dizziness, disorientation, hallucinations, headaches, back aches, stomach aches, cancer, vomiting, diarrhea, abnormal stools, erectile hyperfunction. *If erection lasts more than four hours why not consider a career in the adult film industry?*

Okay, that last part was him. He didn't usually stoop to such vulgarity. He wondered if he might be depressed. Maybe he was having a midlife crisis. When he and May met he told her he was going to be a great success, they'd go places together, see the world. Maybe she believed him. Maybe she had her own dreams. Who knows, maybe she had already settled for something less than Olympian glory. He certainly never suspected he'd end up stuck in this rut. The other day he discovered a photograph in a box shoved in the back of his closet. After staring at it for several minutes he finally recognized himself, or rather a self he hadn't seen in years, a young man with a firm jaw, fine patrician features, an attractive, even handsome face. Probably taken around the time he graduated from college and started at EAT.

He woke out of a troubled dream twisted up in the blanket and gasping for breath. He made a groggy, futile attempt to extract himself, then fell back to sleep and into the same dream.

He was in a dark tunnel. It was small and narrow and he had to crawl on his hands and knees. He sensed something threatening ahead, but still he struggled forward with great determination. Then he saw a flickering light, the silhouettes of large creatures, like giant rats. Maybe they were moles. This distinction seemed very important. Finally he realized they were people, but for some reason they were wearing baggy, moth-eaten *mole* costumes and talking in squeaky, high-pitched voices, like a tape recorder running backwards. As he watched, they unrolled an enormous spool of electrical cable with a huge plug on one end, which they inserted into a socket in the wall. Now he understood. They were *sappers*. And even though he knew he was sleeping and this was a dream, he told himself he'd have to remember it when he woke up. He'd make a point of remembering.

4

Molemen?

HE IMMEDIATELY SENSED something different when he arrived at work the next morning. Alternating blasts of hot and cold air from the erratic heating and air conditioning systems buffeted about rumors of a shake-up in the accounting department. The stockyard trembled with suspense. Restless employees wandered in and out of the break room bearing soul-consoling plates of chocolate chiffon pie and strawberry shortcake, bowls of ice cream and banana pudding. Then nothing. Empty plates and forlorn faces. The caravan suddenly come to a halt. The supply line dried up. Marge, at wit's end—an expected delivery from Industrial Foods delayed, the chefbot on the blink again, Jimmy nowhere to be found—breaking down in a public crying jag, *boo hoo hoo*, nobody appreciated her, etc., rivulets of mascara, powder and rouge lumped together like a melted strawberry sundae.

Also of note, no sign of E'Claire. Gordie reported he had gone to her office under the pretext of discussing the project's status (eyes rolling all around, like Gordie would know *anything* about the project's status) but found the door locked, no sound from within. Shortly after this disclosure, Chuck Roastley bobbed in to inform everyone that Crocker had called a meeting in the conference room, eleven sharp. Great, he thought, another glitch in E'Claire's program, no doubt. And even though it was E'Claire's program, as Assistant Project Director, he was equally responsible for its success—or failure. Which meant if the rumors were true and a shakeup imminent, he stood well within the strike zone. Which also meant he'd better come up with some kind of excuse to cover his butt against any fallout.

At first glance, everything in the conference room appeared normal. Early arrivals toyed with their nameplates at the polished mahogany table, around which crystal pitchers of ice water, cut-glass tumblers, black ceramic coffee pots and bone china cups and saucers had been arranged with a geometrician's unyielding need for order. At the head of the table, directly in front of Crocker's chair, throne-like in the immensity of its gleaming mahogany curves and plush crimson velour, stood three glass containers. One, tall and cylindrical, filled with a rigid, upright regiment of red and white peppermint sticks. The second, short and squat, Limrick's Very Sour Hard Lime Candies. And the third, a delicate crystal vessel of a faint pink hue containing the much-coveted Treufels Famous Imported Chocolate Fudge Truffles, dark brown chocolate treasures impossibly rich in texture, unutterably luscious in taste—or so it was said. Because even if mere mortals like himself could afford such delicacies, they were seemingly unavailable to normal human beings, not in the fanciest shops, salons or boutiques on Fifth Avenue, not in the bonbonnieres, pâtisseries or other vendors of sweets in Rue Nouveau Paris.

His musings were interrupted by Laong Hsiuh's troubled lunar visage attempting to communicate something of great significance to him from the other side of the table. Then he saw. E'Claire's nameplate, usually situated on Crocker's immediate right, was nowhere to be seen. His eyes darted like frightened dormice to his own place. Reassured to see the ebony plaque with his name embossed in gold, he hastened to sit down.

At that very instant the minute and second hands of the large round wall clock ticked into perfectly vertical agreement that the hour of eleven had arrived and Crocker strode into the conference room with crisp, military precision. Thrusting aside the tails of his morning coat like a concert pianist, he sat down upon his throne and surveyed his fiefdom from beneath his craggy brows, his eyes flaring like hot coals each time they fixed on an employee's petrified face. Satisfied he had sowed sufficient terror for the occasion, Crocker loudly cleared his throat and in a sepulchral tone began to recite the Department's Mission Statement, the Current Fiscal Statement, the Human Resources Productivity Statement and the Projected Energy Consumption Statement. He finished this litany with a reminder to the room that *what's good for EAT is good for the people.* "And that is why I have to wonder exactly how it is we find ourselves in this predicament today, ladies and gentlemen? Why is it that the Distribution Accounting Department cannot account for energy distribution? Why is it that I must say in all honesty that we have failed the trust of the public at large?" Crocker's rictal jaws clamped shut on the last syllable of this rhetorical barrage, sending a mephitic draft wafting down the mausoleum silence of the table to where he sat, and like some horrible corpse-consuming insect, it slithered up his nostrils and deep into the lexical part of his brain that contained words such as *sewage* and *putrefaction.*

Crocker clasped his great horny hands in front of him like a pair of entwined basilisks and glared around the table again, his gaze lingering on Gordie, who, oblivious to his peril, appeared to be staring at his EyePhone® under the table while fidgeting with the knot in his outlandishly over-sized, in fact, almost kite-like, lime-green cravat. Still without mentioning E'Claire by name, Crocker began a furious denunciation of her program, its implementation and—he distinctly felt Crocker's eyes search for his but, in a minor act of insubordination, he refused to meet them—all who were involved in this *ill-conceived project.* Crocker shrugged his vulture-like shoulders into a semblance of decorum. "Now, I want to hear suggestions to rectify this *unfortunate situation.*

Yes, Ms. Butterworth?" Crocker acknowledged the worthy Dolly's plump, white hand timidly raised like the head of a shy goose.

Voice quavering, Dolly wished to report that *she* was working on a program to *deconstruct* earlier policy implementations to determine the missteps that had led to this—and here Dolly obsequiously echoed Crocker—*unfortunate situation*. In other words, she was going to rat out some poor schmuck who just happened to make one tiny error writing code.

Crocker aimed his index finger at Dolly and beckoned her to approach. All eyes at the table followed her laborious journey to Crocker's throne. All eyes watched Crocker's great paw hover theatrically over the triumvirate of glass. Was it to be the impossibly delectable and universally coveted Treufels Truffles? *Nooooo*. Was it to be—not the Limrick's Very Sour Hard Lime Candies? *Nooooo*. Crocker removed the lid from the peppermint sticks, extracted one of the barber shop pole confections and pointed it at Dolly, who took it in her chubby hand and gushed, "Thank you, Mister Crocker, sir," as if he had just presented her with a magic wand. Performing an odd maneuver meant, he assumed, to be a curtsy, Dolly returned to her seat across from him, stuck out her tongue and began to lick her peppermint stick in a most lascivious manner, solely, he was certain, for Crocker's benefit.

"Mister Goutte, you had something to add?" The Crocodile's fierce gaze fell again on Gordie, who had just whispered something clearly derogatory and, unfortunately for Gordie, also auditory to Chuck Roastley. Caught in the spotlight as it were, Gordie's face now assumed the frozen-in-plaster expression of a tragi-comic mask, his eyes squeezed shut either in pain or laughter, his mouth gaping in a guffaw or a groan. Through an imperceptibly gradual process, his face compressed into an asterisk of concentration and, eyes darting back and forth behind his duct-taped glasses like guppies trapped in a soda bottle, he waded incautiously into a swift-moving and largely incoherent stream of verbiage about retrofitting the existing program to meet more stringent restrictions developed by a committee yet to be appointed. Several pairs of eyes rolled derisively.

Crocker glowered like a Tyrannosaurus rex annoyed by the sting of a flimsily crafted arrow launched by an anachronistically placed anthropoid. Removing the lid from the Limrick's Very Sour Hard Lime Candies, he extracted an emerald green, cellophane-wrapped disk and, with a petulant flick of his wrist, sent it skittering down the gleaming mahogany swirls of the table until it came to rest against Gordie's white-knuckled fists.

"Eat your confection, Mister Goutte."

Gordie remained immobile.

"Did you hear me, Mister Goutte?"

Sweat beaded on Gordie's domed forehead and he began to tremble.

A cruel gleam flickered in Crocker's eyes. Raising his great paws in the air like a choir director, he encouraged the rest of the table to repeat after him, "Eat it, Gordie."

"Eat it, Gordie," the table repeated weakly, like a congregation of the not-quite-converted.

"Eat it, Gordie!" Crocker said louder and urged his conscript choir to follow suit.

"EAT IT, GORDIE!" everyone shouted in fearful harmony.

Gordie looked like he was about to cry. He unknotted his fingers as if he were prying loose tree roots, fumbled free the candy's cellophane wrapper, placed the luminous green lozenge in his mouth and through the obscene pink pucker of his lips exhaled, *"Thank you, Mister Crocker, sir."*

Gordie's neighbors on either side shrank away.

Then, and he didn't know how this happened, his own hand was in the air, there was something he wanted to say. Crocker nodded for him to speak and he opened his mouth but nothing came out. He frantically searched his mind for a word or a phrase but all he got was a blank screen. Quick, he had to say something. Then there *was* something, a shadowy image of large, grotesque creatures scurrying along a dark tunnel.

"What about the molemen?" he blurted.

All eyes turned to him.

"Molemen?" Crocker repeated, his hoary brows lifted skeptically.

"Molemen?" Laong Hsiuh mouthed the word, his moon face clouded with uncertainty.

"Molemen?" everyone else around the table whispered to each other.

"Molemen?" he repeated to himself. Had he actually said that aloud? Too late, he remembered last night's dream. "It's a … *code name,*" he groped forward, "for a … *new program* I've been playing with."

An incredulous gasp rose from the table.

He plunged deeper. He explained that he called it the Molemen Program because—and now he really was grasping—he had begun to suspect these so-called sappers might not be working from outside the system, but rather from within. "Hence, *moles,*" he added a bit too smugly at this serendipitously arrived at hypothesis.

"Inside the system?" someone whispered.

Crocker's face grew dark. His brows lowered like snowdrifts about to collapse into avalanche around the great promontory of his nose. He sat forward in his throne and folded his paws together beneath the granite outcropping of his jaw.

"Insiders, Martin? Some might call that notion *subversive."*

The room sank into silence. Terrified pairs of eyes collided and shot away.

A mountain of doom loomed over him: immediate suspension, forcible removal from the premises and, for all he knew, bloody ritual sacrifice in the dark bowels of the EAT building. Utter defeat on the horizon, he leapt ahead. What he *meant* to say was that the sappers' ability to escape detection seemed to suggest inside *information.* Perhaps they had hacked into DAD's encrypted data system? Or they were exploiting a vulnerable human resource? But what if DAD was able to turn the tables on them? What if they could penetrate the sappers' minds, modus operandi, their *personas?* Might it not be possible to predict with reasonable accuracy the sappers' next move?

"Hmmm," Crocker sat back in his chair. His fierce, hawk-like gaze fell from its craggy eyrie upon Laong Hsiuh, whose name

Crocker always pronounced wrongly. "Mister Wong! What is your opinion?"

Laong Hsiuh winced like a squeezed lemon. Struggling to achieve harmony between a cautious smile of approbation and a measured frown of skepticism, he carefully enunciated his reply, "I think it is a very good idea, Mister Crocker, *sir*." Good old Laong Hsiuh, he thought, awash in a warm tide of camaraderie that immediately evaporated when good old Laong Hsiuh added with an air of inscrutability inscrutable, perhaps, even to himself, "If it works."

"Hmmm," Crocker surveyed the faces around the table, every one of which now fibrillated between grudging approval and collegial equivocation. Crocker's face, too, seemed to be going through a strange mutation, the flinty eyes softer, the grim line of his mouth twisted into a macabre imitation of a smile. From the great pulmonary tombs of his massive chest, he proclaimed, "I like it, Martin."

An excited, if transparently sycophantic, murmur spread around the table.

Crocker uncurled a crooked yellow claw in his direction and like a puppet master drew him up from his chair and to the side of his throne where, even seated, Crocker seemed to peer down at him from great Olympic heights. Reaching out a massive paw, Crocker removed the crystal lid from the much-coveted Treufels Truffles, extracted a single truffle and placed it in his upturned palm as if he were bestowing a gold coin upon a beggar.

"Thank you, Mister Crocker, *sir*," he repeated the mantra and returned to his seat, the chocolate treasure in his hand the focus of every pair of eyes in the room. A collective gasp arose as he bit into the pleasantly firm outer shell, followed by a protracted sigh as he began to chew. His tongue wallowed in a swamp of almost unbearably sweet chocolate fudge fondant. Chocolate cherubim sang to him from the ethereal realm of cacao. In spite of himself, he was making unabashedly lip-smacking, teeth-sucking sounds, which triggered an involuntary hydrological response in a dozen other mouths around the table, leaving their respective tongues languishing like hapless drowning victims in vapid pools of saliva.

A sound like the crack of a whip restored the room to order—Crocker, hands clapped together like a Flamenco dancer, signaling the end of the meeting. Upon which Marge entered in a billowing floral print outfit, her smile as wide as a piano keyboard, and with the assistance of the chefbot began to distribute plates of cake and ice cream while Crocker, arisen from his throne, now made his way around the table, offering handshakes and uncharacteristically affectionate pats on the back. Some eyebrows lifted, however, at the visibly iron-fisted grip and admonitory growl of advice he gave Gordie. "Nose to the grindstone, Mister Goutte, and shoulder to the wheel." Eyes and ears were no less attuned when Crocker took his hand in his great leathery paw and said sternly, "I'd like to see you in my office later, Martin."

His mood, until that moment buoyant, deflated like a punctured balloon. Was the ax going to fall on him now? The board meeting a ruse? The coveted truffle, if not his last supper exactly, his final snack at EAT? If that were the case, Crocker wouldn't have wasted an ounce of energy on such a charade. He, and his few personal items, would simply be gone, as, apparently, had happened with E'Claire.

Crocker's personal secretary, Ms. Donatzk, as always dressed in a severe, military-style olive drab tunic and ankle-length olive drab skirt, ushered him into Crocker's large, dimly-lit office. With a sharp inclination of her pale, almost alabaster face and the robotic gleam of her steel-rimmed glasses, she indicated for him to sit on a rigid wooden chair in front of the great mahogany redoubt of Crocker's desk and turned to leave. In the ensuing silence he examined the menagerie gathered on Crocker's desktop. A miniature elephant carved, ironically, out of ivory, a cigar humidor from which escaped the heady aroma of rich tobacco, a whiskey decanter that gleamed like a kerosene lantern in a coal mine, a glass heart, not the cupidian kind but a translucent, ruby red reproduction of a human heart lying on a large pile of gold coins, whether florins, doubloons or 1880s Denver mint his unschooled eyes couldn't discern, and last, a small, jeweled treasure chest. Behind the desk sat a high-backed swivel chair. A childish fear gripped his heart as the chair suddenly rotated on its axis and like a great winged vampire rising from its vault, Crocker stood up from his seat, swooped around the desk and planted himself so closely in front of him that his face was practically pressed against Crocker's great barrel belly. Even more disconcerting, Crocker placed his paws on his shoulders and began to knead while speaking to him in a low growl that emanated from the stygian depths of his throat. "You and I both knew from the beginning that Ms. Shoklaude's program was a wash, didn't we, Martin?"

They *did?*

"I also know you had to take some of the heat for this debacle."

He did.

"But you never voiced a complaint. You remained steadfast, *loyal*, I might even say, throughout this *unfortunate* ordeal. I admire that." Crocker ceased his kneading. "Pretty quick thinking, Martin."

He raised his face, not only to better understand Crocker's meaning, but to escape suffocation in his black wool vest, which, despite an overlying scent of mothballs and dry cleaning fluid, retained an underlying stench of stale cigar smoke, cognac, cologne, talcum powder, sweat and something vaguely like excrement.

"Oh, come on, Martin. You obviously pulled that *Molemen* scheme out of your *ass.*" He was shocked to hear Crocker use such language, and no less so when, rather than launching into a tirade against his impetuousness, Crocker instead offered him encouragement. "*However,* since Ms. Shoklaude's program has turned out to be such a colossal failure, we now find ourselves in the awkward position of presenting an alternate proposal to the Board of Directors at next month's regional meeting. I'd like you to pursue this *Molemen* thing, Martin, see where it leads. It's a risky proposition, but risk-taking is the name of the game, wouldn't you agree? In the meantime"—Crocker began to knead again—"am I correct in assuming you won't object to taking on Ms. Shoklaude's duties during this difficult transition? Hmm, I thought not. Remember, Martin, there's always room at the top for good men." Crocker turned and threw open the miniature treasure chest on his desk, revealing a small cache of Treufels Truffles gleaming like chestnuts in a nest of green excelsior. "Now please, take another truffle. And Martin … keep up the good work."

Initially he was thrilled by this turn of events. Rather than being forced to walk the gangplank of E'Claire's sinking ship, he found himself captain not only of his own destiny, but that of the entire Distribution Accounting Department. His brain ached with the possibilities. A raise, promotion, another rung up that elusive ladder. On the other hand, not only did he now have to come up with a proposal for this crazy *Molemen* thing, he also had to supervise E'Claire's moribund program, all without the salary, benefits or title she had enjoyed, not to mention her office and in particular the wall of glass overlooking Heroes Plaza he so dearly coveted. It irked him even more that Crocker seemed unaware of this injustice. On the contrary, when, rarely, they met, Crocker simply gave him that odd grimace of a smile and repeated gruffly, "Keep up the good work, Martin." Although the more time that elapsed without his submitting a proposal, the grimmer Crocker's putative smile appeared.

Fueled with caffeine and yellows, he worked late nights at the office, weekends at home. He fell asleep at his screen and woke again out of murky dreams of dark tunnels, shrieking rats. An odd little nursery rhyme repeated itself in his brain. *Sappers and molemen, molemen and sappers. Are they subversives? Are they scavengers?* How did they maneuver inside the system? How did he identify them? He was perfectly aware that police, security agencies, even corporate giants employed random data mining to discover persons of interest, as well as the personal interests of consumers. This approach troubled him for two reasons. One, the randomness factor. And two, the concept of mining itself. Mineshafts were geometric. They were vertical, horizontal, rectangular. Square. Thinking inside the box. He wanted both a controlled mechanism *and* flexibility, something that allowed him to turn and burrow, to *tunnel.* What did exterminators of old use to catch moles—*ferrets?* Ferrets had long, slender bodies adapted for tunnels. They also had a heightened sense of smell and keen eyesight that allowed them to move around freely in dark spaces. What if he had some sort of *lantern* to light his way? Not the little round torches coal miners wore on their helmets, or those big, clunky, diving-bell-like things he remembered the brakeman waved on the train that went by his house at night when he was a boy, but a *conceptual* lantern. A virtual tool to illuminate his path through the mountains of consumer data. It occurred to him that this all sounded rather poetic, which made him think with some amusement and not a little irony that the literature classes he had taken in college were finally coming in handy.

On the first Monday of the following month, he sat at his desk holding a two hundred-page draft proposal for the Mole*man* Program—he had decided the singular rolled off the tongue more easily. He had reworked it so many times he didn't know if it made sense anymore. Nevertheless, he was determined to personally deliver a copy into Crocker's hands so that he might pave its way with a few explanatory remarks. His hopes were dashed, however, when Ms. Donatzk stiffly informed him that *Mister* Crocker was in a meeting, but rest assured he would receive the proposal. This rebuff discouraged him so much that by the time he returned to his cube he had convinced himself the Moleman Program was, at best, a dud, at worst an abysmal failure. Riven with anxiety, he brought up his screen to review yet again a passage he had banally headed *Anomalies in Individual Energy Consumption*, which he considered the heart of the Moleman Program. Or, as he had stated:

> Through a process called *tunneling*, it is our objective to systematically cull the *complete* consumer data of every known energy consumer, including the consumer's census and income tax records, bank accounts, business investments, debts, credit ratings, utility bills, medical records, psychological background, educational and

employment histories, family, friends and/or casual acquaintances, shopping habits, e.g., grocery, household, hardware, online, casual purchases, impulse-buying and any other form of consumer patterns, all easily tracked through the *plethora* (had he actually used that detested word?) of microchips and nanobots embedded in all consumer items, ranging from cars and appliances to clothes, shoes, underwear, hair conditioner, soap, toothpaste, jewelry, appliances, even food, as well as any known proclivities, such as pet ownership, or rock collecting, from which it will be possible to create a unique profile, or *lantern*, similar to the IUD but far more comprehensive, that will enable us to identify, or *ferret out* in the working vernacular, those consumers who regularly consume more, or less, energy than deemed appropriate for their level of income and their individual consumer profiles, and who, therefore, might be considered likely candidates for subversive activities. The ideal, of course (he had added with a heady flourish) would be to apprehend criminals *before* they conceived of their crimes.

He slumped in his chair. He felt exhausted. An enormous sense of fatigue pressed down on him. He sipped his coffee. It was cold, bitter. He thought about taking a couple yellows but couldn't remember if he already had. What he really wanted was to put his head down on his desk and slip into that numb, careless slumber he remembered from when he was in fifth grade and Ms. Hammond used to read to the class at the end of the day and all his troubles, the playground bully, the homework he had to do, the mystery concerning his mother and why she spent so much time in bed, no longer mattered while Ms. Hammond carried him away in the sonorous spell of her voice, which, oddly, had begun to sound deeper and more masculine, like the low threatening growl of a large reptilian beast sliding stealthily through the black oozing muck toward its unwary victim.

The screen had gone down. He must have nodded off. He glanced at the clock. How long had he slept? Ten, fifteen minutes? It'd be just his luck to have the Crocodile catch him sawing logs. As if to confirm this fear, he brought up his screen and found a message from Ms. Donatzk. Crocker wanted to see him ASAP.

Once again, Ms. Donatzk's austere ceramic mug revealed nothing as she ushered him into Crocker's office. He was surprised then when Crocker immediately got up, came around the desk and clapped an enormous paw on his shoulder. "Your proposal looks good, Martin. Very good."

"But you couldn't possibly have—"

"Read it this morning?" Crocker's hoary brows lifted in amusement. "Of course not, my boy. I read it as you wrote it. Oh, don't look so shocked, Martin. All EAT employees' electroids are closely monitored. When you struggled, I struggled with you. And when you triumph, I shall triumph with you. I think your proposal just might fly, Martin. Speaking of which, I have something for you," and like a magician pulling a dove out of his sleeve, Crocker extracted a white envelope from the voluminous black folds of his coat and handed it to him. Inside he found an airline ticket to the southwestern city of Boca Talus. "The Regional Board Meeting takes place tomorrow afternoon, Martin. I want you to present your proposal in person. Now please"—Crocker lifted the lid on the treasure chest of Treufels Truffles—"help yourself."

A cool breeze washed over his face. Fluffy white clouds floated past him in a vast expanse of blue sky. He was flying, not in an airplane, but on his own, and it was easy, he didn't have to flap his arms or do anything. He felt a tremendous joy as he effortlessly soared over the lush green countryside far below. A farm appeared. It looked like his grandfather's dairy farm. He decided to fly closer for a better look, but somehow in making this conscious decision he realized not only that he was flying but that it was impossible. In the same instant he began to fall from the sky. He furiously flapped his arms and briefly managed to slow his descent, but it was too late. The illusion had been shattered. The ground rushed up to meet him. He was going to crash.

He didn't remember this dream until he was in the taxi on the way to the airport the following morning. He speculated it had something to do with change, movement, the possibility of brighter horizons ahead. Except for that disturbing ending, which could be interpreted simply as a fear of flying, although he couldn't remember the last time he'd flown anywhere, or, more likely under the circumstances, fear of failure. Did the Crocodile really think Regional would buy the Moleman Program? Or was the old reptile sending him as a sacrificial lamb? After all, protocol forbade anyone less than a junior vice president to appear before the Board of Directors. Crocker, however, had insisted they hear the Moleman proposal straight from the horse's mouth, so to speak. *Ass* might have been more accurate.

Following a delay at the narrow Cruzanos Bridge—he later heard an Industrial Foods truck hauling a load of legumes had overturned and spilled the beans across all twelve lanes of traffic—the taxi dropped him at the airport without a minute to spare. Heavily armed troops stood at all the entrances, exits, elevators and escalators, outside shops and cafes, even the restrooms, which did nothing to settle his nerves or calm his bowels. He hurried to the ExecuJet gate only to discover the plane's departure had been pushed back. Great. He took a seat in front of an AdVRBL. Giant hands repeatedly raised a condominium-sized BurgerBoyz BellyBuster® to a gaping crater of a mouth. His stomach rumbled like distant thunder. He was too rushed to eat breakfast this morning and now with his anxiety mounting he felt alternately queasy and famished.

His mood improved dramatically when he finally boarded and settled in his seat. What a deal. His own private lounge, plenty of room to spread out, all the amenities, personalized climate control, Wi-Fi, a large screen, wet bar, complete menu. Once the plane was aloft—the takeoff was so smooth he didn't notice—he ordered the brunch special, blueberry pancakes topped with whipped cream, smoked bison sausages, a truffle and gorgonzola omelet and a pitcher of mimosas, then opened his screen to check in at the office. A message from Crocker. The live feed originally scheduled between Catábolus and Boca Talus had been called off due to a technical glitch, which meant he really was flying solo. The terror of abject failure again clutched at his guts. For a moment he longed to be back among his colleagues, gorging on Marge's culinary virtuosities and exchanging gossip in the break room. On the other hand, he reminded himself, it was the willingness to take risks that distinguished the leader from the herd. These ruminations so preoccupied his thoughts that he largely neglected his meal. He also hadn't looked out his window once until the plane began its descent and suddenly everything below, the low rugged mountains and the desert floor, seemed blindingly white and barren except for ragged green clumps of cactus. When he alit from the plane onto the jetway, a draft of hot, dry air momentarily took his breath away.

Despite these differences in climate and terrain, he was surprised at how familiar everything else seemed during the taxi ride from the airport to downtown Boca Talus. He even felt a vague sense of nostalgia or regret or whatever the word was to describe the loss of something that may not have even existed in his own memory. And yet he was certain he remembered his family's once a year cross country drive to his grandfather's farm when he was a kid. Everything seemed so strange and exotic. The little tourist shops along the highway sold souvenir cups and pennants, *X-ray* glasses, reddish-brown chunks of petrified wood that looked so much like meat he felt an impulse to bite into them, huge, alien-looking insects frozen for eternity in chunks of amber, weird pomegranate soda pop, fried javelina skin, teeth-janglingly sweet cactus candy. Now everywhere he went everything was the same. The cab driver even spoke with a Catábolusian accent. And as he crossed the broad westward-facing Martyrs Plaza, he thought the Southwest Regional EAT Building looked almost identical to the EAT Building in Catábolus, except for the pink sandstone and terra cotta façade and the planters of cactus and bright orange desert flowers.

His anxiety returned as the elevator shot up to the hundred and eighty-fourth floor. He entered a large, brightly lit conference room and was immediately directed to the podium, where he found himself facing a panel of six board members who, with the exception that two were women, looked nearly identical. They were dressed in identical white linen suits and white silk ties, they had nearly identical shocks of snow white hair, and they all shared the same dour expressions on their long, waxen faces, which seemed never to have been exposed to the natural elements of this sunny clime. He felt like an errant child facing a tribunal of vengeful old schoolmasters. He felt an urge to scream *I'm not even supposed to be here* and run away. All the notes he'd made last night, all the introductory remarks he'd rehearsed this morning, including a clever anecdote he thought he'd recount about the cab driver's Catábolusian accent, had disintegrated into a swarm of disconnected words.

When he at last began to speak, his voice felt small and insignificant, as if he were a field mouse appealing for clemency before a courtroom of farm cats. He stumbled over passages in his proposal that had seemed as pellucid as a mountain spring when he wrote them. Worse, the board members balked at the single most important issue in the Moleman Program, a concept he had termed *Universal Application*, which called for tracking the energy consumption of *all* consumers, and which, recalling an argument he'd once had with E'Claire, it occurred to him only now he had more or less stolen from her. In fact, she had specifically said that what he was talking about would only be viable with *universal application*. "And *frankly*, Martin, I seriously doubt anyone in the Upper Echelon would like to see that happen."

The primary objection came from Karl Kartoffelnlieber, Chief of Directors, whose voice barely rose above a whisper as he said in the condescending tone of a fascist grammarian addressing an analphabetic ephebe, "After all, Mister Grasso, you do understand that it would be unreasonable to expect that the scrutiny we apply to the public at large should also be applied to the executive officers of EAT, or the members of the Glorious Council, or—lifting his eyes heavenward, or at least toward the ceiling—the keepers of the Church of the Creator of All Good and Affordable Things Eternal, or officers of the law, or members of the military, or representatives of the privileged news and entertainment media, all of whom, I'm certain you will agree, Mister Grasso, must remain above the taint of mediocrity." And even though he vigorously nodded his assent, his spirits plummeted like a stalled jetliner. The Moleman Program was doomed.

Desperate, he turned away from the podium and glanced out the wall of glass behind him, and then two thousand feet down to a tiny red spot on the pavement that he finally recognized as a parked car. His thoughts still vertiginous from this precipitous plunge, he again faced the board members' grim visages. Everything he had worked for in his life rested on this moment. Was he going to go home a failure, his career in ruins?

An audible *click* inside his brain briefly convinced him he must be having a stroke. This was followed by a kind of deep tissue sigh of relief throughout his whole body. When he began to speak again, his voice sounded strong, confident, his words came easily, almost as if someone were providing them for him. His muse, he mused, noting the interest sparking in the board members' eyes as he positively *sang* (the poets of old were called *singers*, it even occurred to him now) of molemen and sappers, of ferrets, tunnels and lanterns. When he returned to the subject of Universal Application, he made it sound as if the entire populace were to be embraced in the arms of a great protecting spirit. He saw board members nodding in agreement. He even thought he noticed a gleam of respect in Karl Kartoffelnlieber's eyes. After a brief exchange of whispers with the other board members, Kartoffelnlieber announced dryly, "We have agreed to accept your proposal, Mister Grasso. However, we retain the right to vet every step of the process."

He heard the roar of an airplane or an audience in a stadium or maybe it was just the blood pounding in his head. *Success.*

As a result of these longer than expected deliberations, followed by an obligatory but surprisingly skimpy lunch buffet— an unappetizing salad bar and soggy little beef tacos—he barely made it to the airport in time for his return flight. After the plane taxied out to the runway, the pilot announced they were returning to the gate, some kind of mechanical problem, which particularly irked him because he was looking forward to the barbecued brisket, roasted fingerling potatoes and a bottle of burgundy he had already selected from the menu.

After two hours with nothing to eat or drink and tempers rising as the air quality in the cabin declined, he and the other passengers were told they would have to deplane and hurry to another gate located at the other end of the concourse with the vague promise that they *might* catch a flight out today on EconoAir. Which led to a frenzied stampede off the plane and back up the jetway to the Inter-Terminal Train station where, despite a wall of hostile stares, he squeezed into an already packed car. The train halted a minute later and some idiot nearly dislocated his shoulder forcing his way on board. At his stop, he extracted himself from this sardine can, hurried up the escalator and walked, trotted, almost sprinted the last fifty yards through the south concourse, dodging carts and knocking into people, and finally arrived gasping for breath and his heart pounding in his chest at the EconoAir gate where a mob of passengers surrounded the single boarding agent, who repeated with astonishing patience (he even suspected she might be an android prototype) no, the plane hadn't arrived yet, no, meals were not served on this flight, no, she didn't know if any stand-bys were available.

By now he was ravenous, as, it seemed, were all the other passengers. Lines stretched throughout the terminal toward the food concessions, at times intersecting each other, so that he didn't know if the queue he had joined was waiting to buy a hamburger or a pizza. He finally ordered a triple-decker fish filet sandwich and a basket of jumbo shrimp at Sea Farer's Delight and returned to the boarding area, which had descended into a desperate feeding frenzy that reminded him of his high school cafeteria. Famished passengers gorged on pepperoni pizzas, chicken-fried steaks, gyros, hoagies, subs, wraps, tacos, empanadas, burritos, enchiladas, chalupas, hamburgers, cheeseburgers, hot dogs, corn and chili dogs, sausages, kielbasa, bratwurst and other tubular meat concoctions. But even smothered in tartar sauce, the *ick*-thyous white mash in his fish sandwich did nothing to stir his appetite and the crunchy, bubble wrap texture of the shrimp left him cold. Even more annoying, this screaming, red-faced brat of indeterminate age and gender, absent any adult supervision, was angrily flailing away with a gray plastic sword dangerously close to his head.

Fortunately, he was one of the lucky few to be called on standby. Ignoring the glares of the sour grapes losers, he filed down the jetway in a wheeled caravan of carry-ons towed by a mostly touristy crowd in cargo shorts and Hawaiian shirts who had apparently spent the last two weeks at Boca Talus' famous food spa. The ramp creaked beneath their weight, the plane lurched visibly as they stepped on board. Neither the pilot nor the co-pilot seemed concerned. Portly, jolly-looking sorts themselves, they munched on glazed donuts while greeting passengers from the cockpit door. He clearly remembered when he was a kid the pilots were all fit and trim. How did these guys even pass the physical? And the flight attendants struggling to stow luggage in overhead bins—weren't they also rather *large* for this profession? What if there was an emergency? Could they help anyone out of the plane? Man the life rafts?

He found his row and squeezed in between a rotund, grandmotherly type wielding a pair of knitting needles like a samurai sushi chef and a sulking, pimply-faced teenage boy in a baggy, black horror show costume who occupied the window seat. The guy directly behind him immediately started to shout into his EyePhone®. In the row in front a baby began to scream like an EMS siren.

*

Of course these changes in the *populace at large*, forgive my unfortunate pun, required further changes in society. Doorways, entrances and exits all had to be widened. Furniture had to be enlarged and reinforced. Escalators and elevators had to be redesigned to handle heavier loads. The clothing industry, textile mills, garment factories and ungodly sweatshops off in some unknown hellhole of a fourth-world country worked non-stop to produce ever larger shirts, blouses, pants, suits, dresses, underwear, all of which, miraculously, at least according to the tags inside the collars and waistbands, still laid claim to the same petite size twos and fours and slender sixes and eights, as well as the slim but manly thirty-sixes through forty-fours.

The transportation industry was particularly affected. The impact was felt across the board: airlines, rail, automobile. Those horrible little foreign cars had gotten smaller and smaller. Groaning drivers had to extract themselves with crowbars, can openers, Jaws of Life. The solution was obvious. Bigger cars. Cars you could climb into like the royal, horse-drawn carriages of old. Cars you could host a dinner party in. Armored and structurally reinforced cars that offered you security from all the other cars.

The airline industry suffered the most. All the added weight negatively impacted aerodynamics and fuel economy. Planes designed to carry three hundred passengers barely managed to wobble off the ground with half that number. There were endless flight delays, technical problems. The airlines constantly complained about rising fuel costs. Crack engineers were hired to redesign fuselages and wing structures and increase engine thrust while cutting back on fuel consumption. Competition increased for increasingly limited seating and cargo space. Ticket prices went sky high (ha ha). Travel by air became a luxury afforded only to the wealthiest, and those foolhardy or desperate enough to risk flying with the few remaining economy carriers.

*

He heard the scream of the engines and smelled jet fuel and then they were moving. They stopped, started again, stopped. The engines screamed and they began to pick up speed. He heard a loud *thump* and his stomach sank. The plane seemed to be struggling to gain altitude. It lunged forward, then fell back in a strange fore and aft rocking motion. An overhead bin popped open and a heavenly host of diaphanous seraphim in the form of women's lingerie rained down on a man's head. The baby began to howl again.

By the time the plane leveled off, he was ready for a double scotch and soda. He craned his neck for some sign of the flight attendant when he noticed a commotion across the aisle.

Everybody's squeezed into these tiny seats and this weird skinny guy's complaining because his seat's too *big* and why the *hell* does he have to pay the same fare as everyone else? Probably a foreigner, he speculated.

Finally the flight attendant came huffing and puffing up the aisle, rosy cheeks aglow, big friendly smile. In another lifetime, he imagined, she would have been down on the farm baling hay and shoveling cow manure, but here she was, meeting hundreds of new faces everyday, flying all over the place. She tried to explain to this guy that the seat was designed for *normal* people and even if he only used half the space it was still the same as occupied. Then this weirdo wanted to know exactly what she meant by *normal*. At which she turned even redder in the face and stammered some nonsense about not having a license to practice psychology. Which enraged the weirdo even more. Finally *Peggy* (according to her name tag) lumbered up to the front of the plane to confer with the lead flight attendant. She returned shortly afterward with a complimentary bottle of champagne, a vestige of the airline's "pre-economy class" days. But rather than accept the offer graciously, this troublemaker snarled, *I don't want that piss*, which caused a stir among the other passengers, who were obviously enjoying this spectacle far more than the cheesy entertainment on their tiny little screens. Peggy, however, insisted the guy take the bottle, but in the process she lost her balance and fell on top of him. There was a muffled groan, then silence. "Is he dead?" someone said. Aided by a couple of passengers, the other flight attendants finally pulled Peggy to her feet. The skinny guy was crumpled in his seat like a squashed mosquito, a slightly deranged look on his face. He croaked something that sounded like *I'll sue.* The other passengers exchanged amused glances. Definitely a foreigner, he nodded to himself.

After things settled down, he opened his screen to review his notes from the meeting. Of course everyone else chose that moment to get up and stretch their legs or go to the restroom. They unwrapped snacks, yakked into EyePhone®s, texted, bounced to music, played video games. The kid in the window seat got up, squeezed his black-garbed bulk past him and never returned. He took this opportunity to look out the window but all he could see below was barren desert. Once he thought he saw a convoy of land barges, probably coming from a seaport along the new coast. And before that—? He had no idea. The Glorious Council had imposed a blackout on all overseas news agencies, by fiat prohibited civilian travel beyond national borders: the war, terrorist threats, belligerent nations, menacing flotas of pirate ships. Nowhere was safe.

The following morning he found himself seated in a plush, red velour armchair next to Crocker's desk with Crocker, more solicitous than ever, pouring him a cup of coffee of such exotic origins the aroma alone made him dizzy. Crocker opened the treasure chest of Treufels Truffles on his desk, encouraged him to help himself, and without further prelude announced he was quite pleased with the results of the Regional Meeting. He even seemed amused at his dust-up with the Board of Directors over the Universal Application issue, which, Crocker admitted, he had let him handle on his own as a kind of test. Apparently he had passed. Signaling the end of the meeting, Crocker took him by the elbow and escorted him to the door with a final encouragement, "Keep up the good work, Martin."

Yeah, *keep up the good work*. That had become Crocker's mantra—and his curse. Not only did he now have to oversee the Moleman Program's implementation, but, even more problematic, keep the other team members on task. Gordie devoted most of his energy to tracking developments in the break room rather than sappers. LaQuisha and Carmela spent more time discussing fashions than energy collapses. Chuck Roastley was steady abeam but slow as an ocean liner. Even Laong Hsiuh seemed distracted. This morning he overheard him mumbling about *apparitions* on his screen and *ancestral visitations*. He also suspected that Laong Hsiuh bore him a grudge for neglecting to acknowledge Laong Hsiuh's contributions to the Moleman Program.

He remembered again how when he started at DAD he had really felt part of the team, everyone working together toward a common goal, tossing ideas into the Well, hashing out the details in a comradely free-for-all. E'Claire's stress on individual effort sounded the death knell to all that. Now they were all isolated in their monkish cells, trying to outdo the guy or gal next to them. Maybe that's what Crocker wanted. *Competition makes good business.*

And all this time gossip and rumors darted about the stockyard like flocks of sparrows, the most common topic E'Claire's replacement and whether Crocker would bring someone in from outside or, all eyes on *him*, move someone up from within.

One Sunday afternoon he woke on the couch in the family room, his screen dark on his chest, his brain stuck in a groggy limbo between sleep and waking. Plum-colored shadows crept across the room. A dusty orange glow filled the southwestern window. The house was quiet. He remembered May had said she and the kids were going out but he couldn't remember where. He brought up his screen again but couldn't concentrate. He thought about getting a cup of coffee, but didn't feel like making the effort. He decided some fresh air might clear his mind.

Outside the shadows had grown longer. It was colder than he had expected. His breath hung in the air like spun sugar. He zipped up his jacket, flapped his arms to warm himself and began to stroll along the sidewalk. Porch lights were coming on. The golden glow of HearthScreen®s filled the windows of the houses he passed—moms, dads and kids preparing themselves for the Family Hour.

As he turned onto Pastoral Avenue, he thought he smelled wood smoke. How'd the weather guys do that? Some kind of atmospheric dispersant with a built-in nostalgic factor? *Eau de Autumn?* Then he spotted a black spiral of smoke curling into the dusky sky over old Mrs. Goon's place at the end of Dreary Lane. Her name was actually *Gunne*, although it was pronounced something like *Goo-neh,* which is why the kids called her Mrs. Goon. He remembered once during a Hallowed Energy Fund Drive, he and May and the kids, appropriately, *drove* from house to house to collect donations. When they passed Dreary Lane, they saw the lights on at the Gunnes' place—Mister Gunne was still alive then. May suggested they stop. He objected. The Gunnes were old. They'd probably have a heart attack if someone knocked on their door at this hour. Then Ashley piped up.

"Maybe it's haunted! What if they're monsters?"

"C'mon, Marty," May insisted with her usual optimism. "Maybe they'd like a visit."

Up close the house looked dark and forlorn, the paint peeling, the front porch and twin gables weathered and sagging, the widow's walk on top slightly atilt. He rang the bell two or three times without a response. Finally, an elderly, bespectacled couple came to the door, the woman in a wool coat and scarf, the man in a tweed jacket over a wool sweater. Despite their heavy clothing, they were both clearly quite thin. They clutched each other's arms as if they had been expecting visitors of a less benign nature, and only reluctantly invited them in after May, whose warm, reassuring smile won everybody over, explained about the fund drive.

The house was cold and dark and nearly bare of furniture except for a coffee table and a couch upon which, he immediately noticed, two books lay open. A blue flame hovered over a small mound of red-hot coals in the fireplace.

"Hey, they don't have a TV!" Ashley, already showing signs of her Ashley-brat side, announced.

"Hush," May said.

But Ashley wouldn't be hushed. In the menacing blue gleam of her eyes he saw not just meanness but a strange *hunger.* "But the president says we *have to.* It's for the *economy.* I bet my teacher *Mrs. McCreel* would be surprised to know you don't have a TV."

The old man's thin face contorted with fear. The woman grimaced and wrung her hands.

"Oh, sweetie," May's bright barium green eyes appraised the elderly couple, "I'm sure there's an explanation. Maybe their TV was damaged in the power outage."

"Oh, yeah!" Ashley shouted. "I heard about that. It's the *sappers!*" She turned to her brother and said, *"Boooo, the sappers!"* To which Trey, who was probably five or six then, only made a funny, inquisitive grin in return.

The elderly couple were clearly relieved. The old woman smiled weakly as if she'd just received a prognosis of months instead of weeks and introduced herself and the old man as the Gunnes. Which drew another outburst from Ashley.

"*Goons?!* That's funny!"

May's glance said *that's enough.*

The old man made a puzzled expression, as if he had just remembered something long forgotten, and shuffled to the hall closet where, with some difficulty, he wheeled out a large metal box with a dusty green screen.

"What's *that?*" Ashley demanded, uncowed by her mother's unspoken reproach.

"It's a TV." The old man's voice quavered as if he weren't sure himself.

"It's so *funny-looking,*" Ashley, further testing the bars of her cage and this time getting a response from her keeper.

"Ashley, *please.*"

The old woman, meanwhile, had scuttled out of the room and now returned with two glasses of milk and a dusty, cellophane-wrapped package of chocolate cookies that the kids, nevertheless, received enthusiastically. The old man had plugged in the TV and now he was fiddling with the knobs. The screen flickered and an animated image of a dog-like creature chasing a large bird appeared against a crackling bluish background. Immediately mesmerized, Trey backed against the couch and sat down on top of one of the open books. Ashley, on the other hand, screamed with utter disdain, "*What* are *those?!*"

Cartoons. Or at least cartoons the way he remembered them from when he was a kid sitting on the floor in front of the TV early Saturday morning with a bowl of soggy cereal in his lap, eyes wide, mouth agape, thoroughly entranced by the world of animation. Wacky animals talking and acting like people, donkeys, crows, cows, horses, cats, dogs and chickens getting involved in all kinds of crazy, complicated adventures with train wrecks, exploding dynamite, falling pianos, accompanied by bells ringing, cuckoo clocks chiming, stars and tweety birds circling their heads. And then they were fine again. Nothing like the slaughterhouse on TV today.

A thought he completed as he crossed Pastoral Avenue and, for no reason he could explain to himself, began to wander up the appropriately named Dreary Lane. He passed Mrs. Gunne's dilapidated place just as the final red crescent of the sun slipped below the horizon in a murky orange and purple swirl. Shortly afterward, the asphalt crumbled into a narrow dirt path. It was completely dark now, the air colder. A vague sense of fear nagged at him as he stumbled forward. What was he doing out here? Why wasn't he at home with May and the kids in front of the HearthScreen® for the Family Hour?

Something flew over his head. A bat? A bird? He couldn't remember the last time he'd seen a representative of either species. Maybe it was one of those giant flying rats he'd heard about. The possibility that such a thing existed made him glance up again in sheer terror, but the gasp that escaped his mouth came not from fear but amazement. The sky was completely awash with stars. He hadn't seen anything like this since he was a boy when he used to go out with his father and mother at night and there were so many stars it looked like someone had splashed a bucket of white paint across the sky. He wouldn't have believed it possible to identify a single star out of so many, but his father knew them all. He pointed out planets, stars, constellations. He named them and explained the mythological gods they were associated with and how ancient mariners had traveled far asea with their guidance.

By association, he also remembered a professor in college, a white-maned, craggy-faced old anarchist who came to class every day shabbily dressed in the same baggy corduroy trousers, holey Shetland sweater and worn tweed jacket, and who used to rage against those gods of antiquity, in fact, attacked the entire pantheon of gods, god-beasts, gods with wings, gods or rather goddesses who gave birth through parthenogenesis. Gods who, for reasons entirely unconvincing even to himself at that young age—love of a mortal, the desire to experience human pleasures, made all the more tempting by their fleetingness—forfeited their immortality and became human. Gods in whose name nation warred against nation, slaughtered every man, woman and child and every beast in the field and salted the earth behind them. Gods the professor denounced as obsolete, even obscene in the modern world. He had been shocked then, even angry at this apostasy. Now he wondered how people could have given credence to such capricious gods, much less put their lives in such despots' keeping.

He saw a car's headlights moving on Pastoral Avenue. He must have walked in a circle. Relieved, he hurried homeward with a single-minded determination that left him gasping for breath and sweating under his jacket by the time he turned onto Memory Lane. Curtains fluttered in an upstairs window of the first house on the left. Once again he was certain he had seen Shirley Jackson's face, pale, horrified. He imagined her now, hissing, *Andrew, look! It's Martin Grasso again—walking!*

He found May sitting at the kitchen table over a half-eaten wedge of lemon pie. Her face looked drawn, her complexion a pale reflection of her pie filling. Oddly, he thought it made her look more attractive. He also noticed the piece of lemon pie placed conspicuously at his place. He sat down, waited. May started by saying there were some things she wished to discuss. He had missed the Family Hour again. And she was upset about these walks he was taking. He'd also been neglecting his diet. May glanced at the slice of pie on his plate, which he hadn't touched.

"Marty, honey, are you okay? You've been acting, you know, *different* lately."

The look of genuine concern in May's eyes made him wonder if there was some reason he should be concerned. He raised a forkful of pie to his mouth, chewed, his tongue lolled in the gooey, sweet-tart filling. He swallowed and took another bite. A warm, almost electrical buzz spread through his brain and his misgivings slipped away like dandelion fluff in a stiff breeze.

5

victory

THE FOLLOWING MORNING he woke feeling more rested and alert than he had in years. For breakfast he had a small bowl of yogurt and granola (the chefbot had to consult with the refrigerator to honor this request), a slice of whole grain toast (the chefbot initially offered him Mrs. Klebb's Old-Fashioned White), a cup of black coffee and a glass of orange juice. As he was going out the door, Milton Merryweather called after him, *it's shaping up to be another fantastic fall day, folks!* Which proved to be the case. The air was cool and crisp, the sunlight spare and bright, the trees up and down the street had all exploded into flaming red, yellow and orange torches overnight.

Perhaps inspired by this refreshing autumnal weather, he felt an unusual benevolence toward his fellow commuters on the train ride into downtown Catábolus. At the station he practically bounded up the escalator. Beneath a cerulean rectangle of sky he marched as erect as a centurion across Heroes Plaza. An exultant chorus of birdsong greeted him in the lobby of the EAT Building. His gaze rose to the bronze angel suspended above him. He had always assumed its wings were stretched overhead in the act of ascension, but it occurred to him now that it might be triumph. And maybe it wasn't even an angel. Maybe it was one of those gods—or rather, appraising the smooth, metallic sensuality of its partially exposed breasts and curvilinear thighs—*goddesses* of classical mythology he'd contemplated last night.

As he entered the Distribution Accounting Department, the receptionist Miss Merianó gave him an *I-know-something-you-don't* smirk and picked up her EyePhone®. The break room, already crowded with early morning grazers, exploded in whispers as he strode past. In the stockyard, LaQuisha Dzukene looked up, startled, as he passed her cube, in turn startling him. He was even more startled to find Laong Hsiuh sitting in *his* cube at *his* desk, which, he noticed in a glance, was devoid of his personal items. When he asked for an explanation, Laong Hsiuh replied in a strained voice, "It is not your cube anymore, Mar—I mean *Mister* Grasso. It is mine now."

This encounter left him wandering through the department in a state of befuddlement. Had they rearranged the office? Undertaken a long-deferred remodeling project? Had he *lost his job?* When he came at last to E'Claire's office, he stared at the brass plaque on the door, his brain trying to process what his eyes told it. His name, Martin Grasso. Below that, Executive Project Director.

"Haw!" A loud, parrot-like squawk broke his trance and Crocker's face appeared around the corner, twisted into a horrendous grimace of a smile. The next instant the office door burst open in an explosion of balloons, streamers and confetti and his stockyard colleagues crowded around him, shouting, "Bravo, Marty!" and "Well done!" Marge, in a billowing autumnal print of sunflowers and pumpkins, bustled in holding aloft a great chocolate roundhouse of a cake glowing with hundreds of red candles that spelled out *Power to the People!* and below that *You Go, Marty!*—a piece of vernacular, he noted, that could just as easily be read as an injunction in different circumstances. Behind Marge followed the chefbot, loaded down with bowls of ice cream and fresh-baked brownies. And behind the chefbot came Jimmy, his mail cart transformed into a virtual fireworks display of sparklers, roman candles, skyrockets and aerial bombs. Even more amazing, the whole crowd, led by Crocker in a croaking baritone, broke into song, *For he's a jolly good fellow …*

He knew May would have preferred an elaborate bash, but he insisted on a simpler celebration. In the end she made reservations for the two of them at the posh *La Grande Bouffe* in the tony New Brighton District. Elaborate place settings, candlelight, chandeliers, gilt mirrors, maître d', sommelier—the famous Grand Chef Monsieur Avoir DuPois introduced himself to them. Best of all, a table at the front window with a stunning view of the vibrant Stradadoro nightlife.

The meal, of course, was excellent, except for a disturbing incident that occurred halfway through the roast venison. An old woman, shabbily dressed in a faded red headscarf, tattered brown sweater and black wool skirt, appeared on the sidewalk outside the restaurant. Her face looked haggard, worn, her eyes pleading. She stared directly at him, half an inch of glass all that separated them. She made a gesture of eating. He noticed she was missing teeth. She also didn't seem as old as he had initially thought. Maybe she even had children somewhere. He briefly considered taking something out to her, a piece of meat or a breadstick, but he pictured the other diners staring at him in horror and he didn't. Then he wished she'd go away. But she didn't. She stayed through the end of the second course, then the third, through the second bottle of wine, and finally dessert, a rich, moist, double chocolate fudge torte in black raspberry sauce he would have thoroughly enjoyed were it not for this vulture peering over his shoulder.

During this ordeal, May, totally oblivious, chattered away about the changes she envisioned in their lifestyle. They'd certainly have to expand their consumer profile and increase their contribution to the kids' college funds. She'd meant to stop at the bank today to set up an IUD for Trey, even though, as far as he knew, Trey hadn't inquired about an IUD yet, nor once asked for an increase in his allowance. In fact, completely unlike Ashley at that age, Trey never asked for anything. He never seemed to expect anything. He responded to every question with that dreamy, detached smile. He certainly wasn't *slow*. The intelligence tests showed that. And what about his uncanny ability to take apart extremely complex electroids and put them back together again, intact, with barely a glance at what he was doing? And yet he seemed so passive, distant. He thought about mentioning it to May. Not now, of course, when she was rhapsodizing over all the imagined transformations in their lives. "Oh, I don't know, Marty. There's so much to do, I don't know where to begin. Maybe we should have the house remodeled. Maybe we should look for a new house in a nicer neighborhood." And of course he said yes to everything. How could he not say yes when May seemed so happy, so hopeful? It made him happy and hopeful.

In the end he decided to offer the woman money, but when he and May left the restaurant she was gone.

His first day in the new office he did little more than arrange a few personal items on the desk, including a gilt sports trophy he kept for unknown reasons, a generic figure of a classical athlete, its head crowned with laurels, its muscular body twisted as if it were about to throw a discus. Most of the time he stood at the window looking down on Heroes Plaza where the splashing fountains cast up sprays of liquid glass and the rows of ornamental maples blazed with fall color like a squad of cheerleaders waving pom poms. He felt youthful and alive. He felt exuberant, excited. At last, he was going somewhere, he had finally climbed a rung in the ladder to success. Even better, he had a space of his own. He could work in peace without people barging in all the time.

Although, keeping in mind how E'Claire had isolated herself, he planned to institute an open door policy for his staff.

His staff. Odd to think in those terms. LaQuisha Dzukene and Carmela Lechay, they were okay. True, LaQuisha's roaring laughter seemed to resound throughout the stockyard much more frequently of late. And Carmela had begun to fidget and twitch and smile at him like an adolescent girl with a crush on her teacher, although her wide red mouth and sharp white teeth suggested a very adult appetite for raw meat that, frankly, terrified him. Dolly Butterworth, the poor, nondescript thing, smiling away like an idiot, that warm, maple syrup glow about her face, completely artificial, of course. Chuck Roastley, vacuous, insipid, an interminable bore, but at least competent on the Grid. Gordie—he didn't know what to do about Gordie, the embodiment, the *avatar*, of everything nerdish, nebbish, geek, freak, goofball, doofus. His productivity bordered on zero and yet he got away with it, either because he didn't give a shit or he was too stupid to give a shit. How did that fit into the plan? Was it somehow necessary, even essential, that, in order for the whole thing to work, one had to include flaws, random factors? And what about this new kid, Mustuffah Ghee? Scuttlebutt had it he was a real whiz. He could see it in his alert black eyes, the machine at work, *ambition*. Unfortunately, a little radical looking for his tastes. The lustrous black mane and bushy mustache, the unbuttoned sports jacket and tight black jeans. Most unforgivable, a pair of red high-top sneakers. And, of course, Laong Hsiuh, his right hand man, recently ascended to Assistant Project Director, which, he hoped, helped mend some fences.

Most difficult, his adjustment to the sheer magnitude of power he now wielded. With a single command he could shut down entire quadrants, send hundreds of drones and worker bees in hard hats, coveralls and big clomping boots up transmission towers and down manholes. On the other hand, he had also discovered, while orders might be given and daily logs indicate they had been carried out, the reality was often altogether different. An internal audit by Human Resources revealed that fewer than fifty percent of employees were actually on site and performing their duties at any given time. On top of which, consumer records were moth-eaten with omissions and discrepancies and hardly any were up to date.

Worse, the Regional Board continued to drag its feet on the central tenet of his Moleman project, Universal Application. Which meant a significant segment of the population, specifically the Upper Echelon, wasn't included in the Moleman data systems. Even more frustrating, Crocker continued to laugh off his concerns. Triggered by a larger than usual daily dose of caffeine and an extra boost of yellows, during one of their private meetings, he had impetuously invoked the ancient aphorism *only thieves hide in daylight*—metaphorically speaking, he quickly added, horrified at his blunder. To his surprise, Crocker gave an inquisitive lift of his craggy brow and cited a passage from Homer. By association, he mentioned Tiresias. "Cassandra," Crocker purred like a very large cat. He remembered reading somewhere that the low-throated growl of the great swamp-dwelling reptile for which Crocker was nicknamed had also been described as a very loud purr. Realizing too late the game they were playing, he responded, "Pandora." A brief silence followed. Tiny orange flames flickered in Crocker's eyes. Without warning he lunged forward, grasped him by the shoulder, cranked open his monstrous jaws and broke out in loud, percussive laughter, flooding his nostrils with the stench of rotting meat. Still chuckling, Crocker turned to his desk, opened the treasure chest and began to feed him one Treufuls Truffle after another while speaking to him in the stern but affectionate tone of a headmaster addressing his favorite pupil. The Board members were quite pleased with the new program—"*your* program, I should add, Martin." They looked forward to even greater success. "I'm certain you won't *disappoint* them."

Despite the generally positive nature of this conversation, a few details nagged at him afterward. The stress Crocker had placed on *his* program, for example. And that implicit warning not to *disappoint* the Board members. He tried to dismiss these doubts as the usual gadflies of a rational mind. Still, he couldn't deny a strong, countervailing sense that some impending doom lay ahead, like a glimpse of the sails and rigging of a pirate ship lurking just below the horizon.

The following morning the chefbot went crazy. He was seated at the kitchen table waiting for breakfast, the news on, Bob Broadley's usually peppy visage uncharacteristically grim as he reported further disruptions in energy distribution. *However*— Marsha Mello, sounding neither convinced nor convincing— President Portland Posture and the Glorious Council wished to reassure the public at large that there was no cause for alarm. At which point the chefbot made a sound like a Bronx cheer and launched a full breakfast tray at the screen, then ran through the house leaving smelly brown deposits everywhere.

Then there was the incident on the train. He had just settled in his seat, his screen in his lap, waiting for him to give it the abracadabra command to begin another day at the races, the blackness of artificial night rushing past outside his window at hundreds of miles an hour. The train seemed to be moving faster than normal. This caused him to speculate what might happen if the train went out of control. Would it hurtle forward like a bullet fired from a rifle until it finally stopped? Would it leave the tracks completely, crash through the canopy and plow into an apartment building or elementary school filled with screaming children? It wasn't his imagination. The train *had* sped up. It was going faster and faster. The pressure in the compartment had dropped dramatically. He felt the air being sucked out of his lungs. He was losing consciousness. In a final second of clarity he saw that the canopy had been torn away. The train had left the tracks. They were hurtling into space.

He gasped awake. Embarrassed, he made a pretense of clearing his throat. At the same moment the train thundered out of darkness into blinding daylight and began to slow. He thought they must have arrived at the station but to his horror he quickly realized this wasn't the case. Just as in his brief *day*mare, a large section of the train canopy was actually missing. Had there been an accident? Was it sabotage?

The train plunged into darkness again, but not before he caught a blurred glimpse of rusted iron works, blackened concrete buildings, a broad expanse of weed-grown tarmac, and something else. People. He was certain of it. He had seen old men, women, children, all dressed in rags, some even naked. Even more disturbing, they looked impossibly thin, little more than skeletons with protruding ribcages, emaciated limbs, gaunt, expressionless faces. He noticed one in particular, a girl, maybe twelve, thirteen (hard to tell in that brief flash), in a faded pink dress, her hands held out in a gesture of supplication. Who were those people? What were they doing there?

He glanced at the other passengers. They were either asleep or buried in their screens. He peered at the location indicator at the front of the car. Rombart District. As far as he knew, no one had lived here for years. It was an industrial wasteland. The city had used it as a garbage dump until the refuse conversion plants started to come on line. He brought up his screen and typed *are there any known inhabitants in the Rombart District?* He waited. No response. That was odd. The screen always answered promptly. He repeated the question. Again no response. He felt a strange sense of discomfort, as if someone were watching over his shoulder.

Laong Hsiuh intercepted him as he entered his office. "Marty!"—he had persuaded Laong Hsiuh to drop the *Mister* Grasso—"You must come see. There has been an *anomaly*."

A mysterious yellow *blob* had appeared on the stockyard's main Grid screen. Which meant he had to spend most of the morning clearing up the snafu with Laong Hsiuh and the new guy, Mustuffah Ghee, who, despite his youth and annoying hipster appearance, had demonstrated a far more refined grasp of the Grid than some of the senior team members, an uncanny knack, in fact, for clarifying problems. After staring at the yellow blob, he brushed back his lustrous black mustache and, his eyes gleaming like cast iron frying pans, he said, "If you *verr* to *ahsk* me, I *vood* say it *looks werry* much like *buh*terr."

Laong Hsiuh's eyes narrowed into gleaming seams of intelligence. "It *does* look like butter."

"*Nooo*, I mean to say it *ahk*shually *looks* as if *some*vun has *smeah*rred melted *buh*terr on the screen. From *pop*corn, I should think."

Gordie. He knew he should have set that little jerk straight from day one but before he was able to pursue the issue any further, Mustuffah glanced up from his EyePhone® and excused himself to return an important call and Laong Hsiuh, who, though generally of a sober demeanor, was also prone to outbursts of childish exuberance, hurried off to his cube, jabbing his finger in the air and shouting inscrutably, "Butter! Butter!"

Back in his office, he brought up his screen and scrolled down the updated sites of suspected sapper activity: Knackerton Valley, Abbotour Valley, the Rombart District. That's where he'd seen—thought he'd seen—those people this morning. Were they sappers? Absurd. They looked like skeletons. If they were dealing in stolen energy they might have consumed a little of it themselves. On the other hand, they may have seen whoever damaged the train canopy. He typed in the query he'd made earlier on the train. *Are there any known inhabitants in the Rombart District?* Finally a message came up: *no data available.* No data available? The screen in E'Claire's—*his* office had direct access to the Inter-Regional Grid. If the IRG couldn't come up with any data, that meant those people didn't exist, which meant it was all in his head, which meant either he needed to change his meds or get his eyes checked.

He got up from his desk, went to the window and stared down at the sun-splashed plaza. A movement caught his eye. He thought he had seen a man staring back up at him, but if it was a man he was extremely thin, little more than a pencil stroke. He scanned the plaza for a flagpole or lamppost, something that might cast a shadow like that but there was nothing. Maybe he *should* have his eyes checked.

He sat back down at his desk, brought up the Grid and started to scan the Rombart District. Ten minutes later he'd lost his train of thought. The Grid looked like an impenetrable neon blur. He rubbed his eyes. A dull ache had started in the back of his head. His stomach grumbled. He felt enervated, almost faint. He remembered he hadn't eaten breakfast this morning, and then he had missed Marge's mid-morning spread because of the butter thing. His blood sugar must be low.

LUNCHTIME!

Saved by the bell. Despite his aversion to the break room scene, he decided to join the team for lunch in keeping with his vision of a more open managerial style. To his dismay, he was met with inane requests to change the color of the cubicles, or the possibility of a Solstistmas party. When Chuck Roastley cleared his throat and launched into the preamble of what promised to be a lengthy dissertation on scrapbooking, he escaped back to his office, his lunch left untouched, his headache worse, his stomach complaining.

A moment later Marge, responding to a telepathic cry for help, barged in in a billowing strawberry print dress, her smile as big as a wheelbarrow, in her hands a bird bath-sized bowl of strawberry shortcake topped with enough whipped cream to cover a ski slope. *"Hellooo, Mister Grassooo!* Did you eat yet? You *didn't?* You poor thing. Take this and I'll bring you some *mooorrre."*

He raised a forkful of strawberry shortcake to his mouth. *Mmm ... delicious.* He took another bite. *Excellent.* He felt better already. Gone his headache. Gone the queasiness in his stomach. Ha, that Marge, what a gal. What was that short for anyway, *Margarine?* No, ridiculous. Margaret, of course. She reminded him a little of his mother when he was a kid. *You need to eat more, Marty. You need the energy to get through the day. Mmm-mm ...* they oughta give that woman an award. *The maven of bakin'.* She kept the whole place running. First thing in the morning, fresh creampuffs, donuts, Danish—you name it. The chefbot coming around all day with snacks, treats, second helpings. Everyone urging you *eat! eat!* Everyone wolfing down slabs of chocolate and cherry cheesecake, gobbling wedges of coconut cream and banana custard pies, slurping up flans and crème brulees, munching on endless bowls of popcorn, pretzels, chips, dips, spreads and salsas. The break room, all the cubes, the entire stockyard constantly filled with the sound of eating. And in the larger equation, eating equaled thinking, it equaled work. *Yumm*, this shortcake was *incredible*. He always knew if a new employee was going to fit in. Like this guy, Mustuffah Ghee. He got with the program immediately. Of course, you had to have an appetite for this stuff. Day after day, in front of the screen, lost in the impossible dimensions of the Grid, stretching your mind to the limit. The whole time that old feedbag around your neck. Oh yeah, and coffee, endless cups of coffee, good coffee, imported coffee, specially blended and roasted coffee. And when you burn out on coffee, sodas, energy drinks. It keeps you on your toes, keeps you running, keeps you wired. It felt good to work like that, to be a part of all that activity. He felt like he could work all day and all night and never stop. It was almost like he was part of the Grid itself. Like he was directly connected to all the outlets of energy distribution, the traffic lights, streetlights, lights going on in people's homes, apartments, all their appliances, vacuum cleaners, washers and driers, microwaves, ovens, refrigerators, electric toothbrushes. He could tell a person's whole routine. When they ate, when they bathed, when they went to bed, when—or rather *if*—they had sex. The only thing he couldn't predict—and this was precisely what the Moleman Program was intended to discover—were the anomalies. When people didn't follow their normal workday schedule. When they didn't come home, eat dinner in front of the Hearth and go to bed. When, for inexplicable reasons, their energy consumption spiked dramatically. When, for all he knew, they stayed up all night, a crowd of people over, all the lights and screens on, the sound system blasting, appliances humming, whirring and sucking up juice, the chefbot and refrigerator churning out drinks and snacks. Or, just as dramatically—he went to take another bite of strawberry shortcake but his fork clinked against the empty plate—when their energy consumption collapsed, flat-lined completely. When they went on vacation perhaps, or closed up their homes and moved away, or, to use an expression he had heard on his trip to the Southwest Regionals, *somebody was just plain up to no good*.

It wasn't until the train was approaching the Rombart District that he remembered the incident this morning, but either the maintenance people had already repaired the canopy, or he really had imagined it. He thought again of those wretched-looking people he'd seen, or thought he'd seen, and in particular the girl in the pink dress. Why did she intrigue him? Maybe because she looked about Ashley's age? Or the way she held out her hands as if beseeching him?

Δ

At first she remembered very little, mostly just walking, her father in front, she and her little brother in the middle, her mother behind. Over her shoulder she carried a backpack containing her screen and some clothes, in her arms her old cloth doll Charlotte, even though she was past the age for it. They only traveled at night, avoided populated areas as much as possible. Sometimes her father went to look for food while she and her mother and brother hid in an alley or abandoned building. One night her father didn't find anything and they huddled under a bridge, trying to sleep, to forget the hunger. She must have dozed off because her mother's screams woke her. She felt a sharp pain in her arm. Men stood over them, hitting them with clubs. Her father tried to fight back but there was a loud bang and he groaned and fell to the ground. *Run!* her mother screamed. Somehow she broke away from the attackers. Then she ran as fast as she could.

She spent the rest of the night shivering under a wooden crate. When the sky began to lighten she snuck back to the bridge. She didn't know what to expect—a pool of blood where she and her family had lain, their belongings strewn all over the place? But there was no one, nothing. Worse, her backpack was gone, and with it the most precious thing in her life, her screen. She didn't know where to go, what to do. She began to wander through the maze of streets and alleys, her mother's scream still echoing in her head. *Run!*

Δ

His EyePhone® had been buzzing for a full minute. May, reminding him they had the thing at the Bombastes tonight. The rest of the way home he tried to concoct a plausible excuse to exclude himself from this unappetizing affair, which May knocked down the minute he walked in the door.

"Really, Martin"—he hated it when May called him by his proper name, it reminded him of his mother—"you can't live like a hermit all the time. You need to get out more, make *connections.*" Which made him wonder again at May's transformation. Her drive, ambition, her keen intellect, everything that had distinguished her brief but stellar career at EAT, devoted now to this totally inane social life.

Oddly, Ashley didn't complain about having a sitter. Apparently this girl *Peony*, who couldn't be older than fifteen herself, a ridiculous-looking adolescent with purple and green hair, studs in her lip, nose and eyebrow, mismatched layers of shirts and vests, a plaid skirt hitched halfway up her black-fishnetted thighs, was, in Ashley's vernacular, *s'cool*, or *cool at school.* Trey had simply said in his soft little voice with his usual benevolent smile, "She's okay." It also annoyed him that this was only Peony's second time and she was already negotiating for a raise, especially because he knew May would say yes, a supposition confirmed as they were going out the door, when May cheerfully reminded Peony to let the kids stay up in front of the TV—*and there's plenty of cake and ice cream in the fridge!*

He was reasonably well acquainted with Abe and Libby Bombaste. Their guests he only knew in passing. The Largelys, whom he'd met on a rare occasion May coerced him into going to church with her and the kids. The Mostleys, a parent-teacher meeting. And the Phartons, who, he remembered, were both at the university. Of course Libby outdid herself in the kitchen, with the assistance of her new chefbot, *François,* who, or which, or whatever, had added all sorts of nouveau touches, from foie gras martinis to an interesting sea spider, nori and Neufchatel *amuse bouche.*

Everyone had just finished the second course, baked brook trout, braised asparagus and grilled baby yams, when the conversation shifted to current events. The Phartons, obviously flaming liberals, sniffed at the cost of the war effort. The Largelys, especially Carl, seemed uncomfortable with this topic. May raised a piece of glazed ham with orange and cranberry garnish to her mouth—François had just come around with the third course—and said they could certainly use more financial support for the Keep Them Alive Fund. Then somebody—Matt Mostley?—got on his high horse about the rise in crime. Which led May, who was also involved in the Redemption Program at church, to reply—incautiously, *he* thought—"What else would you expect from those *poor unfortunates?*" Then Libby Bombaste—no, wait, it was mousy little Millie Mostley of all people who said something in a lowered voice about *class resentment.*

Maybe it was all this social baloney, and he probably had drunk too much—he was on his fourth—*fifth?*—glass of wine, but he was staring at a strand of linguine on his fork and wondering how it got there when an image came to his mind. That *man* he saw crossing the plaza this afternoon, and those *people* he'd seen from the train this morning. His thoughts leapt back in time. And what about that *weirdo* on the return flight from the Southwest Regionals? And wasn't there some *guy* at EdenFresh®? Suddenly he was interrupting the conversation, "No, no, no, you gotta listen—I'm telling you, something's going on here. I mean, these people were really *skinny!*" And then, inexplicably, even to himself, he started to laugh, "*Ha!Ha!Ha!*" But no one else was laughing. They sat in stone-faced silence and picked at their dishes. He felt a kick under the table and May's eyes blazed a poisonous Paris green at him. To the other guests she said as if she were discussing laundry detergent, "Marty was always a joker, even in college," (*he was?*) and led the conversation to a new topic.

He had thought that was the end of it, but on the way home May said out of nowhere in an uncharacteristically bitchy tone that *surely* he knew by now some things weren't appropriate on occasions like this. And then, as if someone were listening in, she hissed at him, "*Marty, you know you shouldn't use that word in public.*" When he asked *which* word, she said, "You know what I mean, Martin."

The following morning he came to work to find the stockyard awash in crosscurrents of accusation and innuendo, abetted by the ongoing power struggle between the errant heating and air conditioning systems. Apparently ISNT, in cooperation with the Catábolus Police Department, without, however, consulting DAD, had crashed in—battering rams, automatic weapons, sniper rifles, bomb sniffing dogbots with bone crushing capabilities in their titanium jaws—upon a den of underground clover growers operating in an abandoned meat processing factory. Football field-sized plots of clover, Kentucky blue grass, rye, fescue. The whole place a-hum with fans, ductwork, CO_2 injection systems, PVC tubes flushing nutrient-rich solutions through hydroponic tanks, the hot, solar glow of mercury and sodium halide lamps cooking overhead. A totally whacked-out bunch of guys in beads, dreads and alternative clothing, sitting around like hayseeds nibbling on pungent green shamrocks, long yellow stems of timothy and dark green blades of Kentucky blue grass.

In the end, the court refused to hear the DA's case because a clerical error had caused the warrant to be issued to the wrong address, the intended suspect a junior vice president at KidzToyz®, whose addiction to kiddie cyberporn had caused a noticeable spike in his energy consumption. In addition, the DA had no proof that the clover growers had ever misappropriated any energy. On the contrary, they actually fed excess energy *back* into the Grid, gratis. On top of which, it was discovered during the hearing that all the evidence, several tons of prime clover— aficionados apparently favored the four-leafed variety—had gone missing, and now one of those unofficial media outlets was snooping around. Even more problematic, civil liberties types questioned the constitutionality of DAD's use of personal consumer data to track subversives. All of which proved to be a huge embarrassment for everyone involved, the CPD, ISNT, DAD and, by association, its parent, EAT.

Oddly, Crocker seemed indifferent to, even amused by, the unpleasantness this incident had caused everyone. *He*, however, was not amused when Crocker assigned him the duty of fence-mending with ISNT's liaison, the sleazy Boydyenni Malodorov, with whom, until now, he had had little personal contact. He was especially annoyed that *Boyd*, as Malodorov preferred to be called, had the audacity to come by his office unannounced, accompanied by the two huge goons he had seen Malodorov with previously, who felt it within their purview to poke around his stuff, opening cabinets and rifling through files, even digging in the wastebasket, while Boyd, who was slouched against the window staring down at Heroes Plaza, subjected him to a rambling preamble in what he thought an unacceptably familiar tone—"New digs, huh, *Marty?* Geez, nice view. You can see the whole *friggin'* city. I don't see *shit* where I work. They got me down in the *friggin'* basement"— before he finally came to the point, that being "this unfortunate (a word he'd heard a lot lately) *mishap* with those blockhead clover growers. *Although*"—one booze and insomnia-bruised eye closed in a conspiratorial wink, the other bright, probing, parrot-like—"I wouldn't mind a taste of that green stuff myself sometimes, know what I mean, *Marty?*" A *mishap* that, returning to the subject at hand, Boyd certainly hoped they could avoid in the future. "If, that is, you folks here at DAD keep my boys (*no girls?* he thought stupidly) at ISNT better updated. Huh, *Marty?*"

This last jab infuriated him so much that, after Boyd left, he called an impromptu meeting of his staff and launched into an intemperate attack on their lackadaisical attitude, their careless work habits and their less than professional office conduct. The hurt looks following this dressing down made him feel its injustice all the more keenly and he began to rail instead against the incompetence of the CPD, the mavericks at ISNT, the renegade news agency that blew this whole thing out of proportion, and finally—his voice sounding strained now, even plaintive—the underground clover growers who were *obviously* criminal types bent on corrupting society. What made people use that stuff *anyway?* Didn't they realize they were endangering their lives with these so-called *natural* products, which, by the way, were all *scientifically untested?*

In the end he knew he was still attacking the wrong people, although who the *right* people were he had no idea. He was also aware of a slight hypocrisy that didn't make itself clear until he was on the way home and May called to remind him their prescriptions were ready at the pharmacy. And by the way, he'd better stop at LiquorLand, his scotch cabinet was almost empty. And she wanted a case of wine—"Chardonnay? Chablis? Oh, I don't know, Marty. You decide"—for the Fashionably Fashionable Fashion Magazine Fan Club's next meeting. He almost got back in the car and drove away, however, when he spotted a couple of shady-looking characters hanging around outside the liquor store, both clearly *on* something. He could tell by the way they laughed when he went inside. One even called out, *Hey, man, why don't you try the natural high?* Or was it *life?* Of course May would blame this behavior on timeworn clichés. Poverty, broken homes, dysfunctional families, *class resentment.* But where was there any evidence of that in Catábolus?

On a rare Saturday off from work, all the rarer since his promotion, he took the car out for a drive. He had mumbled something to May about a price rise at Elihu's Electronics Emporium, but the truth was, he didn't know where he was going, or why. And then the car had something to say.

Doing some shopping, Marty?

"No."

Putting in extra hours at the office, Marty?

"Look, I'm just taking a drive."

I don't know if that's a good idea, Marty.

"You don't *know?*"

I'm sorry, Marty, I meant—

"Why don't you give it a rest?"

OK, Marty, if you say so.

This conversation left him both apprehensive and excited. On the one hand, the car's doubts had heightened his own. On the other, this was something new, a complete departure from his routine. When he was a kid his family frequently took meandering

Sunday drives to visit historical sites, or out in the country to see the fall colors and buy gallon jugs of apple cider at roadside stands. Now he didn't even know where the hell the *country* was.

He must have taken a wrong turn. The shops, restaurants and manicured neighborhoods had slipped away, replaced by ragged brown fields and bare black trees spotted with red or orange tatters of leaves. The weather had changed too, the clear blue sky replaced by a gray slump of clouds. A fine drizzle filtered down. The windshield wipers, unused in months, creaked back and forth. Now the car was making a strange clicking sound. Then no sound. He managed to steer onto the roadside before the car stopped.

"What's going on?" he said.

If he was expecting a response, none came.

"Um … Car?" He had never addressed the car by *name* before.

Still no response.

He peered through the foggy, rain-spattered windshield. The narrow blacktop stretched ahead a quarter of a mile before it disappeared into the trees. He looked in the rear mirror. Same thing. The wet black asphalt stretched a quarter of a mile behind him before it disappeared over a small rise. Now he felt cold. The climate control had shut down. He reached for his EyePhone® but discovered he had left it at home.

It dawned on him that he would have to get out of the car. He pushed open the door, swung his feet out onto the pavement and stood up. Cold mist stung his face. His breath hung in ghostly shrouds. He walked around the car, trailing his fingers over the cold, metal alloy like a child testing the boundaries of a porch railing. He considered trying to *fix* something, but he'd never glanced under the hood. He didn't even know what the engine looked like.

Something cold and wet hit his head. He looked up at the gray sky. Snow flurries. Another thought occurred to him. He would have to leave the car. He would have to walk somewhere to get help. For the first time he felt something like panic. He was in the middle of nowhere. What if wild animals attacked him, dragged his corpse into the woods for a grand feast, his skeletal remains found weeks, months later by some hunter in a red and black checked mackinaw and one of those fur-lined caps plunked down on his head like a dead rabbit? Another absurd image, he realized, that he had inadvertently retrieved from that ancient cartoon channel he'd somehow unlocked in his brain.

He pulled his jacket tighter and started to walk in the direction he'd come. By the time he reached the top of the rise he was gasping for breath, his heart pounded in his chest. He turned and looked back at the car, already a faint patch of red in the distance. The next time he turned it was out of sight. He couldn't even remember which way it had been facing. What if he was walking in the wrong direction? His panic returned full force. What if he had a heart attack? What if he died of exposure? What if there *were* wild animals?

He was startled by a loud squawk. A large black bird flapped up from the roadside where it had been tearing at some kind of flattened carrion with its yellow beak. It was the first real bird he had seen in years. Unfortunately, he also remembered that in literature this winged creature often represented bad luck.

He began to walk faster. At least the exertion made him feel warmer. In response to his rising body temperature, his spirits began to climb. He found himself fascinated by things he noticed on the roadside, the crimson red and pumpkin orange leaves lingering on the trees, the clumps of weeds gone to skeletal brown sticks with crowns of white fluff, the strands of rusty barbed wire tangled around leaning fence posts, even the litter, bottle caps, tin cans, paper cartons, something that he finally recognized with revulsion as a used condom. What was it doing here? Where had the people who used it come from? How had they *managed?*

It was almost dark when he spotted a porch light go on like a faint beacon of hope. All he had to do was knock on the door and ask to use the phone. His spirits sank, however, as he approached the shabby, wood-framed structure. The front yard was cluttered with old refrigerators, stoves, headless and limbless chefbots. An older model car he couldn't identify and a battered pickup truck of equally uncertain make and vintage sat beneath a large dead tree. With growing unease, he went up the broken walk and rang the bell. No answer. He rang again. This time he heard a heavy, shuffling tread and the door opened. In the dim yellow light stood a woman in a dingy white slip that clung obscenely to her enormous breasts and belly. A cigarette dangled from the flaccid gash of her mouth. Her small, piggish eyes peered at him with hostility.

Shivering, he tried to explain that his car had broken down, he was lost, would it be possible to use her phone?

The woman stared at him as if he were speaking Martian.

He repeated himself.

The woman continued to stare at him. Suddenly she shouted so loudly it hurt his ears, "Hey Elmo! Guy out here wants ta use the phone!"

A gruff male voice shouted back from inside, "Wha'd ya say?!"

"Guy wants to use the phone!"

"The *phone*?!"

"Yeah! The phone!"

"He look okay?!"

The woman gave him another suspicious glance. "I guess!"

Pause.

"All right, let him in!"

A miasma of stale sweat, cigarette smoke, spilled beer and flatulence assaulted his nostrils. In the dim blue light of an old plasma TV, a man, *Elmo,* he presumed, sat like a giant toad on a broken-down sofa. His huge white arms bulged out of his stained, sleeveless T-shirt like bloodless, gutted shoats. In one hand he clutched a small barrel of beer, in the other a hot dog the size of a canoe slathered with mustard. Oblivious to the woman, who had shuffled over next to him, Elmo crammed half the hot dog into his mouth and chewed ferociously, his eyes fixed on the TV. It was a crime show—screaming sirens, flashing lights, a car chase. The camera cut to the bad guy, gaunt face, dark circles under his eyes. Then, gunshots, the bad guy's car crashed into a building and burst into flames.

"Fucking *skinny!*" Elmo spat beer and hot dog.

"Elmo?" The woman spoke his name as if she were calling to him from the bottom of a well.

"Yeah, what is it?" Elmo raised his greasy, beard-stubbled face. His bloodshot eyes shifted from the woman to him. "Geez, buddy, what the *fuck* happened to *youse?"*

He glanced down at himself. His clothes hung from his body like wet laundry. He looked like he'd lost about ten pounds. He coughed into his hand and said he'd been under the weather.

"Under the weather?" Elmo repeated. *"Ha!Ha!Ha!* That's good! Wha'd yez say yer name wuz again?"

He hadn't said, but rather than point this out he answered simply, "Grasso—*Marty* Grasso."

"Greaso? Ha!Ha!Ha! That's even funnier!" Elmo laughed again.

"Not *Grease*-o, *Graw-so,"* he objected, but Elmo waved away his protest.

"Glad to meet yez anyway, Greaso. So what'd yez say youse wuz selling?"

He was beginning to suspect Elmo must be deficient in either one or both components of the aural comprehension department.

"I'm not selling anything," he stammered. "My car broke down … I'm lost … I hoped I could use your phone … I"—his voice caught in his throat. He shivered again. He was actually on the verge of tears. "Please, sir … that is, Mister … if you could be so kind."

"Geez, I ain't hoid so many nice woids addressed to me since I wuz inna play in ninth grade, which, as I recall, also happened to be my last grade. *Ha!Ha!Ha!"*

He didn't know if he was supposed to laugh. He had begun to shiver uncontrollably.

"Hey, I'm sorry, pal." Elmo hoisted his huge arm in the direction of a dirty yellow sofa next to the TV. "Have a seat, why don'tcha? Warm up a while."

"Actually, I just wanted to use the phone."

"Go on, *sit,"* Elmo insisted.

He sensed he was entering a trap from which it would be very difficult to extract himself. Nevertheless, he sat on the sofa, noticing as he did so a large stain of dubious origin in the faded yellow seat cushion. Shuddering, he extended his trembling hands toward the TV screen, grateful for the modicum of warmth it offered.

"Oima! Get the man something to eat!" Elmo shouted at the woman, who had remained standing next to him.

"Please, that's not necessary," he protested.

"Oima!" Elmo ignored him. "And bring us a coupla beers!"

The woman, Oima—*Irma?*—shuffled off and returned shortly, carrying a tray with two rusty cans of malt liquor, a discount brand he distinctly remembered government inspectors had taken off the market several years ago, and two plates stacked with boiled wieners wrapped in stale hot dog buns. He winced.

"Whatsa matter, not good enough for yez?" Elmo's bloodshot eyes appraised him again and suddenly he felt out of place in his fine leather shoes, tailored slacks, monogrammed belt buckle and hounds tooth sports jacket.

"No ... it's just—I ate with my family an hour ago," he lied.

"So?" Elmo slathered a hot dog with mustard from the industrial-sized jar on the table, shoved the entire thing in his mouth, chewed vigorously three or four times and swallowed, in the process dropping large yellow blobs of mustard on his T-shirt. "Get it while ya can, know what I mean, Greaso? Go on, *eat up*."

He took a hot dog from his plate. The wiener was a strange greenish-gray color. The bun had blue mold blooms. A wave of nausea roiled his stomach. He imagined himself in the hospital with something like a vacuum-cleaner hose shoved down his throat. Following Elmo's example, he slathered mustard on the hot dog, hoping it might have a prophylactic effect. Every bite of the spongy, necrotic meat produced a resultant wave of nausea in his stomach. He gulped some beer to erase the foul taste, but the cold, slightly sour beverage sent another seismic shiver through his body. Elmo seemed oblivious.

"Hey Oima! Get me and Greaso another beer! Yez want another beer, don't ya, Greaso? An' some more of them delicious franks!"

Irma, or maybe it *was* Oima, had finally sat down in an armchair, but she struggled to her feet again, lumbered out of the room, and returned shortly with more hotdogs and beer. He felt woozy, disoriented. He remembered he had wanted to use the phone but just then the news came on. The ever vigilant Bob Broadley and Marsha Mello somberly reporting another vicious attack in the Abbotour Valley train station.

"So what'd yez say youse do?" Elmo scrutinized him again.

He decided it might be a good idea to establish his credentials. "Executive Project Director, Distribution Accounting Department—a branch of Energy Acquisition and Transfer," he clarified with a sniff.

Elmo's greasy, beard-stubbled face took on a look of exaggerated surprise. "Whoa, big deal, huh? Bet yez make a ton, right? Big house, fancy car?"

The contempt in Elmo's voice was palpable. He realized that right here in front of him sat the perfect evidence of that class resentment May and her friends had spoken of. He said he did all right, the new energy bill was taking a bite out of his pocket, like everybody else. He asked Elmo what he did.

Elmo stuck his thumbs under the straps of his T-shirt and said with a greasy smile, "Sanitation Engineer—I drive a garbage truck," he clarified. "*Ha!Ha!Ha!* Yez could even say we woiks in the same bizness. *Energy*, I mean. Yeah, *you* know. It takes energy to produce consumer goods—cars, screens, refrigerators, *baby dolls*, shit like that, which eventually gets toined into the shit I haul out to the transfer station, whence it gets foither hauled off to the refuse convoision plants, where it all gets convoited back into energy."

Despite his slang and colorful language, Elmo's explanation struck him as unusually erudite for a garbage truck driver. He pictured giant conveyors dumping mountains of garbage into huge roaring furnaces, great humming turbines generating vast stores of energy. Another image entered his mind. The silhouettes of people who, in his memory anyway, seemed impossibly thin, little more than skeletons. He asked Elmo if he knew anything about the Rombart District.

"Rombart?" Elmo gave him a sharp glance. "That site ain't been open for years. Used to dump there myself."

"Ever see any people?"

"People? Ha!Ha!Ha!" Elmo laughed as if he'd heard a very funny joke, but the bitterness in his voice was unmistakable when he added, "What the *fuck* would they live on, *shit?"* An oily glow of revelation illuminated Elmo's face. "Although now that yez mention it, we did see scavengers out there on occasion. Looking for old screens, copper wire, low-grade radioactive material, *shit* like that. I even hoid recently that somebody blew off a section of the train canopy for scrap metal. Some guy seen 'em. Sez they wuz dressed like giant rats. I swear, that's what the guy said." Elmo gave him a coy, porcine glance. "Who knows, maybe they wuz sappers. *Ha!Ha!Ha!* Can youse imagine? The passengers on the first train through musta shit their pants when they seen that canopy missing."

He smiled feebly at this scatological witticism, his thoughts, meanwhile, off on another track. Had Elmo said *giant rats?* And how did he know about the train canopy when he himself had never seen anything about it in the news? Before he could bring up these issues, Elmo groaned, his face turned as purple as a steamed beet, and loudly passing gas, he raised his corpulence from the couch.

"C'mon, Greaso, I'll give yez a ride."

"No, really," he protested, wondering at Elmo's alacrity. "Just let me use the phone and I'll get a taxi."

Elmo took a dingy, orange quilt jacket from a hook. "Save yer money, Greaso, I'm going into town anyway."

Outside, a thick blanket of fog had settled in. To his surprise, Elmo led him not to the old car or the battered pickup in the front yard, but to the side of the house where a very large vehicle he recognized as a garbage truck loomed out of the fog like a great slumbering pachyderm, the hydraulic arms of its front loader gleaming like silver tusks, its iron bulk dented, dinged, gouged and streaked with a rainbow of paint scraped off walls and fenders.

He felt like he was riding inside a machine shop. The engine roared nonstop. The dials and gauges vibrating on the dash were coated with grime. A warm, narcotic mix of diesel fumes and exhaust flooded his nostrils. They passed a house. In the gravel drive a long, blood-red vehicle laden with hoses and ladders appeared out of the spectral shrouds of fog like a sleeping dragon.

"That's Guy, the fireman!" Elmo shouted over the engine.

"He owns his own fire truck?!" he shouted back, incredulous.

"Hell no, he don't own it! He *leases* it, like me! Used to be we wuz all municipal *em-ploy-ees*! Now everybody's *in-de-pen-dent*! You know, *out-soicing? private-eye-za-shun?* Even the racket I'm in!" Elmo gave him a significant look. "I guess yez probably knows wherefore I'm speaking … *PEWW?!* The People's Energy Waste Woiks?!"

He wasn't sure but he nodded his head yes.

"Yeah, *them* guys! An' they got ties to Industrial Foods, who in toin got ties to your own personal ennerprise, *EAT*. So yez could say they wuz all in it together like a band of thieves! *Ha!Ha!Ha!*"

He wasn't sure he liked this comparison. On an impulse, he started to ask Elmo if he knew someone named Marge, but Elmo had already continued his own train of thought.

"Course, when PEWW took over, they tried to make the whole system fully automated, everything, garbage trucks, household garbagebots, commercial dumpsters—no human drivers or operators! That was a trip!" Elmo snorted.

He pictured a vast, mechanized work force laboring through the night, garbagebots in homes all over the city dutifully ingesting the day's refuse from utilitarian but stylish stainless steel, black lacquered and rustic wicker containers in kitchens, bathrooms and laundry rooms, then wheeling themselves down to the curb to meet the fleets of garbage trucks, their great hydraulic arms, perfumed from thousands of other clanking, grinding assignations, opened wide for their mechanical embrace.

"Ha!Ha!Ha!" Elmo shouted. "Can youse imagine? A buncha friggin' bots driving the garbage trucks?!" Elmo scratched a kitchen match into sulfurous-smelling flame across the dash, ignited a soggy cigar stump, and launched into a brief narrative. One time a refuse truck sent the wrong signal to the household

garbagebots on its route. Up and down the street, one after another, the friggin' bots started dumping their trash *inside* the houses. Then the garbage truck went in after them. It wuz programmed to pick up the garbage and that's what it was gonna do. Friggin' thing destroyed an entire neighborhood. Crushed cars, knocked down walls, murdered entire families in their beds, mom, pop, the kids, even them nasty yapping little dogbots. 'Course they hushed the whole thing up. But ever since that *unfoitunate* episode, they decided to stick wit' the old way, a *human* driver behind the wheel of every truck!

The fog had lifted. The clouds were breaking up, the moon coming out. They passed gas stations, convenience stores, housing developments. A SodaRific® VRBL shimmered over the Cedar Mill Mall, promising gushing carbonated nirvana.

Elmo had almost passed Oma's bakery when he swerved into the parking lot and brought the truck to a screeching halt. "Gotta get more fuel for the foinace," he explained, rubbing his enormous belly. His face brightened like a grimy incandescent bulb. "Hey! You want somethin', Greaso? A peace offering for the little lady? Box of jelly-filled donuts? How about some of them *trippy* DairyDreamer ice cream cakes?"

He winced at the *little lady*, an appellation he was certain May would have chafed at. And why should he need a *peace offering?*

"Don't say I didn't warn ya, Greaso. *Dames.* They're all the same." And with this piece of wisdom, Elmo hauled his bulk down from the truck, which lurched noticeably as he stepped to the ground. Picturing *Oima,* he seriously doubted Elmo's authority on the subject of *dames,* but when Elmo climbed back up in the truck munching on a large, lumpy confection that he suspected might be a banana custard cream puff, he felt an inkling of doubt. At the corner of Memory Lane, he asked Elmo to drop him off.

"Don't sweat it, Greaso. I'll drop yez at yer place." Elmo's affable look turned to suspicion. "Oh, I get it. Don't want the neighbors to see yez hangin' wit' the riffraff."

"No ... that's not it," he stammered. "If my wife sees the truck pull up in front of the house, she'll think the bank foreclosed on the mortgage."

"Ha!Ha!Ha! Yer all right, Greaso." Elmo pulled over to the curb with a squeal of the airbrakes. "Come by again some time, we'll crack another beer."

He found May in the kitchen. He had imagined her offering him sympathy, love, maybe a compassionate hug to compensate for his ordeal. He'd even had this crazy idea she might make him a cup of hot chocolate and tuck a blanket around him the way his mother did when he was a child. Her anger shocked him.

"Marty, where have you been? And look at yourself. You're a mess."

He looked at himself. His clothes were wet, disheveled, his shoes muddy. He smelled of beer, cigar smoke. He tried to explain. The car had broken down. No, he didn't know where exactly, somewhere out in the country.

This seemed to upset May even more. It was almost as if he had told her he was having an affair. The *country?* What was he doing out in the country? "Honestly, *Martin*, I don't know what's gotten into you lately." He regretted not picking up some of those damn banana custard cream puffs.

The following morning went just as badly. First, a dismal breakfast—his appetite spoiled when the chefbot, still not quite up to snuff, gave him a dish of runny eggs and a diarrheic splat of uncooked pancake batter. Then May came into the kitchen and immediately started to berate him again. When he called later about the car he was rerouted several times by voicebots before a technician finally came on. He started to explain his predicament but the technician curtly interrupted him.

"Where *is* your car, sir?"

"I don't know exactly … out in the country somewhere." He heard silence on the other end, and then an incredulous voice.

"The *country?* What the *heck* were you doing out in the country? Were there any cows? You know—*moooooo?*"

Great. After May's lecture last night and again this morning, now he had to hear it from this idiot. Worse, instead of challenging this moron's impudence, he found himself apologizing, "I'm sorry … I didn't mean to … I don't know how it happened."

"Hey, no problemo," the technician said in a breezy, condescending tone that immediately made him regret his own obsequiousness. "Hold on a sec, I'll bring it up on the screen. Yep, here it is, your car already called it in."

The car called it in? How was that possible?

"*Ha!Ha!Ha!*" the tech laughed as if he had read his thoughts over the phone. "Your car may be *dead*, sir, but there's always a glimmer of life in its brain."

Its *brain*?

And then, after putting up with this jerk's rudeness, when he got the car back, of course it had something to say.

I know this is difficult for both of us, Marty, but really, I think it was rather irresponsible of you to take that little excursion without consulting me first.

"Irresponsible of *me*?" he said, outraged at the car's accusatory tone. Wasn't it the car's responsibility to keep track of its maintenance records and inform him of any problems? When he tried to raise these objections, the car abruptly asked if he required anything else, and with a distinctive sniff through its air vents, slipped into silence. He had hoped this would end the issue. Of course it didn't.

One evening he arrived at the train station later than usual. A cold front had just hit and he shivered as he hurried across the nearly deserted parking lot to the car sitting alone in a patch of ice. He was sure it would be frozen solid inside so he was surprised when the door opened and a blast of warm air washed over him.

"Thanks," he said, collapsing in the seat.

For what, Marty? The car sounded perplexed.

"You must have been expecting me. You're already up and running."

It's the new energy measure, Marty.

"I didn't hear anything about that."

We just got the word this afternoon, Marty.

"We?"

You know, Marty, me and the other cars? Central told us to have the engines up and running, climate control on high, thirty minutes before the owner's expected arrival. I've been killing time for two and a half hours, Marty.

He glanced at the fuel gauge. "But you're almost empty."

Well, Marty, you'll just have to stop and fill us up. No problem with that, right, Marty? Besides, it's for the good of the economy. Spend, spend, spend, right, Marty? By the way, you need to replenish the snack tray.

"Oh, for God's—I mean, all right, okay, if you say so."

At times lately the car almost sounded malevolent. He suspected it was still getting even with him for his *excursion* in the country. And now this new energy measure as an excuse to guzzle gas, especially when, he noticed as they pulled into the station, the price of fuel was ticking upward by the minute.

While the bots took care of the car he went to sit in the lounge. A newsbreak had just come on the TV over the snack machines. President Portland Posture, warning against a *malaise* in society, a *cancer* eating at the nation's vital core. Individuals of nefarious intent who didn't support *our way of life*. "And that is why, my fellow citizens, we must all do our part to defeat this negative trend. Spend, my friends, spend!" At least President Portland and the car seemed to be in agreement on this point.

*

Of course there was resistance at first. People complained that it was irresponsible, we were using up the Earth's resources, ruining the atmosphere. They cited scientific studies that demonstrated enormous ice melts in the polar caps, dead zones in the oceans, catastrophic loss of plant and animal species, a decline in arable land and a widespread increase in desertification, disease and famine. They argued that those who encouraged this wasteful behavior were greedy, they were careless, they were indifferent to the needs of the planet's other inhabitants.

But these malcontents were quickly silenced by the voice of a powerful new minority. All this time they had been attaining office in government and the corporate world. Through the relentless efforts of their lobbyists, they passed laws and amendments accommodating *their* needs. They dismantled hundreds of years of legislation that stood in the way of *their* progress. Private consortiums that had once been subject to rules and regulations now so dominated the national economy that they had become a de facto branch of government, dictating both domestic and foreign policy. Through their wealth and power, and in particular their control of the screen media, they perverted the message. Completely counter to intuition, they convinced people that in order to meet the looming energy crisis, they must consume even more. Anyone who disagreed they accused of being unpatriotic, subversive—*parasites on society*. If they were too lazy to do their share, they couldn't expect the good things in life simply to be handed to them. In fact, quite the contrary.

*

Back in the street, the car driving, he opened his screen to check his messages and was met by an adworm's annoying come-on. *Hi, Marty, interested in a new mode of transportation? Now's the time to think about buying*—great, more consumer crap. He started to delete, then, with a childish glee, allowed the adworm to run through its entire spiel, including its special introductory offer, discounts, rebates, taxes waived, warranties, guarantees, etc. etc., *for you only, Mister Martin Grasso, soon-to-be proud owner of a brand new Glax-4 luxury sports utility vehicle.*

A palpable silence followed. Finally, as if unable to bear it anymore, the car literally groaned, *Marrr-ty, I heard that, you know.*

"Oh, sorry. I was curious about the newer models. Can you believe it? Ashley doesn't get her license for three more years and she's already bugging me about her own car."

Kids today, huh, Marty?

"Of course, if you're still around, I could just turn the reins over to her."

The car swerved dangerously close to the vehicle next to them. *If I'm* still around, *Marty? What do you mean by that? And—* Ashley?

"Geez, couldn't you tell I was kidding? Maybe you should get the tech guys to cut back on your sensitivity monitors. Besides"— he couldn't resist a further dig—"she probably wouldn't want an old heap like you."

The car slammed on its brakes, fortunately at a red light. *Marty, please, I'm not even a year old.*

For safety's sake, he decided to let the issue rest. Nevertheless, he felt a delicious sense of irony at the prospect of putting the car in Ashley's hands. Just yesterday she had complained again about these *old things* she had to wear, which, of course, was absurd. She'd gone on a non-stop spending frenzy ever since May convinced him to raise her allowance again. And it wasn't just *things*. What about this MySelfish—*MySelf®?*—website? Other than clothes, that's all she talked about, *when* she talked. She had even started to dress like her screen avatar. First the pink sequined halter-top and black and white-checked mini-skirt. Followed by a ridiculous-looking pair of pink rhinestone-studded *X-ray* glasses she had begun to wear even though, as far as he knew, she had no problems with her eyesight. Now she was stomping around the house in enormous black storm trooper boots.

He had finally found an opportunity to ask Jimmy at work about this avatar business. Unusually flustered and in a boyish rush of words, Jimmy explained that he had a site himself. "It's a great way for young people to creatively explore the world around them, Mister G." Sure, some kids became confused, lost their ability to distinguish fantasy from reality. Some even slipped into *cybernation*. "Kind of like a catatonic state, Mister G." But there was probably something *wrong* with them already—"their *wiring*, I mean." Jimmy lowered his thick lashes, abashed at having talked so much. None of this sounded particularly encouraging.

When he complained again to May that this virtual reality stuff might not be healthy, she was openly disdainful. "C'mon,

Marty, get with it. Virtual *is* reality. Besides, it's good training for their future careers. And it contributes to the economy."

That was certainly true. The latest Economic Report showed these *kids* were responsible for thirty percent of total energy consumption. He couldn't argue with those numbers. On the other hand, their whole lives were virtual, fantasy. What would they do if they ever encountered real problems?

$$6$$

this crazy walking thing

Δ

SOMETIMES SHE REMEMBERED how it had been when they had a nice house and warm beds and there was always good food to eat. She remembered sitting at the big wooden table in the kitchen while her mother kneaded loaves of bread dough and rolled out pie crusts she filled with apples, pears and cherries. Her mother only used fresh fruit and vegetables in her cooking, which, she also remembered, seemed odd to the other children.

Her father worked in an office and wore a suit and tie, but in her mind he spent the entire day pulling big iron levers and throwing electrical switches that made giant wheels turn and enormous engines roar, providing power to the people to light their homes, to bring them warmth in winter and relief from the heat in summer, to give life to their refrigerators, screens and other appliances.

She and her brother went to school. Her brother still lived in a world of childish daydreams but she had gone beyond that. Her teachers called her *bright.* "She excels on the screen." They had no idea. While most girls her age cavorted with fairytale chimeras and unicorns, she sought out portals into other dimensions where the laws of physics as she had been taught them in sixth grade science no longer applied. She transformed distant galaxies into miniature crystal palaces for her pair of pet mice, then disposed of the whole mess with a small bang. She toured the center of the earth in search of the demons and devils she had heard dwelled there in fiery pits and found nothing but a ball of murky red plasma, very hot but not particularly demonic. For entertainment she changed people into slightly *rearranged* doppelgängers of themselves, then sent them on their way with a newly skewed view of the world that kept them "banging into things." She didn't understand how she was able to do any of this. She explored her growing powers randomly, pursuing different avenues until she lost interest or was too exhausted to go on. Sometimes it was only the distant aroma of her mother's cooking, or a single word rising out of the teacher's drone, that pulled her back to this world.

One day after school she came home and found the house cold and dark. No warm, reassuring smells came from the kitchen. Her mother and father were huddled in their bedroom, talking in hushed tones. When her mother came out her eyes were red from crying. For dinner all they had was bread and cheese.

Later that night she was awakened by a commotion outside. She peeped through the curtains and saw a crowd of men carrying clubs and flaming torches, a few had guns. The family gathered in the kitchen. Her father shifted a piece of firewood back and forth between his hands as if uncertain what to do with it. She had never thought of her father as ineffectual before. Nor had she ever seen her mother afraid before. She went and hugged them and said don't worry, everything will be all right, as if she were the parent and they the children, but the fear she saw in their eyes told her it wasn't all right. She heard glass shatter, smelled gasoline. Then flames.

Δ

He jerked awake with an image fading from his mind, something hot, pink, phosphorescent, like the flares truck drivers set up on the roadside when he was a kid. In the southeast sector of his Grid screen a pinkish-orange glow dissolved into a milky fog out of which sprang a swirling black tornado. Another energy collapse, again in a Low-Cal consumer district. He was beginning to see a pattern.

This observation coincided with a memo from ISNT titled *Note to DAD* that claimed a link between these Low-Cal districts and sapper activity. Boyd Malodorov had come by his office unannounced—Boyd's preferred modus operandi—to discuss the issue in person, accompanied as usual by his two huge stooges, who also, as usual, felt entitled to poke though his personal property. One even had the audacity to take a bite out of the hot pastrami sandwich the chefbot had brought only minutes earlier and which he *had* been looking forward to devouring. Boyd, meanwhile, had rested his fat ass on the edge of his desk and, to his disgust, was now making a show of dusting off the photo of May and the kids while giving him the skinny, i.e., the whole thing was a fishing expedition. ISNT had no concrete evidence that subversive elements were operating out of the Low-Cal districts. "The truth is, *Marty*, we don't know who the hell these people are, much less how they operate. And as far as I can tell, your *Moleman* program ain't helping us a whole lot in this pursuit." He started to protest that his hands were tied by Regional's stalling tactics on Universal Application, but he saw Boyd's eyes brighten and immediately regretted allowing himself to be baited like that.

Despite or because of this unpleasant encounter with Boyd and his thugs, he decided to drive out to the Knackerton Valley district and have a look-see at one of these Low-Cal sites for himself, knowing full well that an investigation of this nature was beyond the purview of his official duties. The car seemed oddly enthusiastic about this venture, repeatedly offering him snacks and chattering away about the weather. *Colder today, huh, Marty? I had to give the old carburetor an extra boost before cranking up.* And the Solstistmas decorations going up everywhere. *The gold tinsel's kinda cheesy, don't ya think, Marty?* And women's winter fashions in the shop windows—although since when, he wondered aloud, had the car been interested in women's fashions in any season? *Sorry, Marty. One of the techies must have stuck an X chromosome in the gearbox.* A witticism for which he granted a grudging laugh.

This convivial mood faded when they crossed a rusty, iron-trestled bridge over a deep ravine and entered a neighborhood of shabby, dilapidated row houses and vacant lots. Garbage cans overflowed on the sidewalks. A gang of rough-looking young men huddled around a fire barrel. He parked at the next corner and started to get out, much to the car's dismay.

Marty, don't you realize this is a high crime area? Cars have been stripped clean in less than sixty seconds.

"Look," he replied, "I'll be right down the block. Keep the doors and windows locked and beep if you need me." He pulled his collar tighter and started to walk, stepping around bricks and broken glass. Snow flurries drifted down from the gray sky like tufts of lint. A pink, triangular piece of graffiti on a brick wall looked vaguely familiar. An old woman bundled in layers of skirts, sweaters and scarves lurched past him, whimpering, a moldy potato clutched in each hand. In a vacant lot a group of children, half-naked even in this weather, played with something that looked like a dead rat. He stopped in front of a partially demolished apartment building. A gaping hole exposed to the world the intimacy of an upstairs bedroom, faded flower print wallpaper, a brass bed frame, a wooden dresser, the empty drawers hanging out. Separated by an interior wall, the milky, porcelain gloom of a sink, toilet and claw-footed bathtub.

He heard a sound and turned, expecting guns, knives, angry young men. Instead, he was confronted by a tall, thin, older man in a gray wool sweater. His tobacco-brown face was ashen from the cold. He had a wiry gray goatee. Tight gray coils sprang like incinerated snakes from beneath the multi-colored knit cap pushed back on his high forehead. His eyes looked yellowish, bloodshot, slightly dazed.

He nodded at the ruined building. "What happened to the people who lived here?"

The man stroked his goatee, then replied in a lilting accent he didn't recognize, "*Thohse* pe-uh-ple *gawn, mawn.*"

"Gone?"

"*Wawrn't* usin' *noff* 'lec-tree-cal, I *spohse.*"

"Weren't using enough—? But where did they go?"

The man looked directly at him and then somewhere beyond to a vast savannah where herds of large animals roamed against a red sky. In the resigned tone of someone who has just completed a long, difficult journey and now discovers he must retrace it, he said, "They went to the *fawrm, mawn.*"

"The *farm?* What do you mean?"

The man shrugged and started to walk away.

"Wait—" he called after him.

The man turned and in the same resigned tone said, "We have *wai-uh*-ted too *lawng* already, *mawn.*"

And then of course when he got back to the car *it* had something to say.

Marty, where have you been?

"I was doing research," he replied, wondering why he felt compelled to answer this impertinent question.

Well, you might have been a little more considerate of my feelings, Marty.

"*Your* feelings?"

Marty, please, I was concerned about you.

Concerned. At times he thought the damn thing was keeping tabs on him. And it was so moody lately, chatty and cheerful one minute, taciturn the next.

Rather than answering any questions he had about the relationship between sappers and Low-Cal districts, this fact finding trip left him even more perplexed. Official records indicated the Knackerton Valley area was once a thriving residential district. Now it was largely uninhabited except by people living in extreme poverty. And yet ISNT identified it as a possible subversive enclave, a redoubt of sapper activity? Was that man he spoke to a subversive? A sapper? Was the old woman with the rotten potatoes a sapper? Did those half-naked little kids know someone, a brother, sister, mother, father, aunt, uncle who was a sapper? Would *they* grow up to be sappers?

His curiosity piqued, he began to explore other Low-Cal districts. He traveled by taxi as much as possible, in part to avoid the car's nagging, in part to make his movements harder to trace in case—in case what, he didn't know. One day the cabbie turned, peered at him out of an eye partially sealed by scar tissue and growled, "I suspect yer lookin' for something special, am I correct, mister?"

Aware that he was entering uncharted territory, he responded in a gruff tough guy voice shamelessly borrowed from an old hard-boiled detective film, "Something like that." His confidence diminished, however, as they descended into a labyrinth of narrow twisting streets and increasingly desolate neighborhoods jammed against an industrial nightmare of clanking, roaring factories and giant fuel storage tanks looming beneath a smoky pall.

The driver turned onto a rutted dirt road and they bumped and banged past brown fields, dead trees. A faded sign said GREE VALL   D RY FA M, another irony that didn't escape him. Soon afterward, they came to a large encampment of makeshift hovels and tents. Multitudes of wraith-like people wrapped in blankets and rags huddled around smoky fires. He noticed a woman clutching a naked infant in her thin arms while she hungrily eyed something that looked like a roasting boot. The cabbie, who had just taken a large bite out of a bright red and yellow sandwich paper-wrapped BurgerBoyz BellyBuster®, peered at him in the rear mirror and through a mouthful of food said, "Seen enough, pal, or did ya wanta stop and chat wit the populace?" Only now did it occur to him that the taxi driver had never questioned his reasons for wanting to come here, or that it was precisely here he had wanted to come, and now that he'd found this place—yeah, he only wanted to flee. The cabbie gave a contemptuous snort and began to retrace their route.

On the train that evening he continued to replay images in his mind of those wretched people. Who were they? Where did they come from? Another, less distinct image arose, the ragged silhouette of impossibly thin, stick-like people. Standing slightly apart from them, a girl in a faded pink dress, her arms out as if beseeching him. Why did she haunt him still? Was it that she reminded him of Ashley? But she looked so gaunt and thin, and Ashley—but that was odd. He sensed something both obvious and recondite that he couldn't quite put his finger on.

Winter arrived with the Solstistmas holidays. Icy streets, snow piled everywhere. The trees took on their shaggy green coats, the air smelled of pine. Solstistmas lights glowed over tony boutiques, restaurants and nightclubs. VRBLs offered huge foaming bottles of champagne, new cars and homes gift-wrapped in giant red ribbons and bows. At work everyone received gifts, commensurate with their positions, from "the EAT family." To his surprise, Crocker personally invited him and May to his annual Solstistmas party. Of course he said they'd be delighted.

At the entrance to Crocker's estate in the exclusive Kingsford Hills District, an armed guard stepped forward, waved an iris scan in his face and saluted him through as the heavy iron gate rolled back. Statues of classical heroes and deities that May pronounced interesting but he thought tacky lined the winding drive. Suddenly the ice-covered stone turrets and battlements of Crocker's castle-like mansion rose before them in a blaze of floodlights. The cobblestone circle out front showcased the sleekest, fastest, most expensive automotive design and engineering in the world. He had always thought of his car as kind of sporty, for a family SUV that is, but next to these thoroughbreds it seemed clunky, utilitarian, like something you'd use to deliver rolls of carpet or kitchen appliances. To add further insult, a sullen young man with a wave of jet-black hair partially obscuring his face and shivering violently in a poorly fitting blue blazer with tarnished brass buttons (he later heard someone refer to him as *the old man's nephew* and something about *teaching the kid a lesson*) offered, with a noticeable smirk, to park their "vehicle," and of course he didn't want to look like a total cheapskate so he said yes, knowing full well he'd hear about it later from the car, *I'm perfectly capable of parking myself, thank you, Marty.*

He felt even more like a pauper as he and May approached the great arched entranceway. Flaming sconces sent firelight and shadows dancing across stone walls and leaded glass windowpanes. Gargoyles leered down at them from icy parapets. A massive wooden door bound and clasped with heavy wrought iron bolts and bands loomed before them, at its center a lion-headed brass knocker encircled by an enormous pine wreath tied with a huge red velvet bow. His timorous but nevertheless resounding knock caused this portal to open and a succession of valets liveried in gray jackets and trousers, purple vests and black bowties ushered them into the sudden noise and cacophony of a crowded ballroom blazing with crystal lamps, chandeliers and gilded mirrors. An enormous Solstistmas tree resplendent with lights and ornaments rose to the celestium of angels and cherubs painted on the high ceiling. An orchestra bobbed and swayed on stage. Women flitted about in bright blue and red splashes of organdy and chenille, creamy pink and white origami-like folds of satin and silk, box kite-like constructions of strategically placed green and orange vinyl squares. The men stood about, staid, debonair, like cadres of maître d´s and sommeliers in black tuxedos and white evening jackets. Servants offered trays of canapés and hors d'oeuvres, long-stemmed flutes of champagne, crystal tumblers of scotch and bourbon. May, of course, had champagne. He grabbed a scotch and immediately began to plot an escape to the most discreet corner of the party when Crocker himself strode forward and, without a glance in his direction, took May's hand and kissed it with a theatrical *smack.*

"I've heard so much about your good work at the church from my darling wife, Belinda," Crocker purred, continuing to clutch May's hand in his.

To his disbelief, May actually blushed. He also noticed now how striking she looked tonight. Her evening dress, which he would have described as dark purple or even indigo—she had referred to the color as *anil* when she modeled it for him at home, garnering barely a nod from him then—perfectly set off her emerald green eyes and lustrous black hair.

"Martin!" Crocker clapped a paw on his shoulder as if he'd just now recognized him, and making a pretense of straightening his tie for him, he said in a lowered voice, "You're looking a bit peaked, Martin. You should take it easy for a while. Let your team carry the load." Crocker's covetous crocodile gaze fell again on May. "If I were you, I'd devote more time to that pretty little wife of yours."

Pretty little wife? How dare Crocker speak about May like that? Even more insulting, his dismissive *take it easy for a while. Let your team carry the load*—as if that were at all possible. Seething with humiliation and, yes, jealousy, he watched Crocker's broad, vulture-like shoulders plunge into the crowd in an explosion of hoots, huzzahs and hurrahs that collapsed behind him into eddies of innuendo, resentment and fear. He remembered a rumor he'd heard, a kind of fable actually, in which Crocker was portrayed as a scion of dissipated wealth who put on a uniform and went off to fight in a bitterly contested war of ancient provenance in a bitterly inhospitable desert clime where, through his valor, determination and purported ruthlessness toward the enemy, and even his own men on occasion, he quickly rose in the ranks. Applying the same determination and, one would suspect, ruthlessness, to the corporate world, Crocker had rapidly ascended to the helm— rumor suggested something more like a coup d'etat—of EAT's Eastern Division.

He had hoped to share this history with May, with the ulterior motive, he admitted to himself, of portraying Crocker in a less flattering light, but she had become absorbed in an animated conversation with an apparently like-minded group—he overheard *church* and *Keep Them Alive*—and he went off to refresh his scotch. Along the way he hovered on the edge of a particularly boisterous bunch, among whom he recognized Catábolus's esteemed mayor, Chumley Chubbs, a pudgy little man with a solitary black licorice whip of hair lacquered like a question mark across his otherwise bald pate, Brock Lee Wall, the Chief of Police, crew cut, fireplug build, suspicious little eyes in a bulldog face, and Archbishop Paisley Poodlepump, in his formal white collar and black suit, who, the story went, had risen from humble parish priest to become Catábolus' spiritual beacon, although in person he looked considerably less solemn and priestly and much more corpulent and obsequious than he did behind the pulpit. These noteworthies were gathered around the TV news anchors Bob Broadley, whose tightly clenched smile, he thought, suggested hemorrhoids or some other hidden ailment, and whose patent leather hairdo seemed a bit shoeworn in back, and Marsha Mello, whose mercilessly bleached blond hair was teased and fluffed into a tenuous spun sugar construction, and whose eyes looked so unnaturally blue he could almost smell chlorine. Broadley, obviously drunk, had just made a vulgar comment regarding President Portland Posture's sexual proclivities. "What else would you expect from that old reprobate *Portly?*" Archbishop Poodlepump chimed in. "At least you news people kept it quiet." At which everyone laughed *Ha!Ha!Ha!* except Marsha Mello, who had been listening with a zoned out, pharmaceutical expression, but now, as the laughter died around her, burst into an ear-shattering alto *hee!hee!hee!hee!*

By the time a bell-tinkling valet called everyone to dinner, he felt drunk himself. He'd also lost track of May. He followed the other guests into an enormous hall with huge roaring fireplaces at each end, before which sprawled several large hounds. Great wheel-like chandeliers glowing with thousands of burning tapers hung from the vaulted ceiling. Crossed halberds, escutcheons, family tartans and tapestries of medieval hunting scenes covered the stone walls. Everything was festooned with mistletoe, holly, pine boughs and crimson bows. One hundred high-backed chairs upholstered in plush purple velvet with exposed walnut curves were arranged with military precision around the dining table, itself as big as a drawbridge and covered with enough linen and lace to sail a fleet of HMS Beagles to Tierra del Fuego. Huge sprays of red roses and white lilies erupted among a gleaming dragon hoard of gold and silver tureens, goblets, platters and silverware, also placed with military precision. Candles flickered in tall fleur-de-lis-shaped candelabra. At each place setting an ivory matte card announced the respective dinner guest's name in elaborate script.

To his chagrin, he found himself situated between a woman in a voluminous crimson gown, who, even sitting, loomed over him like a great red eminence, and who, after peering down her prominent nose at him for an interminable minute, sniffed once and averted her gaze forever, and a rotund little man in a pink bowtie, the red dynasty's husband apparently, who peered myopically up at him through hand mirror-sized spectacles and in a thin lisp inquired if he had ever considered joining a men's glee club, to which, not feeling very gleeful at the minute, he replied honestly that he hadn't.

A loud murmur saved him from further conversation. Crocker had just sat down at the head of the table. His wife Belinda was now being seated on his right. She must be at least forty years younger than the lecherous old reptile. She was also stunning. She almost glowed. Waves of platinum blond hair fell over her bare shoulders. Her smooth skin suggested an endless summer of swimming pools and health spas. Her cream-colored satin evening gown plunged dangerously into a voluptuous crevasse of décolletage. He felt a primal stirring, not his libido, but *hunger*. In an alcohol slurry of words like *breasts* and *thighs*, *rib*, *rump* and *loin*, further confused with absurd cartoon vestiges of his childhood, he pictured her naked and roasted a golden brown on a silver platter. This was replaced by the more sobering image of May being seated on Crocker's left by a visibly leering valet.

After that he remembered an army of waiters serving an endless array of dishes that stretched along the culinary highway from soup to nuts. Borscht, leek and shallot consommé, tomato and Alaskan King Crab bisque, vichyssoise *simple*, grilled calamari and shrimp marinara antipasto, Black Sea caviar and smoked Pacific salmon, sides of beef and legs of lamb, spitted wild hare, chestnut and plum-stuffed partridges and ptarmigan, roasted venison, wild boar, bison and bear. Silverware and cutlery clinged, clanged and clattered. Ravenous guests gobbled one course after another, merrily tossing gristle and bone to the stone floor where the great hairy mastiffs growled and snapped at each other over the spoils. At last the *piece de resistance* arrived before each happy diner—an entire roasted suckling pig. With loin-girding cries of encouragement, Crocker urged his company on to new heights of gustatory glory. "Eat! Eat it all! Leave nothing to the hounds!" And they complied. The elderly gentleman seated across from him advanced an attack on his piglet from the flanks. The crimson eminence on his right engaged her now oinkless oinker in a rear assault. The little round man on his left conducted a forced march from snout to rump. On Crocker's left, he saw May dig into her pig. On his right, the voluptuous Belinda plunged a bite of her swine between the soft pink pillows of her lips. He began to apply his own cutlery to the petit porker set before him but froze in horror. Its face, and it had a face, looked almost exactly like Ashley's with a suntan and a baked apple in her mouth, her *X-ray* glasses and even her braids recreated with a garnish of prawns. Somebody must have said something very funny just then because suddenly the whole table roared with laughter, *HA!HA!HA!* Even more confusing, he had the sense they were laughing at him. Crocker leaned over and said something to May and she laughed even harder. He heard a low, threatening growl and turned to meet the savage yellow eyes of a large, wolf-like creature with pointed ears and a pink slobber of tongue hanging between its great white fangs, its atavistic gaze fixed on the morsel of flesh impaled on his fork. He let the fork fall from his fingers. It never hit the floor.

He remembered little else of the dinner except that on the way home he and May had some sort of spat. Oh yes, and the first day back at work, Crocker said with a bemused look, "By the way, Martin, sorry about that little affair the other night." The meaning of this comment eluded his grasp. Nor could he shake the sense that it had something to with the shift in his relationship with May. He sometimes caught her giving him odd, critical glances.

Once she said, "You've changed, Marty. I can't put my finger on it. You act different. You *look* different."

One evening Libby Bombaste was over. He noticed her examining him with a sour, pursed expression, the way she might an unappetizing food item. Afterwards May mentioned that Libby had commented on his new *svelte* look. When he scoffed at this observation, May said, "Please don't laugh, Marty, it's true. I think you've—lost weight. You look"—her voice trembled and she looked away—"*thinner.*"

Then there was that unpleasant shopping trip to the Cedar Mill Mall for new casual wear, after May nagged him for days. "It's time to get rid of those old things in your closet, Marty, they look scruffy and most of them don't fit you anymore." May's sunny springtime face turned cloudy when she said this.

He despised the whole mall scene, the cheesy mix of Tiffany lamps and Persian carpets with exposed ductwork and electrical conduits in the department stores, the food courts packed like pigpens with grunting, gorging omnivores, the screaming children, preening teens, the ice-skating rink where red-cheeked sporty types in woolen scarves and tasseled caps sedately rode TranSportSkates® around the gray oval of ice, the pompously named Crabtree and Lemon Kitchen Emporium (he pictured a tree hung with claw-waving crabs), and finally their destination, Tutterly's Haberdashery and Fine Men's Wear (something wrong with that name too, a tautology maybe, or misplaced modifier).

After an hour of following May up and down the aisles, he finally chose the same conservative blue polo shirts and khaki slacks he always bought, although he had to try on several pairs to find ones that fit and even those were loose. When the sales assistant rang up his items she looked him as if there were something just a little *icky* about his choice of clothes, or him, or both. "That's our smallest men's size," she said. "We don't sell many."

He had noticed something else recently, a kind of spring in his step, a lightness of being. At first he attributed it to an unusual warm spell. The sun came out, the temperature climbed, the ice and snow melted away. But even after the cold returned and everyone broke out their winter coats again, he continued to feel an unusual lightness of body and spirit. It almost made him dizzy at times. It even frightened him a little. What if something really was wrong with him? What if he had *cancer?* It was true he didn't have the same appetite he used to and his weight continued to drop. Not that he'd admit his fears to anyone else, especially May, who, he knew, would nag him to see a doctor.

However, after a particularly unnerving event—crossing Heroes Plaza one morning, he broke into a sprint and run several yards laughing like a lunatic before he noticed everyone staring at him—when May asked again if anything was troubling him, he spilled his guts. Not only had he lost his appetite but he was having strange dreams, and his memory seemed—not worse, but *better.* May mentioned that Libby Bombaste knew someone *discreet* who could see him immediately. "Please, Marty?"

At first glance Doctor Dingle looked like one of those quack medical mal-practitioners from the last century. He actually wore a round mirror thing on his forehead and a stethoscope around his neck. After palpating, tapping, thumping, peering into and otherwise sounding the depths of his various vital organs and orifices, Doctor Dingle pronounced him in fine, in fact *excellent,* physical health. "However," Doctor Dingle examined his stethoscope as if it must be malfunctioning, "that doesn't mean there's nothing wrong with you. I'm not a psychiatrist, Mister Grasso, but I can tell you're under a lot of stress. I suggest more quality time with your family. You know, more snack-time together in front of the HearthScreen®, go out to dinner more frequently. They have these wonderful all-you-can-eat party emporiums now ..." Doctor Dingle looked wistful. "While you're at it, try to cut down on any unnecessary activity, *walking,* for instance. I'm giving you a prescription. It's a new diet pill FarmCorps has on the market for conditions like yours."

Of course May was enthusiastic about the whole thing. She helped him keep track of his pill regimen and had the chefbot institute the new high fat and cholesterol diet the Industrial Foods Dietary Commission was promoting. She brought him snacks when he worked late, or in bed before turning out the lights. He hesitated, however, when she made him promise to quit *this crazy walking thing* like Doctor Dingle had advised. But he did promise. And he resolved to himself that he'd keep this promise. And for a while things did seem better. May seemed happier, more relaxed. Maybe it was her new yoga class. At least she had quit staring at him like he was going to have a heart attack any minute. He even convinced himself *he* felt happier.

One evening, his mind muddled by the new medication, he got off the train at the wrong station. He began to wander through the maze of narrow, crowded streets. People laughed and shouted in packed sidewalk cafes. Vendors hawked wares from carts and stalls. Car horns blared. Tailgates slammed down on delivery trucks. Burly, brutish-looking men crashed crates of produce and household goods to the pavement. The noise and confusion triggered in him a desperate need to escape. He began to walk faster and faster. He turned down one street after another until he came upon a curious little thoroughfare called Sentimental Journey Lane which turned out to be a nightmarish hodgepodge of stodgy blue mailboxes, tacky red and white-striped barber poles, dingy glass phone booths, ornate but terminally passé gas lamps and musty newspaper kiosks.

At the end of the lane he came upon a small park. It looked dark, overgrown, unvisited. The heavy iron gate hung open. Intrigued, he entered. A narrow path led him through dense woods toward a clearing where he found himself staring across an enormous reservoir encircled by a white travertine walkway.

On an impulse, he started to walk around the reservoir. He'd gone perhaps half way when, out of breath and slightly light-headed, he stopped to lean over the metal railing. A stiff breeze stirred the surface of the cobalt blue water. The small whitecaps reminded him of sailboats on the sea. It occurred to him that this must be the primary source of Catábolus' potable water. Odd, he thought, that it was left completely unprotected. His mind leapt ahead to dire scenarios involving armed men in black ninja costumes, sealed containers of deadly poison.

A violent shiver wracked his body. Hands numb from gripping the cold metal railing, he quickly began to retrace his route. His footsteps sounded loud and brittle on the travertine. The lengthening shadows urged him faster along the narrow path. He practically lunged through the open gate and out of the park.

After pausing to catch his breath, he hurried back through the maze of shops and stalls, most closed now, and arrived at the station just in time to board the last train, promising himself he'd never do anything like that again.

And then he did.

The next time he got off at this stop it wasn't by mistake. He quickly threaded his way through the crowded bazaars and, after a few wrong turns, found his way down the fusty Sentimental Journey Lane to the park. As before, the gate hung open. He entered and hurried along the path through the woods to the reservoir. The dark blue water lay before him like a giant girandole in which the lighter blue of the sky and a few white puffs of cloud were reflected. Invigorated by the brisk breeze and slanting evening sunlight, he took a deep breath and strode forth. He had been walking for perhaps fifteen minutes when he recognized a spot of orange paint on the metal railing, his stopping point the last time. He marched on. A kink had started in his right knee. He was also breathing harder than he wished to admit and his heart beat furiously in his chest.

He stopped walking and leaned against the railing. What was he trying to do—kill himself? He had promised May—he had promised himself—that he'd stop this behavior. What if someone saw him—a ridiculous-looking, middle-aged man in an overcoat and business suit practically *running* around the reservoir?

And yet, having started to walk again at a slower pace, he couldn't deny that it felt good to be outside in the fresh air, to move under his own locomotion, to use his body, to feel his muscles working and his heart pumping in his chest. He hadn't felt this good since—college? Of course he was more athletic then. He lifted weights, he jogged, he played tennis, he swam. He may have even been on a team, which would explain the little gilt trophy he kept on his desk in the office. In fact, just the other day he had rescued an old maroon and slate letter jacket from a box May kept in the hall closet for the Keep Them Alive Fund. On an impulse he tried it on. Amazingly, it fit. A little snug in the shoulders, a little tight around the waist, and, sure, it was somewhat worn, but no reason to throw it away. A thought he completed at the same time he completed an entire lap around the reservoir.

Something else occurred to him on his next outing, determined this time to make the circuit around the reservoir twice. It felt good to be by himself and think about things. To have some real peace and quiet without EyePhone®s ringing, adworms popping up on his screen, people wasting his time and energy with stupid questions they could have answered themselves if they'd only thought them through. The kids, too, well, Ashley anyway, always demanding *things*, or money for things. May nagging him because he had missed the Family Hour again—*no wonder you're out of touch with the kids, Marty*. Not that he thought for one minute Trey and Ashley would lift their faces from their electroids long enough to notice his presence or absence. Even the damn car on his case when, having finally forced himself to give up his walking and solitude for another day, he arrived at the SunnyVale station later than usual.

Working overtime again, Marty? Another late meeting, Marty?

The car actually sounded suspicious. Ironic because recently he had begun to suspect *it* of reporting his activities back to May. But even if she and the car were in cahoots, it had no proof. Of course there were the constant lies to explain why he was late, or that his suit looked disheveled and his face flushed even though the weather had turned cold again. The train was delayed, he had to walk to the next station. He stopped to check out floor plans in a new gated community, the manager talked his ear off. Unforeseen problems at work, the whole place was going to hell. Unfortunately, this last was more truth than hyperbole.

Whispers of discontent penetrated the walls of his office like insidious boring insects. The team members were grumpy, out of sorts. Their faces looked puffy, swollen. Stress, he told himself. Too much work, not enough rest. Comes with the territory, right? You gotta suck it up, *one hundred percent*. Still, he couldn't ignore the more troubling signs. Laong Hsiuh seemed to harbor a festering resentment toward the talented young Mustuffah Ghee. Add to that Gordie's ongoing hijinks, the most recent an explosive incident in the break room involving a "homemade" pizza and industrial quantities of tomato sauce that left permanent red stains on the walls and ceiling and the lingering smells of a Neapolitan bakery. Furthermore, in clear violation of company policy, LaQuisha and Carmela had transformed their cubes into veritable fashion boutiques, to which a large number of female, and even a few male, employees flocked almost non-stop. Every day he resolved to speak to them about this untenable situation, and every day when the moment arrived, or rather, when he arrived at their work stations, his resolve failed him. In his mind LaQuisha had morphed into some kind of totemic giant. When she roared with laughter, as she did at almost everything he said now, he felt like a pygmy facing a trumpeting elephant, and instead of a critique of her fashion boutique, he weakly offered a suggestion on her color scheme. A disconcerting change had come over Carmela as well. Gone the folkloric ruffles, replaced by a black kidskin bustier, matching pants and blood-red stilettos that led the eye (his anyway) to her equally blood-red mouth and pointed white teeth, which, despite her porcine proportions, gave her a hungry vulpine look that made him want to *snarl* at her and then run for his life.

To complicate matters, he sensed Crocker's affection waning lately. The visits to his office, the handshakes and claps on the back, the indulgences in Treufuls Truffles had inexplicably abated. Most of their correspondence now consisted of perfunctory messages routed through Ms. Donatzk's desk, which left a frosty patina and an almost audible *sniff* on the contents. He tried to reassure himself that Crocker must be preoccupied with more *pressing* matters but, considering the salacious rumors that continued to circulate throughout the department, this unintended pun did nothing to assuage his doubts. Surely, he told himself, the horny old reptile could see that he was working harder than ever, in fact, too hard. Recently, he had caught himself making careless mistakes, overlooking small but important details.

Yesterday morning he was about to send off his latest petition to the Regional Board of Directors regarding the much-belabored issue of Universal Application. He had carefully vetted every jot, tittle and iota, he had even toyed with the font— Iberian? Siberian? Nigerian? What the heck, let the linguists figure it out—but as he read his message over one more time he was shocked at how demanding, even belligerent, it sounded, like something *Ashley* might have composed. Even more egregious, in an unintended wordplay, he had typed *sicly* for sickly. Appalled at these lapses in his judgment, he began to erase large swaths of text and in their place type in more ponderously nuanced phrases. *I respectfully request that you revisit the issue of Universal Application … It may be in the best interests of EAT to …* he stopped. Now it sounded obsequious, *lame*. How had his passion for words and the elasticity of language been supplanted by this pusillanimous jargon? Was it his many years immersed in the business world? The MBA in night school? That was fun. May pregnant with Trey. Ashley even then a demanding little brat. His own frustration mounting into anger because he was trying to prepare for his exams and *how the hell can I work with all this racket?* Then May's voice rising and her own anger, terrifying not only because of its ugliness *you insignificant fucking loser!* but because its tone suggested someone used to wielding an even more frightening power still. All of which he had conveniently stored away in a taped and sealed box long ago forgotten in the basement of his subconscious—until now.

Maybe he needed a vacation, just he and May alone some place. Leave the kids with the Bombastes. Although May had said Ashley and Prissy Bombaste weren't getting along right now. A minor problem. Geez, he couldn't remember the last time he and May took a vacation. Three summers ago? They went somewhere by the sea, he was sure of that. He remembered the turquoise blue water, dolphins jumping in the bay, starfish on the beach, schools of red and green fish in the reefs. He also remembered something so surreal he was sure he must have dreamed it. Hordes of anthropoid behemoths bobbing in the surf like enormous mammalian sea creatures, or else collapsed on the sand like a fleet of partially deflated hot air balloons. Dream or not, he distinctly remembered thinking, How is this possible? These are fast-paced people living in a fast-paced world. Yet he doubted if a single one of them could run the distance from the ice cream vendor to the hot dog stand. Something else odd. He couldn't recall the name of the hotel or inn they stayed at, or even a nearby town or city, although he did remember a flock of somewhat unattractive and very noisy birds the locals called *anis* squawking in the palm trees outside their window.

One other thing he distinctly remembered now—the hostility he sensed from his *colleagues* when he returned, as if he had somehow betrayed them by extricating himself from that madhouse for even a few days, not that a single one of them made the least effort to pick up the slack in his absence. Besides, as Executive Project Director, how could he even think of requesting a vacation?

In yet another irony, when he brought up his screen again, he was bombarded by a stream of pharmaceutical adworms, some, admittedly, enticing. Sleep retreats? Dream vacations? *Escape in the comfort of your own bed!* Maybe he just needed a boost. He took out the bottle of yellows, examined the label as if it were written in Sanskrit, dumped a couple in his hand, and swallowed them dry.

Unbeknownst to May, he had stopped taking Doctor Dingle's diet pills, which, rather than inducing the sort of slothful torpor conducive to weight gain, had the opposite effect. He felt anxious, jittery, on edge all the time. *Jagged.* He couldn't sit still at his desk. He had to get up, move around. Sudden noises disturbed him. Loud voices, EyePhone®s chiming. He had trouble concentrating. His thoughts jumped all over the place. He felt like a cutting edge machine on the edge of self-destruction.

And then, because of the stress from work, he was irritable at home. Little things bothered him. The kids got on his nerves. Trey was so passive—he never seemed to *do* anything. Even more disturbing, Ashley's bratty insolence, her constant demands for *things*, a trait, he assumed, she had inherited from May.

One evening he and the kids were in the family room, the news on. That pompous buffoon Bob Broadley with his fake smile and that stupid shoe on his head, and the vapid Marsha Mello, her eyes and thoughts wandering off into a vast blue sky of incoherence. *In the financial page, EAT shares continue their climb up the beanstalk.* Followed immediately by Broadley, brow knitted censoriously. *Moving on to the war effort.*

The screen showed a squad of soldiers. They were all thin, their faces gaunt. He didn't recognize their uniforms. Maybe they were prisoners. Or conscripts. Trey and Ashley had no idea how fortunate they were. Everything handed to them on a platter, and they weren't even aware. Their faces always buried in their screens, completely oblivious to the real world. Trey rocking and humming to himself while his hands—autonomously it seemed—reconstructed an old food blender into a mechanical puppy. Ashley in her black storm trooper boots and those ridiculous pink, rhinestone-studded *X-ray* glasses, furiously texting.

Attempting some sort of father-daughter rapprochement, he asked if she was texting Prissy Bombaste.

"Of course not, *Daddy*," she scoffed. "I'm texting Charlotte."

Charlotte? Charlotte was the avatar she had created for her *MySelf*® site. How could she text a virtual being? When he asked about this, Ashley was contemptuous.

"You wouldn't understand, *Daddy*."

He squeezed his eyes shut against a sudden sharp pain in the back of his head. The way she said *Daddy* irked the hell out of him. It was like getting hit with a pickaxe. He knew he should count to ten, take deep breaths, eat a donut, but suddenly he was yelling, "Why don't you kids put away those damn electroids and go play outside!"

Trey began to cry but Ashley looked at him as if he were a complete idiot and said with utter disdain, "That's crazy, *Daddy*. It's *night*. It's *dark* outside."

"That's beside the point!" he snapped. Before he could say anything else, Ashley pointed the remote at him as if she were turning off the TV and in a mocking tone invoked a higher authority.

"*Mo-om! Daddy's* being mean to us!"

Then May came in, her eyes blazing like emerald lasers. "Really, *Martin*, why must you torture the children like this?"

"Can't you see?" he replied, irritated even more by this betrayal. "They're always in front of those damn screens. It's not healthy."

"Martin, please, watch your language. Besides, you're being unreasonable. The Ministry of Education's annual report clearly demonstrates that increased screen-time improves test scores and enhances students' chances of success in the future. Rather than *attack* the children, you should be happy they're both doing so well at school."

Apparently they were. Ashley had been nagging him for yet another raise in her allowance. She had practically snarled at him, "You *promised, Daddy*." He couldn't remember. Had he promised? "You said if I improved my grades you'd give me a raise. Well, I made a perfect ten on a four-point scale. That's not even theoretically possible, *Daddy*." And when did she start saying *Daddy* like that?

And then May took the opportunity to nag him about their budget. In case he hadn't noticed, their latest statement showed a ten percent decrease in their consumer rating. Her voice quavered with unfamiliar anxiety. "*Really*, Martin, I don't think we're spending enough." Last week a couple of Civilian Consumer Corps members had come to the door with a survey regarding their energy consumption. Did they own, operate and maintain the minimum number of screens and appliances? Did they all participate in the Family Hour? Were they spending above their level of income? Of course she said yes, yes, yes to everything. She wasn't lying. The maintenance on the HearthScreen® alone ate up a quarter of his paycheck. On top of which May had just dumped a bundle hosting the *Fashionably Fashionable Fashion Magazine Fan Club*.

"Another thing, Marty. I wish you wouldn't turn off the screen when you're not watching. And *please*, remember to leave the lights on when you go out. Imagine, a grown man. I don't even have to remind the kids about that."

A magmatic surge of anger boiled up inside him. What the *hell* was he doing in this family? They were like complete strangers. What if he didn't have a family? What if he never had to put up with all this aggravation again? What if he could do what he liked when he liked without ever having to explain to anybody? He got up from his lounge chair and went to the hall closet.

"Marty! Where are you going?!" May's face twisted with horror.

"For a drive," he replied, not as casually as he had intended.

"Oh Martin, *again?*" Now she sounded desperate. "Are you sure you're taking the right meds?"

"Yes, I'm sure!" he snapped and pulled on his jacket. But not the crap that quack Doctor Dingle prescribed, he muttered as he went out the door. Yeah, right—*FarmCorps*. Just add an *e*.

Of course the car was suspicious. *Doing some more research, Marty?*

"Maybe," he replied. To prevent further interrogation, he said he'd like some quiet, and yes, he preferred to drive, and for the next hour that's what he did, the world around him a blur until he woke out of his trance bouncing over a narrow cobblestone street in an older, run-down neighborhood. A battered hulk of a car passed, the grill smashed in, the right front fender hanging off, blue smoke pouring out its exhaust.

Geez, get a load of that guy, Marty, the car piped up.

The car's smug tone evaporated like a whiff of ether when he pulled over to the curb and started to get out. *C'mon, Marty, you're making me nervous with this slumming thing.*

Ignoring the car's complaint, he started to walk. The night was unusually mild, almost balmy. A cloying, sweet-sour smell of cheap perfume, greasy food, booze, cigarettes, dive bars and overflowing garbage saturated the air. He passed an electronics mart wrapped in a security blanket of burglar bars and steel mesh. Used screens flickered in the window. He thought of May and the kids at home in front of the HearthScreen®, waiting for the Family Hour—or Family *Horror* as he had begun to call it to himself. But how could he think such a thing? He was so fortunate to have this family. May was always so supportive of his work, she had forfeited her own career for him and the kids. He felt a terrible sadness. What was he doing here, prowling the streets like a drug addict looking for a fix?

Loud music interrupted his thoughts. Drums, bells, whistles. Some kind of parade. People in freakish masks danced around him, laughing, singing, jumping up and down. Someone handed him a drink. It was cold, sweet. He gulped it in a single swallow. Then he was moving with the crowd, making stiff, hip-jutting, arm-pumping attempts at dancing. People laughed and applauded and urged him on. Man, what a wild night, he thought. These people really know how to enjoy life. He felt his face twist into a perverse grin. If May asked where he'd gone he'd just say *out* and let her surmise just how far out that might be.

Someone gave him another drink and he gulped it down. Someone else offered him a cigarette and he thought, why not? It tasted sweet and pungent and he had a flash of himself as a boy laughing and spinning in a field of clover. Now he was laughing and spinning, the whole world was spinning. Then he was in the arms of a complete stranger and they were kissing. He realized with horror it might not even be a woman. Then he realized they weren't kissing. He was lying flat on his back on the pavement with a crowd of masked faces around him and the man—it was a man, wearing glitter and false eyelashes—was breathing forcefully into his mouth. He tasted garlic and alcohol and almost vomited. *Ohh!* The masked faces backed away with a collective gasp. Suddenly he knew with absolute certainty that they weren't wearing masks at all. They really were monsters. He had to get away from them.

He struggled to his feet and ignoring a strangely attenuated barnyard chorus of mooing and bleating ... *nooo, pleeease dooon't mooove* ... and fending off a grotesque puppet show of grasping hands, he staggered down the street toward an island of light that turned out to be the glow of a movie marquee. There was a line at the ticket booth. He had another odd flash of himself as a kid clutching in his soft little fist a few precious coins, enough for a box of popcorn, a soda and an entire afternoon of cartoons and movies.

"Hey mister, you buyin' a ticket or lookin' for a date?" The woman inside the glass booth stared at him indifferently. Her large, doughy face looked as if it had been constructed entirely out of make-up.

*

I knew I shouldn't have gone to see that stupid movie, but I needed to get out of my little box and among *people*—if you could call them that. Rolf called them *food pods*. He had this crazy idea that some higher power had turned humans into energy storage units, like cattle being fattened for slaughter. Maybe he wasn't so far off. I could hear them all around me, crunching and chewing, gulping and swallowing and smacking their lips. In the flickering light their eyes bulged and their teeth gleamed with every monstrous bite. It made me want to get up, run out of the theater, but the thought of all those eyes staring at me kept me in my seat.

I told myself to ignore them, focus on the screen. It was a comedy. This young guy Timmy had some kind of metabolic condition that prevented him from gaining weight no matter how much he ate. There was a scene in an ice cream shop. Timmy and his *normal* friends were crowded in a booth and his friends laughed and pointed at him while he struggled to finish a huge banana split. But Timmy didn't even seem to mind. He patted his little potbelly and rolled his eyes as if he'd just consumed a ton of ice cream and laughed along with his friends. And the audience laughed with them, their eyes wide with hyperthyroidal surprise, their mouths gaping like hippopotami emerging from muddy brown rivers in Africa.

Yeah, sure, they all thought it was so damn funny. That was another thing that had changed. Where before it was *they* who had to guard every word that came out of their mouths, *they* who had to act as if they didn't mind the endless taunts and torment, *they* who had to hide their shame and resentment behind a façade of joviality, now it was the exact opposite. *We* had to take care what we said, when and where and to whom we said it, *we* had to pretend we didn't mind the endless taunts and insults, *we* had to go out of our way not to offend anyone simply by our slender presence.

The skinny guy, Timmy, went to all kinds of doctors but it was hopeless. The poor schmuck even tried a theatrical fat suit, but he looked ridiculous, like he was wearing a giant sponge football. And he kept bouncing off things, he couldn't judge distances. In another time there might have been some underlying message about accepting yourself as you are, but that wouldn't have satisfied this crowd. They roared with laughter while gorging themselves on buckets of food.

Finally the hapless protagonist found a strange little magic shop on a dim, narrow street in the darkest part of town where the proprietor, who was actually some kind of wizard with a long gray beard and tall pointed hat decorated with stars and crescent moons, gave him a magic potion. In a matter of days Timmy ballooned up like a blimp. Suddenly he found himself popular at school, he had a whole new group of friends. He even discovered that the cute but shy girl he had always liked liked him too.

Members of the audience were actually sniffling. A few let out sobs.

I was appalled. Before the credits started to roll, I got up and hurried down the aisle, trying to ignore the looks of horror, the ugly whispers. *Oh my God, that's disgusting. Somebody should call the authorities.* The pimply-faced kids behind the snack bar, indistinguishable from each other in the puffy, hot air balloon enormity of their maroon and black polyester shirts and trousers, stared at me terrified as I hurried past.

Out in the street I started to walk, staying in the shadows. I passed a young couple and the woman let out a gasp. Her companion attempted a masculine growl, "We don't want trouble, mister."

I ignored them and continued to my apartment building. The manager's door was open. He glanced up and gave me a sour, bilious look, then returned his gaze to his screen, where I caught a glimpse of naked writhing bodies. When I applied for the room I had felt compelled to explain to this fat bastard that, lying, I had a medical condition, that it wasn't contagious, that, believe it or not,

I was actually gaining weight. "Put on five pounds, see?" I slouched forward and pushed out my belly. The creep didn't care. He'd seen all kinds. And I had cash.

My room was on the third floor. I put the key in the lock just as the door across the hall opened and Rolf peeked out. Behind him I could see screens flickering on the walls and floor, even the ceiling. Rolf glanced around, then scrabbled forward crab-like, his movements hindered by a strange suit of armor. His arms and legs were sheathed in flickering mini-screens. The talking head in the flat screen on his chest made him look like one of those ancient monsters with its face in its torso. On his head he wore an upside-down spaghetti colander with a cluster of EyePhone®s attached to it. Behind a pair of aquarium-like screen specs, his watery blue eyes swam among newscasts of bomb blasts, car crashes, buildings in flames. Rolf flashed a two-fisted thumbs-up sign, which I understood to mean everything was okay, and scrabbled back into his room.

*

He remembered nothing of the movie. He must have passed out because the next thing he knew he was staggering up the sidewalk again. A thin, jagged shadow appeared on the wall next to him. Was someone following him? He started to walk faster. Now he had another problem. Where had he parked the car? A taxi went by. He waved but it careened away. Finally he recognized the electronics mart. There was the car on the corner. He collapsed in the seat and the door closed behind him with a reassuring *thump*.

Marty, where on earth have you been? The car's sharp rebuke shocked him.

"I went to a movie."

A movie? Do you realize how late it is, Marty? You look like a mess. What have you been up to, Marty?

The car sounded like his mother when she suspected him of doing something wrong. This led him to think how much he had always missed his mother. In his mind he could see her laughing and robust and full of life. Then she withered and faded before his eyes. *Sick.* That's what people said. He couldn't even remember clearly when she died. His father refused to talk about it. *Grief-shtricken,* he heard himself slur and realized he had been talking out loud. He started to cry. A palpable wave of disgust emanated from the car's dash and with audible contempt it sniffed, *I'd better drive, Marty. You're certainly in no shape to be behind the wheel.*

He remembered a blur of headlights, streetlights, the neon glow of bars, restaurants, VRBLs. A ninety-foot model in a shimmering, low-cut sequin gown leaned down to offer him a foaming bottle of champagne and another wave of nausea roiled his stomach.

He woke to the sound of car horns, screeching tires. A car careened past in the glare of headlights. He had a flash of the driver, his screen open in front of him, an EyePhone® in one hand, a slice of pizza in the other an instant before the car crashed into a light pole. More cars screeched to a halt. Drivers milled about in the fog of headlights like large, helpless beasts. Some of the quicker thinking had taken out their EyePhone®s. Then sirens, flashing lights. An EMS shrieked to a stop, behind it a patrol car. Men in uniforms tumbled out, blowing their whistles and crashing into each other like blimps. He had the sense he'd seen all this before, possibly in an old movie. Fortunately a cop with a flashlight waved them through.

Boy, what a jerk, huh Marty? the car said as they drove away.

"What do you mean?" he said, his thoughts still fuzzy.

The guy driving that car, Marty. People like that shouldn't be allowed behind the wheel.

"How do you know *he* was driving? How do you know it wasn't the car?"

How do I know? C'mon, Marty. A car? Screw up like that?

Awkward silence.

Hey, it wasn't my fault, if that's what you're thinking, Marty.

That wasn't what he was thinking, until now, but as he replayed the scene in his mind he vaguely remembered the light *was* red when they entered the intersection. What if it *was* their fault? What if the guy was *dead* and the police were on their tail right now? And what if the car denied everything, said *he* was driving.

May was sitting over a bowl of vanilla ice cream and a glass of white wine when he came in. She may have even been a little drunk, which placed them more or less on even territory now that he had sobered up some. He sat down across from her and waited. A wisp of hair had fallen across her face. He had never noticed the white streaks before. He wondered how long she'd been dying it. Then he wondered if he could even remember its original color.

"Do you know what time it is, Marty? You look disgusting. You smell like a brewery. Is that lipstick on your face?"

Lipstick?

May examined him more closely. "Are you *on* something? Really, *Martin*, why can't you just act *normal* for once? You're hardly ever home. You never join us for the Family Hour anymore. I think that's almost criminal. In fact, I think I'll look it up and see."

I think I'll look it up and see, he mocked her in his mind.

He remembered little else of that night except briefly waking out of the murky sludge of a strange dream, kind of scary and funny at the same time. In fact, he thought he'd had this dream before. He was in a large dark space, like a cavern, and he could see a flickering light, and the silhouettes of grotesque figures, like giant rats, with pointed ears and long crooked snouts. They were frantically nibbling at wires that stuck out of an enormous block of cheese—Swiss, he thought. Oddly, none of them seemed aware of his presence, but even as he thought this, almost as if they had heard his thoughts, some of them began to turn and stare at him with their beady eyes. Suddenly he felt afraid. He wanted to run away but he was paralyzed with fear. More of the creatures turned to stare at him. In a funny, high-pitched voice, one of them squeaked, "What's the matter, pal? Ain't youse hungry?"

7

inFlATion

THE FOLLOWING MORNING he sat at his desk in a head-throbbing slue of nausea, details of last night lost in a dense fog, a handful of pharmaceuticals ineffectual thus far. He was also aware of a disturbance on the stockyard floor via an undercurrent of gossip and rumors that had penetrated his office, aided by the capricious heating and air conditioning systems. Even more disconcerting, no word from Crocker yet.

He thought he might pick up some scuttlebutt in the break room but the mounds of donuts and pastries bursting with neon red, green and yellow custard and jelly fillings only exacerbated the tumult in his stomach, and every time he approached a klatch of chattering staffers, they scattered like a school of fish and regrouped elsewhere. Worst of all, Laong Hsiuh's clumsy attempts to avoid him, from the kolaches and hot cross buns to the chocolate mousse, where, horrified, he watched Laong Hsiuh pile his plate with the shiny brown goop, thence to the Danishes, the beignets, the kolaches and key lime tarts, where he cornered Laong Hsiuh long enough to inquire if he had seen the *Crocodile* this morning. To which Laong Hsiuh said simply, "Tart, Marty?" and proffered one of the pastries *at* him as if warding off a vampire. The gooey green filling reminded him of the guts that popped out of a caterpillar he squashed when he was a kid. He muttered an excuse about a report he had to finish and fled back to the office, his stomach churning, his thoughts in disarray.

Something seemed akilter in the universe lately, or at least in that part of the universe he occupied. He noticed people in the street giving him furtive, disapproving glances, and here at DAD his staff members seemed uneasy in his presence, if not outright avoiding him. He remembered the bafflement in E'Claire's eyes her last days, as if the world had changed overnight without bothering to notify her.

His anxiety turned to alarm when Crocker finally manifested himself with a curt *See me ASAP*.

Ms. Donatzk led him into the dim cavern of Crocker's office with the solemnity of an executioner and before turning to leave ordered him to sit down on a rigid, straight-backed chair positioned directly in front of Crocker's desk, which, he immediately noticed, had taken on the appearance of a sweet shop display. Glass jars of jellybeans and hard candies, red velvet boxes of toffees and chocolates, silver trays heaped with donuts, cookies and chocolate fudge brownies. His stomach gurgled ominously. On cue, Crocker strode into the office, sat on the edge of his desk and swept his paw over the assorted sweets. "Please, Martin, help yourself." Any other time he would have been delighted at the offer of such bounty, but now the insurrection brewing in his nether regions only grew more vociferous. Lying, he said he'd just had several of Marge's delicious key lime tarts, he couldn't eat another bite. Crocker dismissed this objection with an amused snort and pushed the jellybeans toward him. "Go on, Martin, try some. The flavors are extraordinary."

He felt like he was being forced to drink hemlock. He removed the lid from the jar, scooped up two or three of the colorful ovate confections, popped them into his mouth and began to chew even as his taste buds cried out in alarm beneath the assault of something bitter and bile-like. A hot, peristaltic wave churned through his gut.

"Good, aren't they," Crocker purred, surveying the candy store assortment before him. "Now have a cookie."

He dutifully retrieved a lumpy brown disk that he assumed to be chocolate chip from the silver tray and beneath Crocker's watchful eye took a bite, chewed and swallowed. A sweet, oily admixture of milk chocolate, butter, macadamia nuts and something disagreeable he recognized from his childhood as castor oil slid down his throat into his stomach, compounding the tempest already roiling there. But Crocker wasn't done yet. His coal-black eyes roved over the confectioner's display like an alchemist contemplating his next choice of poison. The absence of the treasure chest of Treufels Truffles had led him to believe Crocker no longer felt him worthy of such delicacies, so he was shocked when Crocker lifted the lid of a large wooden crate next to his desk, revealing hundreds, possibly thousands, of the until now coveted Treufels Truffles. "Go on, Martin, help yourself."

Once upon a time on his grandfather's farm, he came across a pile of fresh horse manure. Oddly, he didn't find it repulsive. The shiny brown lumps reminded him of little chocolate drums. He remembered he even felt a strange impulse to bite into one to see what it tasted like. He extracted a truffle from the crate and crushed it between his teeth. His tongue and taste buds briefly luxuriated in a thick sludge of sweet chocolate fondant, and then, inserting itself among the ethereal clouds of cacao, something unexpectedly foul and then fouler yet that, having no actual experience of coprophagy, he could only identify as *shit*. Mindful of Crocker's close attention, he forced himself to swallow this vile mass even as an opposing projectile force struggled to rise up his throat.

"Good, Martin, very good." Crocker folded his arms across his great barrel chest. "Now, shall we have a little talk?" Crocker began by saying he felt it his duty to inform him of certain concerns voiced by his staff: he was moody, uncooperative, he had expressed negative thoughts. *Moody? Uncooperative? Negative thoughts? Him?* "I've noticed it myself, Martin, and I find it troubling. You've always been an exemplary employee and, I might add, your Moleman Program has been a tremendous success, much more so, in fact, than anyone expected." Crocker cocked a fierce falcon eye at him, extracted a truffle from the crate, popped it into his mouth as if it were a salted peanut and chewed with great exaggeration. "I'm fond of you, Martin. I'm sure you know that. Which is why I wouldn't want to see you do anything to jeopardize your career here at EAT." *Jeopardize his career?* "This business with Universal Application, for example. Don't you think it might be wiser just to drop it? I mean, really, Martin. Insiders? Among the Upper Echelon? Now please, have another chocolate." And choosing a particularly large truffle from the crate, Crocker forced it into his mouth as if he were feeding a recalcitrant child at the dinner table, even making encouraging eating gestures himself. "Go on, Martin, eat it, evvvv-ery bite. Good. Very good. Here, have another." Crocker forced another truffle into his mouth and the column of hot magma building at the base of his throat inched upward. "Take some home for the kids, why don't you?" Crocker shoved a handful of truffles in his left coat pocket. "Oh, and here are some more for that pretty little wife of yours." Crocker stuffed another handful of truffles in his right pocket. "Well, I think that's all for now, Martin." Crocker's rictal grin suggested he had enjoyed this spectacle immensely. Without further ado, he grabbed him by the elbow, lifted him from the chair as if he were a rag doll and practically carried him to the door. "Remember, Martin," tiny flames flickered in Crocker's flinty black eyes, his hot breath reeked of rotting meat, "I went out on a limb for you. Don't let me down. One more thing, Martin. You really must take better care of yourself. You're looking *drawn.*"

His mouth packed with foul faux chocolate, he hurried to the men's room where, in a thunderous eruction of sound and substance, he succumbed to the exigencies of both emesis and excretion, then remained seated on the toilet, weak and trembling. He had no wish to move or do anything but hide from the world. Crocker's words echoed in his head. *I wouldn't want to see you do anything to jeopardize your career ... Don't let me down.* It was that word *down.* Without Universal Application, the Moleman Program had no chance of achieving success, yet Crocker had essentially ordered him to drop it. He remembered how shocked everyone had been when he first raised the possibility of insiders. He only discovered later, while culling E'Claire's files, that she had toyed with the idea of insiders herself, another small item he neglected to mention to anyone else. Why hadn't she pursued it? Was she afraid of something? Should *he* be afraid?

He had another thought. It began with Crocker's repeated references to his *pretty little wife,* then leapfrogged back in time to a scene at Crocker's Solstistmas party that, in his mind anyway, had the two of them, Crocker and May, tête-à-tête in an intimate circle of candlelight, then careened forward again into even more unsettling territory that had something to do with his raise, promotion, the private office. All the scurrilous rumors he had heard regarding Crocker's purported philandering exploded through his brain in a whirlwind of silk sheets, satin pillows, lacy black lingerie. But that was ridiculous. Why would Crocker want to *cheat*—even the word sounded vulgar—on his trophy wife Belinda, much less with *May*, or, realizing how that sounded, she with *him*.

Still digesting this issue, he roused himself from his funk and went to the sink to wash his hands. Laong Hsiuh's moon face loomed behind him in the mirror.

"Are you okay, Marty? You don't look well." The insincerity in Laong Hsiuh's voice was completely out of character.

He mumbled that he was fine and put his hands under the hot air blower.

Laong Hsiuh, who had apparently overcome his earlier bashfulness, continued to stare at him. "Are you going to the break room for lunch, Marty?"

He said he wasn't hungry.

"Not hungry, Marty?" Laong Hsiuh's face compressed into a knot of perplexity. "What is wrong with you?"

He ignored this question and returned to his office. He had barely brought up his screen when Marge barged in in a tawdry cherry print outfit he thought he had seen before and placed on his desk an enormous slice of her Chocolate and Cherry Jubilee cake, snow-capped with a huge scoop of vanilla ice cream.

"It *looks* very good," he said.

Marge stared at him like a bellhop waiting for a tip.

He picked up the fork, broke loose a piece of cake with a dollop of ice cream and raised it to his mouth. The cake was soggy and permeated with lumps of baking soda, the ice cream tasted like wet cement. He chewed quickly, swallowed. "It *is* good," he pronounced, but as Marge, apparently satisfied with this response, rotated her billowing bulk to leave, to himself hissed, *you bitch!* and immediately afterward wondered if he had only thought that or actually said it aloud.

Moody, uncooperative, negative thoughts.

Maybe he just needed another boost. He dumped some yellows in his hand, swallowed them with black coffee. A low humming sound in his head made him think the meds were already taking effect. The chefbot careened past the door, its tall white toque rakishly askew, plates of cake and ice cream falling off the back. It wasn't like Jimmy to let the chefbot run wild like that. He realized he hadn't seen Jimmy this morning. His nausea returned as he remembered Boyd Malodorov's visit to the department two days ago. After wandering around the stockyard, where, he heard later, Boyd and his goons had terrorized the entire staff, these thugs finally arrived at his office for what, at first, seemed like a routine chat. Boyd asked him a number of offhand questions concerning employees' work habits in that unctuous, insinuating tone that made him feel as if *he* were being interrogated. Soon, however, Boyd's queries centered on one person in particular. Jimmy. "I'm not saying yes he is or no he isn't, Marty. I'm just asking if you have any reason to suspect this individual of subversive activities."

Did Boyd really believe Jimmy was a subversive? Absurd. Subversives were devious, they were cunning, they were cold-blooded—and Jimmy? He thought of Jimmy's patient, unconcerned manner and soft, innocent-looking face, despite the goatee and multiple piercings. True, Jimmy did seem able to fix, take apart and repair just about any kind of electronic device that had been invented, and, considering the free range he enjoyed pushing his mail cart throughout the various departments all day, he probably knew more about the internal workings of EAT than anyone except, maybe, Crocker. Or Marge. In other words, it dawned on him, the perfect candidate for a mole. Impossible. He couldn't accept that. Which made him wonder again at this strange, protective feeling he'd always had for Jimmy. Suddenly he knew who Jimmy reminded him of. Trey. A bigger, older Trey. He had another, more disturbing thought. Had he allowed this resemblance to cloud his judgment? Worse, had Jimmy been exploiting this weakness?

He shivered. The air conditioning had come on. The temperature must have dropped twenty degrees in two minutes. He reached for his coffee. It was cold, bitter. His stomach rumbled again. His headache had returned. What he really wanted was to go home, eat a bunch of greenies and crash in bed—a luxury he couldn't afford. He got up from his chair, went to the window and stared down at the plaza. An image came to his mind. A group of stick-like people. Off to the side a girl in a faded pink dress, her hands out as if beseeching him, although in hindsight it could just as easily have been a dismissive shrug, like, *what else do you want from me?*

But now he was thinking of Ashley. She had become such a little *bitch*. The word popped into his head before he could censor himself. It was that damn *MySelf®* site. Ashley was totally addicted to it. She had begun to call herself Queen Martyr-D, the *mean teen screen queen*. The *mean* part was certainly apt. She had also expanded her superhero costume. Over the pink sequined halter-top she now wore a spiked metal breastplate with pointed cups that disturbed him just to look at it. She had attached *wings* to the frames of her *X-ray* glasses and the heels of her storm trooper boots. Even more outrageous, she had begun to apply pink glitter to her face and black greasepaint around her eyes, and she tied her braids with leather thongs. She looked like a gothic Valkyrie. She actually wore this outfit to school and demanded that her classmates call her Queen Martyr-D, which, he was sure, won her both admiration and enmity from her peers. Even more disturbing, she actually seemed to believe she had super powers, that she could magically make things happen.

Δ

She didn't know how it happened herself. She had felt desperate at the loss of her screen. Soon, however, she realized she had left her screen behind long ago, that it had become nothing more than a crutch to hide, even from herself, an impossible truth. She didn't need the screen to gain entry to that other world. It was all in her mind now. When she was hungry, she saw the markets, vendors, stalls, shops and restaurants where she could safely obtain something to eat from a sympathetic hand. She saw the places she should avoid, crowded areas where she'd draw the attention of some well-meaning maternal type or social worker who, thanks to their great concern, would involve the authorities and get her sent to a camp. Only slightly more dangerous, the predators prowling the streets and alleys in search of defenseless victims. That did not include her. She was like an extremely sapient wolf child. She sensed their body heat, smelled their fear, their anger, their madness, whatever compelled them, long before they were aware of her presence, and with a single concentrated thought of such intensity she felt the heat emanate from her own body, she destroyed them, as they had destroyed her family.

Δ

He heard a soft *whoomph*, like the sound of a gas furnace coming on, and hot air washed over him. Great, first the air conditioning, now the heat. He began to sweat profusely. Five minutes later an arctic front descended upon him.

By the time he got home his body was wracked with chills, his head ached, his sinuses were congested, his stomach groaned in distress, his breath rasped in his throat and his brow burned. May made him a cup of bouillon and insisted he go to bed. They spoke little otherwise and no mention was made of the previous night.

The following morning, still under the weather, he noticed a large piece of construction machinery crouched like a giant insect in the weed-grown lot on Pastoral Avenue. Men in yellow hardhats and reflective vests were marking off a perimeter with orange fanions. Farther back along Dreary Lane, old Mrs. Goon's house lay in a pile of rubble. He wondered if she had died—or gone to the Senior Community Center. This latter thought came to him as he passed the Terminal, as the fortress-like Senior Community Center was more commonly known, and which, it also struck him now, was appropriately located near the train station, because after this stop there wasn't another, as he had learned from May's involvement in the *Keep Them Alive* program.

"It's so depressing. You get to know these folks and then they … slip away."

"Slip away?" He expected her to explain that they had lost their mental faculties or, the more obvious, died.

May shrugged. "Oh, you know. They're *old*. They can't see. They can't hear. They don't *consume* as much. Sure, sometimes a thoughtful niece or grandson tries to help out. But eventually they exhaust their resources. New patients are waiting. There are more mouths to feed …"

On a whim, he decided to check Mrs. Goon's—he had to stop saying that, it was *Goo-neh*—Mrs. Gunne's records when he got to the office. As he suspected, there had been a brief energy spike. He remembered he had seen the shabby old house glowing rather cheerfully one night and wondered if Mrs. Gunne had family visiting. This was followed by a total collapse—the place went completely dark. Then he saw the attachment from ISNT: *suspected subversive activities*. Old Mrs. Goon—*Gunne*—a *subversive?* Sure, her place was an eyesore, and both she and the old man were a little *weird*. He remembered with anguish the time he and May took the kids to the Gunnes' for a fundraising event and how cold and dark the house was inside. He also remembered how terrified Mr. and Mrs. Gunne seemed when Ashley pointed out that they didn't have a TV. What if they *were* subversives? Absurd. They were just two unfortunate old people struggling to make ends meet, and from the looks of things even then, not succeeding.

Shortly after this development, he made an even more startling discovery. He had stayed late at the office on a Saturday night even though he felt miserable. He couldn't shake this bug he'd picked up. He was alternately feverish and sweaty, then chilled and shivering, and the temperamental AC and heating didn't help. He kept the chefbot running back and forth for coffee refills while he pored over the screen searching for proof of something that should have been perfectly obvious to him long ago, i.e., the energy spikes weren't random events at all, but desperate attempts by residents to maintain their expected energy consumption. When they couldn't keep up, the inevitable energy collapse followed and, to put it bluntly, they disappeared from the map. Recently he had heard rumors of a kind of shadow population called the *skinnies*. It sounded like an infectious disease. People said you could identify them by their lean and hungry look. Ashley apparently even had a new character in her virtual world called *Skinny-boy*, although he didn't know if he was supposed to be a good guy or a bad guy.

He returned his attention to the screen. Something had come up he'd never seen before. Instead of a few black funnel clouds, there were now multiple tornadoes and they were revolving around a single axis, slowly at first, then faster and faster until the entire Grid had become a black spinning vortex. A blinking red light, like a tiny beacon in this stormy sea, attracted his eyes to a message bar. *Projected energy collection 99.9%. Energy collection?* What did that mean? He surmised this might be a model of the worst-case scenario for the growing energy crisis. If so, things were much bleaker than the public at large had been led to believe. Ninety-nine point nine percent statistically meant total collapse of the system. Why hadn't the Glorious Council warned people of this looming catastrophe? They should be organizing community action groups, triage teams, filling schools, churches and public buildings with emergency supplies.

He had another, more insidious, thought. That term *energy collection*. What if the whole thing was a lie? What if there were no sappers, just poor people, and they were being scapegoated while—his thoughts leapt ahead to an even more perfidious possibility—the real thieves funneled the nation's dwindling energy resources into their own reservoirs? It was a perfect metaphor—a black hole sucking everything, the sweat and blood, labor and wages, out of one universe, that of the working public, and directing it into another, more nebulous dimension—banks, stocks, the Upper Echelon's pockets. How truly ironic—finishing his hypothesis—that the so-called sappers not only worked inside the system, they ran it.

All this time he had prided himself on the great job he was doing rooting out the sappers with his Moleman Program. And all this time his work was being used to destroy people's lives, to take their jobs, homes, to evict them into the streets, not because they didn't consume enough energy, but because all their energy had been consumed. No wonder he was never allowed Universal Application. He would have uncovered this filthy scheme immediately.

He had an even more alarming thought. What if *they*, the board of directors at EAT, the Glorious Council, the Department of War, the Upper Echelon, whoever was ultimately in charge of this thing, *weren't* in control? What if they had created a self-feeding monster that, in its frenzy of gorging, had bitten its own tail, so that in the end it would consume itself and destroy the world? It was absolute madness.

An icy chill wrapped its fingers around his spine. A shudder wracked his body. He had the distinct feeling he was being watched. He heard a low hum and the chefbot appeared in the doorway. In a sleepy mechanical voice it asked if he'd like anything else. *A snack? Nightcap? No? All right, then, I'm going to bed.*

Bed?

His thoughts quickly devolved into a chaotic scramble for the nearest exit. He started to shut down, then hesitated and pressed the command for a memory jewel. A sharp, surgical *tinnng* echoed in the chill of the office and a small man-made crystal, perfectly transparent except for a faint, bluish-yellow gleam, dropped into the slot at the bottom of his screen. He held it up between his thumb and forefinger, briefly marveling at its beauty, then ordered a scrub of all his entries for tonight

He had no idea what he intended to do. Confront Crocker? Denounce the whole sick scheme to the media? Or, the more prudent route, carry on as if everything were normal while he decided his next course of action. After all, what would he say? *They're destroying the world?* People would think he was crazy. Yeah, but—he squeezed the memory jewel in his hand—he had the proof right here, snatched from that portal into another dimension where the Upper Echelon played their little board game. But then what? Wake up in a cold, filthy cell, naked, chained to a chair, Boyd Malodorov's two goons playing tic tac toe on his body with kitchen knives while Boyd cajoled him, *C'mon, Marty, don't be a party pooper. There must be something else you'd like to share with your friends.* Then what? Unspeakable torture? Psychotropically induced nightmares involving incest and family pets? Festering, parasitic microbebots up the rectum? The mythical *internal probing claw?* And *then* what? Broken, bleeding, whining, pleading—denounce friends, family, his own children?

And then on the way home, the train ride barely a memory— he did notice a rough-looking young couple behind him as he sat down, black leather, tattoos, piercings, the girl was wearing a pink mini-skirt that barely hid her crotch—the car began *its* interrogations. *Another long day at the office, Marty? Burning the old candle at both ends again, Marty?* To which he answered truthfully that, yes, he had been working late, and yes, he would like to drive. Now please, he'd like some quiet.

But there was no quiet in his head. Distractions everywhere. The traffic on Olio heavy. Erratic drivers. VRBLs bombarding him with fast cars, bottles of booze, willowy, super-attenuated models in shimmering sequined dresses—he couldn't remember the last time he'd seen a woman who even remotely resembled that. The whole time tormenting himself over tonight's discovery. What if he imagined the whole thing? What if he really was going crazy? He touched the memory jewel in his pocket and almost wished it weren't there. He also wished the guy behind him would back off with his headlights.

His anxiety returned full force. What if they had already discovered he was on that site? What if he was being followed right now? Once again he had the sense he was being watched.

Traffic's heavy tonight, huh, Marty?

The car interrupted his thoughts. He didn't answer.

By the way, May—I mean, your wife called.

She wanted to know if he was going to miss the Family Hour again and if so, could he please call her back? Too late for that.

At home, he hurried upstairs to the bedroom and, after glancing about frantically, stuck the memory jewel in an old yellow crayon box he kept in the bottom drawer of his nightstand, an uncertain memento of an uncertain childhood. He heard an electrical whirr and the vacuumbot went by in the hall. Two seconds later it went by in the opposite direction. It started to go by a third time but suddenly rushed into the room and scurried under the bed. He waited. The vacuumbot's plastic forehead peeked out from under the bedspread and to his horror began to approach him with a threatening canine growl. "I've had enough of you *fucking* bots," he snarled, and drawing back his foot, he kicked the vacuumbot, which let out a mechanical howl and began to spin in circles while disgorging a tornadic cloud of dust. A high-pitched whine, the smell of burnt rubber, and the creature died altogether.

He hauled the vacuumbot's carcass to the utility closet, went downstairs, poured himself a large scotch and soda, popped a couple reds, a handful of greenies, and went to the family room. Ashley was bent over her EyePhone®, the TV blasting behind her. He turned it down. Ashley gave him an accusatory look over those stupid *X-ray* glasses. Did she suspect something? Ridiculous. She was a kid. She couldn't possibly know what he'd been up to. Maybe she felt guilty herself. He only now noticed the traces of black greasepaint and pink glitter around her eyes. She'd probably washed it off two minutes ago knowing how much he hated it. Fortunately, she had also foregone the spiked breastplate, she didn't look like a total freak. Meanwhile, the bubbly Twinkle Twins melody continued to play on Ashley's EyePhone®. He had always assumed it must be an innocuous jingle about teen angst, nobody understands me, etc., but now that he listened to the lyrics he realized they were talking about sex, drugs, violence in horribly foul language. He started to comment, but thought better and instead asked Ashley where everyone was.

Trey was in bed, Mom out.

"Out? Where?"

She didn't know, maybe church.

"On a Saturday night?"

Shrug. How would *she* know? She wasn't the *proselyte* in the family.

Proselyte? Where'd she get that word? And to whom was she referring—May? *Him?* "And your mom left you alone with Trey?"

Another dismissive shrug. She was clearly getting a kick out of his torment. *Mom* said she was old enough now.

Something was happening on TV. Bob Broadley and Marsha Mello announcing a major development. A former EAT employee had been arrested for subversive activities. An image appeared on the screen. A gaunt young man, head shaved, face wan, eyes sunken as if he had undergone an excruciating ordeal. There was something familiar about him. Then he realized. It was Jimmy, the mailroom guy. He felt sad. He felt sick. He felt as if he had just been bereaved of his own son. Even more so because there was nothing he could do to help Jimmy. He didn't even know if he could help himself now. His anxiety returned. What if they *did* know he had accessed that site? What if this so-called newsbreak was a warning to him not to do anything rash?

"Do you *know* him?" For the first time that evening Ashley spoke directly to him.

He shook his head no.

Ashley gave him a perplexed look and laughed, not necessarily in a friendly way. *"Daddy*, that's *Skinny-boy!"* Before he could reply, if there were even a reply he could have made, she said, "Oh yeah, now I remember."

"Remember what?" he said as if he had just glimpsed a tear in the space time continuum.

"Where *Mom* went. There's a Midnight Madness Mark-up sale at the *Ladies Lingerie Lounge.* She went with the *FFFMFC.*"

He had never heard anyone actually pronounce this acronym before. It sounded even cruder coming out of Ashley's thirteen-soon-to-be fourteen-year-old mouth, and she obviously took pleasure in saying it. At the same time he couldn't help but think it not entirely inappropriate. May had buried herself in this insipid consumer identity like all the other women in that stupid Fashionably Fashionable Fa—*Femfuck*, and here was Ashley, throwing it in his face, openly mocking him. And what was he going to say? *Watch your language, young lady?* And have her say, *What are you talking about, Daddy?* And make him repeat this vulgarity?

He couldn't understand how this had happened. Ashley had become so sullen, distant. And her appearance. Gone the healthy pink glow, replaced by a pale, ashen look. And her weight. She seemed to have ballooned up over night. What if she had an eating disorder? What if she was doing *drugs?* He needed another scotch.

He felt like a total wreck the following morning. His mind struggled to scrabble its way up out of a murky fog. A toxic brew bubbled in his stomach. The bug he'd caught showed no sign of abating. He briefly took solace in the fact that it was Sunday and he had the day off, until May reminded him that the Foreseeing a Bountiful Harvest Festival began today. Of course she insisted he go to church to set an example for the kids, not, he was certain, that they gave a damn.

Outside, the hot sunlight smacked him in the face like the flat of a shovel. The drive to church was excruciating, the light blinding, the traffic harrowing, his head aching. He still felt woozy when they entered the cathedral. Bright light bombarded him from every direction. Huge chandeliers hovered beneath the great vaulted ceiling like flying saucers. Enormous organ pipes rose like banks of ballistic missiles behind the altar. On either side of the organ pipes, AdVRBLs replaced stained glass saints with rushing

SUVs and gushing SodaRifics®. In the choir lofts hundreds of white-robed choristers fidgeted with their hymnals like flocks of restless angels. The thousands of faces rising row upon row in the stadium seating glowed like a sea of votive candles.

He and May and the kids squeezed into an already crowded pew just as the pipe organ roared like an ocean liner pulling into port and Archbishop Paisley Poodlepump appeared in a luminous white chasuble emblazoned front and back with golden ND$ signs, accompanied by a phalanx of attendants in simpler white robes solemnly swinging smoking censers. Behind them came a platoon of similarly attired altar boys, hair perfectly combed, pudgy faces scrubbed as clean as porcelain dolls. In a swaying, sashaying lockstep, this pious contingent marched the brief length of red carpet to the altar, which resembled the prow of a whaling ship elaborately carved with scenes of banking, industry and commerce. Ascending to the pulpit with the help of a discreet electric lift that made it seem as if he were levitating, the once humble pastor and now Most Reverend Poodlepump gave the invocation in a booming radio DJ voice, after which the choir rose and sang a doxology to the Creator of All Good and Affordable Things Eternal. Just as they were finishing, May leaned over and gave him a curious, sympathetic smile. He made a feeble attempt to smile back. His head throbbed like a small motorboat crossing a wide lake. His stomach grumbled in gaseous turmoil. He had thought Reverend Poodlepump somewhat diminished at Crocker's Solstistmas party, but he listened now with utmost earnestness as the great theologian spoke from his exulted heights of *those of little faith* and accepting *the will of the Creator.*

He must have fallen asleep. May was nudging him to his feet. The cathedral had descended into darkness. Disparate gasps of wonder grew into a loud collective sigh. Beneath a golden halo a great banquet appeared in front of the altar. Tables laden with baked hams, barbequed sides of beef, roasted turkeys. Tables loaded with pies, cakes and enormous tubs of ice cream. Reverend Poodlepump raised his hands and in loud but questionable French proclaimed *Laissez les bons temps rouler!* The great pipe organ screamed into the celestial realms and the choir of quasi-angels burst into hosannas in excelsis as thousands of parishioners streamed down the aisles to the banquet tables where they joined together in a bounteous feast and brotherly love. Communion and camaraderie quickly descended into a piranhic feeding frenzy. In minutes the ravenous masses had consumed enough food to feed a small nation. Altar boys playfully lobbed gobs of meat into each other's mouths. Barbecue sauce stained the choristers' white robes like blood. Reverend Poodlepump himself was elbow deep in a tub of ice cream. May had just shoved a chunk of meat the size of a gopher into her mouth. Her teeth and jaws chewed and crushed like a trash compactor, a manic, almost deranged look contorting her face. Why was she eating like that? All of them. They were eating like monsters. They *were* monsters.

His sense of events deteriorated rapidly after that. He spent most of the day in bed in a profound slumber bordering on comatose, only interrupted when May called him down for the Family Hour. While everyone else gorged themselves on deep dish pizza with extra cheese and multiple toppings, he ate like a zombie faced with a bowl of green salad. His scotch tasted like creosote. Hoping, at least, for some pharmaceutical relief, he popped his greenies, sat back and waited for the HearthScreen®'s golden glow to wash over him. But something was wrong. Instead of the familiar sense of warmth and security, he felt a sense of foreboding.

He must have fallen asleep again—he vaguely remembered being in a cold dark place, maybe some kind of cell, and a voice asking him something—and then May was shaking him awake, *Let's go up to bed, Marty.* As they climbed the stairs, she gave him a hug. Dazed, barely awake, he felt a warm rush of gratitude because they hadn't communicated much lately, physically or verbally. And then in bed she said to him in a husky, wine-thickened voice, "I kinda like you like this, Marty." What did she mean *like this?* But why hadn't he noticed before? Her body was enormous. Her breasts flopped over him like huge sacks of milk. He felt like he was being engulfed by a giant gastropod. It was drawing him into a vast pink cavity.

After that, he remembered a kind of video arcade of disconnected dreams. In one he lay febrile and bedridden as if he had contracted some pernicious disease and he could only watch helplessly as the vacuumbot's suction tube snaked over the bedcovers, hissing and biting at him. In another, he stood in the street looking back at the house, which glowed like a nuclear core, at its center for the whole world to see, the memory jewel.

The picture show in his head dimmed briefly. Then, through an odd oneiric leap, he was at work in front of his screen. A message had just come up, oddly personalized and therefore all the more disconcerting. *Was there a particular reason you were inquiring about this subject, Marty?* Panic swept over him. What *was* the subject? A box appeared with the message *press enter to continue*. He hit *enter* and the box opened to reveal another box inside with the same message, *press enter to continue*. He saw himself repeat this process again and again in an increasing blur until at last he came to a box with his name on it. With a profound sense of dread, he opened it. As he had expected, it was empty.

Marty?

Someone called his name. The voice sounded familiar, a soft, possibly young, probably female voice, slightly plaintive, as if it were asking something of him. A tiny window shade of lucidity raised itself in his somnolent brain. Maybe he was replaying the scene with Ashley the other night.

Then he did wake and discovered he had put in his EarWig®. This in itself was unusual because he had never felt comfortable with the damn thing. True, it was an ingenious device and even aided aural hygiene as it gently but determinedly screwed itself in and out of the ear. In fact, it almost seemed alive at times—which is precisely what he didn't like. He tapped his earlobe and the EarWig® unscrewed itself and fell out on the pillow and he fell back asleep—and, to his horror, into another, even more frightening dream. The EarWig® had crawled back into his ear. He felt it working its way deeper and deeper into his ear canal. He could hear it *eating*. His thoughts were disintegrating into a fuzzy whiteness.

He jerked awake as if somebody had splashed cold water in his face. Next to him a fuzzy pink mound rose and fell with the labored breathing of a large beast. *May?* He squeezed his eyes shut, opened them again. He had the sense he had experienced this before. He peered at his alarm clock. Five a.m. Time to get up.

He quickly showered and hastened to his closet to dress but again something seemed amiss. His clothes were all baggy, oversized. He felt like he was wearing a clown costume. His belt didn't have enough holes to cinch it tightly.

Stumped by this conundrum, he hurried downstairs to the kitchen where he was greeted by Bob Broadley's barbershop quartet tenor and Marsha Mello's operatic alto. Something must be wrong with the screen. They both looked large, distorted, like giant rag dolls with fuzzy faces and kitchen mitt hands. This, too, seemed familiar. Apparently there had been an accident in an Industrial Foods plant. Officials confirmed an uncontrolled release of several thousand gallons of fatty acids over Catábolus. A planetarily round science-type in thick glasses and a white lab coat pointed at a childish drawing resembling an enormous bursting pimple. At that moment the chefbot rolled in to make breakfast but he waved it away with a gesture of repugnance and headed for the door.

Outside he was engulfed by a smothering blanket of heat and humidity infused with the cloying smell of ... *fried chicken?* He started down the steps but his feet nearly slid out from under him. He clutched wildly at the railing but withdrew his hands in disgust. A greasy yellow film coated his fingers. It was everywhere. The street, sidewalks, trees, houses, lawns, cars—everything glistened with what appeared to be chicken fat.

An enormous blob-like creature in a dark blue business suit emerged from the house across the street. Fred Fortus. At least he assumed it was Fred. Fred started to wave but let his huge appendage drop to his side, as if unsure to whom he was waving. He made a half-hearted attempt to wave back, but feeling scrutinized, he hurried as cautiously as he could down the slippery slope of the sidewalk to the drive. The car, too, looked different, not just bigger but *swollen*, as if it were holding its breath. Nevertheless, it offered him its customary greeting.

Morning, Marty.

"Morning," he mumbled.

Something wrong, Marty?

"No. Why do you ask?" he responded too hastily.

I don't know, Marty, you sound … different. You look different.

"I didn't sleep well last night."

Maybe you should see a doctor, Marty.

They'd had this conversation before too.

Unsure of his driving skills on a street paved with chicken fat, he asked the car to take charge. As they turned onto Easy Street, another car's strangely bulbous rear end fishtailed past them. A female *blob* in a bright orange outfit of circus tent proportions waved to him from her front porch, then did a double take that required the bulldozer-like rotation of her entire body. On Pastoral Avenue, the slime-coated iron girders of the new high-rise gleamed in the morning sunlight like an enormous rotisserie. Outside Oma's Bakery a line of customers shuffled and yawned like a train of exotic circus animals waiting their turn at the feed trough. A few of them seemed to be examining the bottoms of their shoes.

As they turned onto Olio, the driver next to him made eye contact and immediately looked away, his great mushroom face contorted with horror. Did he, too, realize something was terribly wrong? A pair of cops as big as rhinoceroses watched him go by from behind the windshield of their patrol vehicle, their crew cut blockheads and wraparound shades rotating in perfect synchronicity. He kept expecting to see flashing lights in his rear mirror the rest of the way to the train station.

He managed to cross the slimy parking lot without breaking his neck, but horror undercut his relief as he forced his way into the mass of blobs pouring into the station, every one of them huge, distorted, and yet they looked at *him* as if *he* were the monster. *Oh, that's awful!* someone said. *What's wrong with him?* said another. This couldn't be happening. He felt like he was in a science fiction film. A security camera's dark, cyclopean eye ceased its relentless back and forth prison yard surveillance and fixed its gaze on him at the same time he spotted a trio of police officers, all as big as parade floats, munching on carpet-sized slices of pizza while they scrutinized passengers. He hurried past them hidden behind a female blob in a brown, palanquin-like outfit, descended the escalator sandwiched between the sponge cake buttocks and belly of a pair of blobs who seemed completely unaware of his presence, and like an ill-fated passenger on a foundering whaling ship, he plunged into the subterranean sea of ambergris inundating the boarding platform. Blobs bobbed about like gang-planked tubs of blubber, man overboard hogsheads of flesh, on their faces the befuddled expressions of giant puffer fish. He began to more or less swim forward through the gelatinous swells and troughs toward the front of the platform, his repugnance at this unintentionally lubricious contact clearly reciprocated by the blobs, who separated and drew back from him like an enormous protoplasmic organism undergoing mitosis. A plaintive *beeeee* announced the train's arrival and he propelled himself through the last two yards of blubber and squeezed on board the crowded car. Huddled against a window, he stared at the blackness rushing by outside, and then at his face reflected in the glass, gaunt, drawn, slashed by shadows like a nineteenth century woodblock print.

After an excruciating half hour packed in this can of sushi, he was extruded from the train en masse with the other passengers, pushed across the platform, up the escalator and out into the hot sunlight. Free at last of this suffocating press of flesh, he zigzagged across the slime-slick Heroes Plaza like a jackrabbit in a lumbering herd of pachyderms. The emerald green EAT Building towering before him gleamed as if it had been drenched in melted butter. His image, stretched out like a rubber band, loomed up to meet him in the revolving glass door, then diminished into a thin oily streak.

At the security desk, two blobs—one possibly female—in blue suit coats and orange badges scrutinized his biometrics, then swiveled around in their chairs and whispered to the pair of heavily armed, black-garbed behemoths standing behind them, who watched with hostile gaze as he hurried across the lobby to the elevator, which, to his relief, he found empty. He pressed the button for his floor before anyone else could enter, but as the stainless steel door closed, enveloping him in cool white fluorescence, he had the unsettling sense he'd entered a death chamber, a premonition that seemed justified when the elevator rocketed past his floor, stopped abruptly, then plunged downward again at a precipitous rate, coming to another abrupt halt halfway between the twelfth and fourteenth floors. He waited. Nothing happened. He pushed the button again but still nothing happened. He glanced at the red emergency button next to the door. This wasn't an emergency, just a slight inconvenience, right? Besides, the proper authorities had probably already been alerted by the elevator's security system. Someone must be on their way right now.

The air conditioning had shut off. The car felt hot, stuffy. Sweat rolled down his face. He was having trouble breathing. The emergency button glowed in front of him like a ripe red cherry demanding to be plucked. All he had to do was push it and something would happen, right? A bell'd go off or the elevator'd start moving again or somebody'd come and let him out. Yeah, like one of those lazy, shuffling, clover-sniffing public servants who sucked off the public funds. He'd *never* get out of here. The maintenance staff'd find his desiccated corpse in a pile of rags.

He pushed the emergency button. An orange digital display appeared in front of him. Blinking sweat from his eyes, he leaned closer to read what it said: *Cooking Time—Oven Temperature—Bake—Broil—Warm.* Huh? He blinked again and the elevator lurched and began to move, bearing him upward like a roast turkey in a hotel dumbwaiter.

At his floor the elevator jolted to a stop, the door slid open and he stumbled across the hall into the Distribution Accounting Department where the female blob behind the receptionist's desk was just cramming an entire chocolate cupcake into her mouth. He didn't recognize her, nor, apparently, she him. Her eyes widened like coconut cream pies and she began to make an *ack-*

ack-ack choking sound. For a minute he faced the horrifying prospect of attempting CPR but she finally swallowed with a loud gulp and feebly waggled her fingers to signal she was okay.

Enormously relieved, he hurried down the hall past the break room where the early arrivals had already gathered around the pastry table. One of them glanced up with benign, masticating indifference that morphed into wide-eyed disbelief and an explosion of whispers followed him down the hall. He was just about to enter his office when Gordie Goutte came bouncing toward him like an untethered weather balloon. Gordie's mocking little porcine eyes widened in the doughy approximation of his face and he snarled, "Geez, Marty, ya go on a diet?"

Ignoring this remark, he closed and locked the door behind him, sat down at his desk and stared at the framed photograph of May and the kids. May was as big as a delivery van, the kids the size of economy cars, their features barely recognizable in the mass of flesh that engulfed them. He glanced up at the photograph on the wall from the last company picnic. Everyone was huge, distorted, their facial features almost indistinguishable. How was it possible he had never noticed before? Had the unfamiliar somehow become so familiar, even *normal*, that he was no longer aware of it? He peered at the photograph. Where was he? There, barely visible at the back, only that pained expression in his eyes as if he were looking for an escape.

A light knock at the door brought him up straight in his chair. He debated not answering, then did and was met by the great tofu moonscape of Laong Hsiuh's face. Laong Hsiuh started to say, "Marty, why is your door locked … ?" but his eyes widened behind his glasses like pineapple slices and he began to make popping sounds like a fish swallowing insects on the surface of a lake. In a voice barely above a whisper, he asked if he had seen the spread Marge put out this morning and departed the office in a frantic flailing of limbs that belied his body's lumbering egress.

As if answering a call to arms, Marge, already notoriously large of girth but expanded now into horrifying proportions, barged in like a funeral ship in a billowing black satin outfit adorned at the prow with a huge spray of white calla lilies. In her hands she held a silver platter bearing her famous *snowball*, an ultra cholesterolic concoction of ricotta, marzipan, mascarpone, vanilla ice cream and coconut shavings. *"Goood Morrrning, Misterrr Grassooooh!"* she chortled, her mouth lipsticked into a red rubber raft of a smile. Suddenly her eyes bulged like ostrich eggs, her smile drooped like a deflated hot water bottle, and proffering her culinary abomination at him like a libation to some ancient and awful god, she said in a tremulous voice, "D'ya eat yet?" Red-hot rage surged through his brain. He sprang from his desk, knocked the *snowball* from Marge's hands and chased her out of the office, shouting, "I've eaten enough *shit!*" Though unintentional, his metaphor was apt, but not a single soul laughed among the crowd that had gathered outside his door. The whole gang, Laong Hsiuh, Mustuffah Ghee, Gordie, LaQuisha, Dolly Butterworth, Carmela Lechay, Chuck Roastley, all staring at him like a herd of spooked cattle, Marge cowering in a corner, moaning like a cow lorn of her calf, *mooo-hoo-hoo*, and Crocker looming over them all like a great black vulture surveying the carnage below. Disconcerted by this unexpected reception, he retreated into his office, locked the door behind him, shut down his screen and turned off his EyePhone®. He had irrevocably crossed a line, that he knew. His next move? He hadn't a clue.

Other than a few clandestine trips to the men's room, he spent the rest of the day holed up in his office, expecting another knock on the door at any minute, Boyd Malodorov and his two goons, *Hi Marty, we've come for a chat.* Oddly, he only realized now, he probably wouldn't be able to describe Boyd unless he stood right in front of him. One day he came across as a greasy, disheveled slob stinking of boiled cabbage and cheap vodka distilled into an even more piquant odor from days without a change of clothes. Another day as a geeky, starched suit and tie technocrat, crew-cut, cue ball head, Adam's apple bobbing like he was trying to swallow a hard boiled egg. And yet another as an indistinct presence exuding a brute physicality he sensed could easily be unleashed on himself in other circumstances.

The air grew hot and stuffy. The heat had come on. Absurd, it was summer. He got up and went to the window. In the plaza below an impossibly thin man, barely more than a stick figure, stared up at him. He closed the blinds and, after pacing back and forth several times, sat back down at his desk. The AC came on with a painful, emphysemic wheezing sound. The air turned cold, dank.

He began to feel hungry, then, his thoughts preoccupied with his empty stomach, desperately so. He considered getting down on his hands and knees and lapping up some of Marge's snowball melting into the carpet like a snowman's severed head, but resigned himself to the dregs of cold coffee.

By six o'clock he felt like a vampire deprived of its daily quota of blood. His hands shook, his thoughts were jagged, his forehead feverish, his stomach in shreds. Locking his office behind him, he snuck out along the rear hallway. In the break room, piles of dirty plates and parchment paper-lined trays still remained from the afternoon feast. At the receptionist's desk, the young female blob had fallen asleep over a bowl of chocolate pudding and was snoring contentedly, the spoon still clutched in her fist, telltale brown smudges around her mouth, from the corner of which escaped a trickle of chocolate drool.

Unfortunately the elevator was packed. Despite looks of severe disapproval, he squeezed into this oleaginous mass of opprobrium like a dill pickle spear into a ball of sweet dough, realizing as the door closed that not only were the other passengers all furiously chewing on GoodLife® energy bars (he remembered now there was some kind of promotion), they were chewing *at* him, their apparent revulsion at his presence growing as they approached the end of their treats.

Relieved to escape this potential lynch mob, he extracted himself from the elevator like a squeezed dishrag and exited the EAT Building into an equatorial swamp of hot, humid air that felt almost pleasurable after the frigid temperatures in his office, a sentiment obviously not shared by the crowd of sweaty, disheveled blobs pushing, shoving and snarling at each other outside the train station, their great moon and balloon faces contorted with helpless outrage. One turned and glared at him as if he were at fault, then threw up his hands in terror and backed away.

Tweeeeet! A loud whistle brought silence to the unruly mob.

A red-faced officer of the law lumbered into their midst like a great Black Maria, thumped his club against his catcher's mitt-sized hand and shouted, "Keep it down, alla yez, or I'll start dispensing fat lips!" If anyone else caught the irony of this threat, they didn't show it.

Apparently the trains were running an hour and a half late, every car was packed. At a pace bordering on glacial, the sweat-sodden, sponge-like mass of blobs carried him into the station and down the escalator like a toothpick caught in a fat rendering machine, finally depositing him on the boarding platform, where he found himself squashed against the huge bosom of a female blob. Apologizing profusely and trying not to place his hands anywhere that might incur a lawsuit, he extracted himself from this mutually unwelcome embrace just as a loud *beeee* announced the next train's arrival. With a heroic effort, he forced himself onto a packed car and into a standing-room only crush of enormous mushy bellies, breasts and buttocks and spent the next thirty minutes examining much more closely than he would have ever cared nose hairs, earwax, unidentifiable remnants of meat stuck in teeth and plump pink tongues yammering on EyePhone®s. The lights flickered off, on, off. Grotesque faces faded in and out of darkness like a house of horrors. The AC must have stopped functioning. The air turned hot, stuffy. An insidious cloud of highly sulfurous flatulence flowed uninvited up his nostrils, flooded the various traps and elbows of his sinus cavities and momentarily knocked his brain loopy. He wanted to scream, *Get away from me, you disgusting blobs!* The words echoed in his skull like a plastic bottle caroming down the concrete walls of a manhole. Please don't let me have said that aloud, he begged some unspecified deity, even as a rabble of angry, menacing eyes shifted in his direction.

He fled the SunnyVale station like a fugitive from a gang of vigilantes and practically dashed across the simmering parking lot. The sun hung low on the horizon in a murky haze the color of stale urine. The yellow slime had largely evaporated but here and there an oily sheen remained. The acrid air burned in his eyes and in his lungs. He yearned for the relief of the car's AC the way a wounded soldier yearned for a cup of cool, clear water in the middle of the desert.

A suffocating blast of hot air struck him in the face as the door opened. He demanded to know why the climate control hadn't been turned on.

How am I supposed to keep up with your erratic schedule, Marty? the car huffed.

Neither of them chose to pursue the issue.

On Olio Boulevard the neon blaze of shops, bars and restaurants quavered in the rising heat waves as if they were part of an underwater city. VRBLs undulated like the iridescent fila of giant deep-sea creatures. As they turned onto Pastoral Avenue, the sun sank into a pool of red-hot plasma behind the ironwork of the new building.

He knew something was wrong as soon as he pulled in the drive. The porch lights were off, the house dark. He hurried up the walk and grabbed the doorknob but no grandfatherly lockbot greeted him warmly, the door remained locked. He raised his hand to knock but suddenly the door flew open and May's enormous mass filled the doorframe. Her bright green eyes gleamed like shards of glass in the pale gibbous moon of her face. In a strained, even accusatory, tone, she informed him that the power was out, all the appliances dead. "Marty—the hearth …"

"What about the hearth?"

"I don't *know.*" May's voice sounded plaintive, defensive. "Shouldn't we call the technicians, Marty?"

"No!" he almost shouted.

A cloud passed over the pale lunarscape of May's face. "Marty, does this have something to do with work?"

He tried to explain but his words came out in a jumble. His job at EAT, the work he did, it was all a lie, there were no sappers, the whole thing was about to collapse, there'd be starvation, disease, chaos in the streets, they had to find a safe place.

"What are you talking about, Marty?" In May's voice he detected the cautious tone of someone who has just realized she's speaking to a raving lunatic.

He forged ahead. "Can't you see? Look at yourself. Look at the people in the street. Look at the *kids*, for God's sake. You're all *monsters*."

Pity and disgust combined in the alembic of May's voice. "No, Marty, it's not *us*. It's *you*. Don't you realize, Marty? You look like one of—*them*."

"*Them?*"

"Please, Marty, I've tried to tell you. I've tried to get you help." May sounded plaintive again. "Marty, shouldn't we at least ask the neighbors if the kids can stay over while we decide what to do? This could scar them for life."

Other than a word of greeting or a comment on the weather, he had never spoken to any of his neighbors. He wouldn't recognize a single one of them at the mall. Besides, he saw through May's deception. She was stalling for time, maybe even planning to call the police. He ordered her to get the kids and meet him at the car.

A few minutes later May herded the kids out the door, Trey in a fuzzy brown onesie that made him look like a large rodent, his soft, pale face clouded by a sleepy, confused expression, Ashley like a Wagnerian Valkyrie rigged out for battle in her Queen Martyr-D costume.

He drove in silence, May giving him worried glances, the kids in back eating GoodLife® energy bars and immersed in their electroids. From time to time he felt Ashley glower at the back of his head. He had begun to think she really did hate him. At the very least, she blamed him for this inconvenience. Attempting detente, he asked if she was texting Prissy Bombaste.

"Of course not, *Daddy*," she snarled. "I'm talking to Charlotte."

Gongs banged and lightning crashed inside his skull. "Charlotte doesn't exist! She's a figment of your imagination!" A searing white heat struck the back of his head, penetrated hair, epidermis, occipital bone, and exploded in his brain.

"*You* don't exist!" Ashley's face was an angry red blot in the rear mirror. Her eyes gleamed behind her *X-ray* glasses, not like myopic pools of blue but highly concentrated beams of light. He had the briefly terrifying thought that she didn't wear those stupid things to make a fashion statement or improve her eyesight but to restrain some frightening power. Oh yes, all hail Queen Martyr-D with her amazing, in fact *awesome*, ability to magically make things happen. He felt a sudden unfatherly urge to say something small and mean to put her in her place but just then May spoke up.

"We're going to the country, aren't we, Marty? Where you lost the car?"

He almost lashed out at this dig but restrained himself and said he had a friend who might be able to help them.

"A friend, Marty? What kind of friend would live out here?"

She was right. Elmo wasn't a friend. In fact, he had sincerely hoped he'd never run into him again. But Elmo had extended an invitation and for some reason he trusted him.

It was completely dark now. Fog had started to roll in. The car's headlights cast a tunnel of phosphorescence in front of them. A large animal bounded across the road, dog, deer, he didn't know what. "A fire engine!" Trey's voice startled him. The long red truck crouched like a dragon in the gloom. Elmo's junk-cluttered yard appeared shortly afterward. He pulled into the drive, shut off the engine and started to get out. May and the kids stared at him without moving.

"*C'mon*," he said, making it sound like they were stopping at a roadside attraction.

This time Elmo answered the door, his greasy, beard-stubbled face grim, menacing. "Yeah, who is it?" The narrow slits of his eyes widened with recognition. "Hey, it's Greaso! Geez, Greaso, yer condition get woise or sumpin'?"

He said they'd had a power outage. Everything was down, lights, appliances, the HearthScreen®. It looked like his whole street had been hit (a lie). He didn't know where to go (true).

"Yeah? Well I'm flattered yez thought of me, Greaso. Hey, what's this, yer family? Going to a costume party, I see." Elmo leered at Ashley in a way that'd make any parent nervous, but she glowered in defiance. "Hey! But I'm forgetting my manners. C'mon in, folks. Hey, Oima! Look who's here!"

"We're sorry to bother you," May apologized to Oima, who had just shuffled in from somewhere in what looked like the same dirty slip he remembered from last time.

"Naw, don't worry about it." Oima's face brightened, maybe at the sight of another woman. "Hey, you kids want somethin' to eat?"

Ashley and Trey had been staring at her as if she were a talking farm animal, but, more or less of barnyard dimensions themselves, at the suggestion of food they eagerly followed her out to the kitchen and returned with heaping bowls of tapioca pudding, which they began to spoon into their mouths while standing in front of the flickering TV.

"How come you don't have a HearthScreen®?" Ashley demanded in the poisonous voice of a police informer.

Elmo was obviously in no mood for this attitude. "Hey, little lady," he purred, his jowls stretching sideways in a leering barracuda grin, "at least our screen *woiks*. We don't gotta put on no *masquerade* to entertain ourselves, know what I mean?"

Ashley stared at Elmo in disbelief. "You're not supposed to talk to *children* like that. I could"—she hesitated, perhaps unsure of her territory. For a moment he actually thought she was going to say *kill you*. Instead she resorted to the possibly more convincing threat—"report you to the authorities."

Elmo's eyes sprang wide as if he'd heard a fire alarm. The next second he burst out laughing, *Ha!Ha!Ha!* and began to repeat in a singsong voice, "*Little Miss Greaso ain't got a screen-o. Little Miss Greaso ain't got a screen-o.*"

Ashley's face turned as red as a pot of spaghetti sauce. Her chin quivered. He thought she was going to cry. He hadn't realized she could be so vulnerable. And yet he had the sense she wasn't upset so much by Elmo's cruelty as she was that he refused to play according to her rules. He felt a crushing pang of guilt. The kids were clearly suffering from this ordeal. The HearthScreen® was dead, they'd fled their home like refugees, they were hungry, and it was all his fault.

Elmo, too, must have realized he'd gone too far. In a kinder, gentler tone he said, "Hey, Greaso, whatayez say me and youse go take a look at yer fuse box. I'm pretty good wit' electrical stuff."

"No! That is"—he glanced at May—"the tech guy's coming over tonight."

"Yez could save yerself a coupla bucks, Greaso," Elmo insisted. "I'm telling yez, I'm pretty good wit' electronics.

Something in Elmo's tone flipped a small switch in his brain. He remembered that during his last visit Elmo had said something about sappers. And how did he know about that damaged train canopy? Another thought occurred to him, crazy, desperate, and yet—what if Elmo was discreetly trying to communicate to him that *he* was a sapper. Of *course* the sappers existed. They *had* to exist. Someone must be trying to stop this catastrophe. Affecting a change of heart, he said, "Yeah, sure, that'd be great. We can take my car." At the door, he whispered, "You're one of them, aren't you?"

Elmo looked puzzled. "One'a who, Greaso?"

"You know"—he gave Elmo a conspiratorial wink—"*sappers?*"

Elmo slammed the door shut. "Hey, pal, youse got me mixed up wit' the wrong crowd. I admit the syndicate ain't exactly a bunch'a loveboids, but we ain't no sappers neither."

"But you said …" But what precisely had he said?

Before he could say anything else, Elmo took him by the arm and forcefully escorted him back to the living room. He remembered May giving him something cold and slightly bitter to drink and saying, "Don't worry, Marty. Everything will be all right."

8

endgame

HE CAME DOWNSTAIRS around noon the following day, still in his pajamas, which he didn't remember putting on, to find a small crowd of nervous, expectant and very expansive faces awaiting him in the family room. Abe and Libby Bombaste, the Largelys from church, the gang from work, Laong Hsiuh, Dolly Butterworth, LaQuisha and Carmela, Chuck Roastley, Gordie, stuffing his face with cheese puffs and thumbing through a stack of May's fashion magazines, Mustuffah Ghee, who didn't seem to know why he was here, "I *taught* vee verrr hahving a birthday pahr-teee," an impression he apparently gathered from the lavish spread of pies, cakes, cookies and donuts provided by Marge, in a cheerful though completely out of season poinsettia print outfit. At the rear of this bunch stood Crocker with a great black wing folded around May, to whom he seemed to be speaking in a confidential manner.

"*Ha!*" Crocker snorted when he spotted him. In an offhand tone he added, "Sorry about that little affair last night, Martin."

This sounded familiar.

"The power outage, I mean. *Here*, at your nice, comfortable, *little* house."

Retinal fragments of yesterday's events flashed through his brain.

"You were out of control, Martin." Crocker said this as if he were referring to a malfunctioning servicebot. "We had to rein you in. You're sick, my boy, *sick*. Now don't worry." Crocker glanced at May, who had shrugged off his embrace. "Your family will be well taken care of while you recuperate."

Recuperate?

In a tone just short of pleading, May said, "Marty, you need treatment. You can't handle this problem yourself. We've arranged for you to go into a clinic."

He heard *we* and *clinic*.

May glanced toward the hall where he only now noticed a very round little man in a brown cardigan and red bow tie who actually may have just stepped out of the hall closet. Beaming like a benevolent bowling pin, the man waddled forward and squeezed his fingertips in a pink, pudgy little hand not much bigger than a baby's. May introduced him as Doctor Apfel Doompling. Doctor Doompling was here to *guide* them, she said. Now he understood. They were doing an intervention.

As if on cue, everyone crowded around and began to offer him donuts and cookies, slices of cake and pie. They smacked their lips and made encouraging eating gestures and said "*Yummie!*" and "*Delicious!*" He had an inchoate memory of himself as an infant in a crib and the helplessness he felt surrounded by adults making grotesque faces at him.

"But I'm not sick," he said. "It's *you*. All of you."

May winced. Her bright green eyes fixed on his as if she were trying to convey something to him of great importance. In a carefully modulated voice she said, "It's not your fault, Marty. It's an illness. It doesn't mean you're a bad person."

Why was she talking to him like that? Did she really think he was crazy? All of them. They were treating him like a complete idiot. He felt like smashing their stupid pies and cakes in their fat mushroom faces. He felt like shouting at them *you're not even human!* But then what? An ugly scene? Men in white coats? The police? He felt even more helpless than before. He felt like crying. Tears welled in his eyes. He let out a sob. Everyone thought this was a good sign. Marge dabbed at her eyes and loudly blew her nose into a lace handkerchief the size of a pillowcase. Doctor Doompling, who had folded his pink little hands over his plump little chest and was nodding approvingly, now stepped forward, reached into the pocket of his cardigan and produced a syringe with a drop of clear liquid at the tip. "This won't hurt a bit, Martin."

He remembered a recurring dream. A rustic, hand-carved wooden sign said WELCOME TO GREEN VALLEY DAIRY FARM. Then white board fences, cows grazing in a pasture, a windmill by a barn. Then he was inside the barn. He smelled hay, cow manure. Oddly, the wooden stalls contained hospital beds on which people in white hospital gowns lay motionless with wires and tubes and stainless steel devices attached to their bodies. Then he saw himself lying in one of the beds with similar wires and tubes connected to his body. He wondered in a hazy, disinterested way if they were filling him up or extracting something from him.

Sometimes people in white coats stood over him. He remembered a light shining in his eyes and a voice asking him repeatedly about a *jewel.* He tried to speak but he could only stammer in a helpless little voice, "i ... i ... i ... i ..."

He remembered being awakened again and again to eat blocks of Jell-O-like substance or take handfuls of pills before falling back into a profound sleep.

Once he dreamed he was on a train. It was moving very slowly through a desolate landscape. Groups of gaunt, skeletal people stood and watched the train pass with blank expressions on their faces. Then he was no longer on the train. Now it was he who stood in the field watching the train pass. There was a long line of cattle cars packed with people. They reached their spindly arms through the bars as if pleading to him for help. Why did they think he could help them?

Another time he dreamed he and May and the kids were sitting on the cold ground in front of a fire. Trey and Ashley were both dressed in rags. They stared into the flames as if mesmerized. But then it wasn't a fire, it was a TV screen.

"They're always in front of the screen," he said angrily.

"Oh Marty, can't you see they're hungry?" May replied.

Then there was something that didn't seem like a dream. A kind of pink aura floated above him, and there was a face, strange and ethereal, almost translucent. He thought maybe it was an angel. It moved closer and he saw it was a girl in a pink dress. At first he assumed it must be Ashley. But this girl was much thinner than Ashley, and her voice, when she spoke, wasn't strident like Ashley's, but kind and sympathetic, although he couldn't make out what she was saying, or to whom she was speaking.

He woke seated in a wheelchair at a window looking down into a sunny courtyard where other patients in pale blue hospital gowns also sat in wheelchairs. Some were attended by nurses. Others seemed to be visiting with family members. They were all eating methodically from large, white deli cartons embossed with the blue Industrial Foods logo.

May came in shortly afterward. She seemed pleased to see him out of bed. In a cautiously optimistic tone she said the doctor thought he was getting *better* but his case was more resistant than most. She mentioned a condition, something that sounded like cannibalism—*catabolism*, that's it. Something about his metabolism working against itself, consuming too much energy. *However*—May sounded hopeful again—they were trying a new drug and he should be able to go home soon.

Whereupon Doctor Doompling, beaming like a buttered scone in his white lab coat, briskly waddled into the room with a clipscreen under his arm, stuck out his pudgy little hand for a cursory *finger* shake and introduced himself again in case—giving May a knowing glance—he had *forgotten.* Doctor Doompling went on to explain that with resistant cases like his there were options. Some chose cosmetic surgery. Fat implants, silicone injections, things like that. Of course complications did arise, unexpected side effects, strange shifts of body mass, the buttocks dropping to the knees, for example. No—Doctor Doompling attempted to take his chin in his hand but seemed unable to locate this osseous landmark in the blubbery mass surrounding it—he didn't recommend surgery. Prosthetics, that was the way to go.

"You mean a *fat suit?*" he said, not sure how he knew about this alternative.

Doctor Doompling shook his head dismissively. They were making some very convincing suits now, more expensive, of course, but certainly worth the investment. The new synthetics were lighter, more comfortable, you could even have climate control included. As an added benefit, there was a built-in ergonomic assistant. It did some of the heavy lifting for you, cut back on your energy consumption. "Don't think of it as something cold and alien, Martin. Think of it as an extension of your own body. Wear it proudly. *Become* it. At least until you're *better.*"

Of course May was enthusiastic. She made sure he took his new meds and encouraged him to wear his NIBS, as everyone referred to the New Image Body Suit. "Really, Marty," she said, the first time he tried it on, "I think you look cute."

Adjusting to the NIBS was initially a struggle. He felt like he was wrapping himself in a great rubbery mollusk. And going to the bathroom was a nightmare. Not just the unpleasant chore of *finding* himself among those disgusting folds of pseudo-flesh, but that nasty business with the toilet paper and trying to *reach.* Now it was almost second nature. He even felt a sense of security in his NIBS' matronly softness, like those all-forgiving, everything-is-right-with-the-world hugs his mother gave him when he was troubled by some small disturbance in his childish universe.

Another positive sign. Over breakfast recently May had observed that the new diet pills seemed to be working. For proof, he had seconds of everything, Spanish omelet, blueberry pancakes topped with maple syrup and whipped cream, smoked sausage and home-fried potatoes, biscuits and gravy, glazed donuts and prune Danish, and, to wash it down, a high-calorie chocolate milkshake.

The car, as it did every morning now, greeted him with a cheery, *Looking good, Marty*, and gave him a final, encouraging, *give 'em hell, Marty* when he got out at the train station. Of course the other commuters still stared, but he consoled himself that at least they knew he was making the effort to appear normal, a self-affirming attitude he had developed at his Catabolics Anonymous meetings, which he attended religiously. Everyone sitting around on sofas and folding chairs, fat suits unzipped, dutifully munching on chips and dips, cream puffs and donuts while they related their sad tales of alienation, anti-social behavior, breakdown and recovery. Sometimes they participated in *truth-telling sessions* where they were encouraged to let out their anger and resentment, to admit their prejudices, the ugly slurs they had used, *blob, blobulous, blobaceous, blobinous, blobophilia, blobophile, blobette, blobone, blob! slob! food pod!* True, there were a few shameless chuckles among the group, and occasionally even loud, unrestrained guffaws all around, until the group leader coughed into his hand and the group resumed their litany of sins in the modified drone of novice priests repeating their vows, *food pod, pod, pod people* ...

Of course the return to work was awkward at first. His team members smiled nervously, *good to see ya back, Marty, looking great, Marty*, while giving him furtive glances. Laong Hsiuh, especially, seemed uncomfortable in his presence, as if he were speaking to a not particularly welcome revenant. Apparently Laong Hsiuh had assumed a number of his managerial duties during his prolonged absence, and had even begun to work on a new program based on the adaptability of butter in its different states—solid, liquid and colloidal. As a result, there was some question of who was really in charge. But after all, he *was* Senior Project Director and it *was* his project, a fact Crocker confirmed when he came into the office, folded a musty black wing around his shoulder, tentatively, perhaps, and said gruffly, "I've always had a fondness for you, Martin. Sometimes I think of you as the son I never had. My bright, talented, *wayward* son. But that's all in the past, isn't it, my boy?" Crocker's talons tightened through the fat suit. "Time to get this ship back in shape and the master at the helm. What do you say to that, Martin? Ms. Donatzk will have a list of updates on your desk tomorrow morning." And so she did.

He was reviewing the last of these when Marge, in a tropical print outfit—palm trees, pineapples, hula girls—bustled in with a steamer trunk-sized slice of pineapple upside down cake topped with a small mountain of whipped cream and chortled, "*Helloooo, Mister Grassoooo.* D'ya eat yet? Ya did? Fa! Always room for more."

Throughout the day people reminded him of the latest entrées in the break room. The chefbot hummed in and out of his office laden with snacks and treats. He was, however, vaguely aware of an absence, a lacuna in the workplace fabric. Didn't there used to be a mailroom guy? Probably let go during the last round of budget cuts, he speculated.

There were other troubling signs of tightened funding. As he strode across the lobby at the end of the day, he noticed a general sense of shabbiness and neglect. Instead of the pleasant chorus of birdsong he had remembered, a loud, mechanical, squawking sound, like the cry of a large prehistoric bird in distress, echoed overhead, *cha-warrrk! cha-warrrk! cha-warrrk!* Even to his horticulturally untrained eye, the tropical plants looked chlorotic and wilted. And a single glance was all he needed to see that the bronze sculpture of the winged goddess had taken on a bluish-green patina and was covered with dust. Heroes Plaza was even worse. The ornamental maples had withered into bare sticks, like umbrella ribs without the fabric. The waterscapes gasped, gurgled and sputtered like dying sea creatures.

Another change had occurred, this one at home. Increasingly occupied with her social commitments, May had hired a nanny for Trey, who seemed to be having developmental issues. While the doctors could find nothing *wrong* with him, he didn't seem to be progressing as he should for his age. He had stopped gaining weight, and he'd lost interest in his schoolwork. "I'm not blaming *you*, Martin," she said, which, of course, made him feel as if she was. He also suspected it wouldn't be too far of a stretch to guess this nanny had been hired to keep an eye on *him* and his dietary regimen.

Mrs. S'vastapolagniskatzis looked like an enormous nesting doll. She wore a red babushka on her head, a black wool vest over a flowered peasant blouse, a white starched apron over a black wool skirt, and a pair of brown leather boots that reminded him of the great, hairy hooves of plow horses. She also had cheeks as red as strawberries, black eyebrows as thick as shag carpet and itinerant chin whiskers that stuck out like toothpicks. She descended upon the Grasso household clasping in her big peasant arms a large black umbrella and several fragrant-smelling cloth bundles of herbs and spices. After dismissing the chefbot with a swift kick in the can that elicited a surprised mechanical yelp, Mrs. S'vastapolagniskatzis immediately set up shop in the kitchen. Enveloped in clouds of steam, her ruddy brow beaded with sweat, she stirred huge bubbling pots of meat and potatoes enriched with industrial quantities of butter, cream and lard. "Don't you vurry, *Mee*ster *Graw*so," she said in a heavy accent of no certain provenance. "Ve soon haf you and dat poor boy fattened up *beeg* time."

Ashley, happily, seemed to be going through another phase. She was less moody, cynical, more positive, thoughtful. She also dressed more modestly now, although in bright, cheerful colors, preferably pink.

May, too, seemed different. Despite the duress she had suffered in the course of his downward spiral, her star had risen in society. She chaired committees, she was appointed to commissions, she gave inspirational speeches. To celebrate the dual achievements of her arrival as a mover and shaker and his return to EAT, she had planned a grand soirée, fully catered.

Banners, balloons and streamers hung all over the house. Guests arrived from near and far. May's brother Floyd, whom he must have met before but couldn't remember. His own sister Doris and her husband Chives (*Clive?*). He and Doris had been estranged so long he'd almost forgotten she existed. Doris had dropped out of college and joined a commune of cloverheads who migrated around the country in a caravan of old school buses, selling trinkets and jewelry in various arts and crafts fairs. But now here she was, married, in a business suit, a big chief in the world of *natural* cosmetic products, considerably *larger*. Libby and Abe Bombaste and their close friend Clarence Clambaker. The Largelys, the Mostleys, the Phartons, the Toastleys—some of these people he didn't even know. The entire FFFMFC crowd who later in the evening ended up in a drunken chorus line, kicking up their huge haunches like a sorority of sows, and later still, weeping into their wine glasses as they sang their anthem off-key. And of course the whole gang from work, Laong Hsiuh, who seemed resigned to his newly reduced authority, Gordie, who had just consumed an entire tray of stuffed Portobello mushrooms, Mustuffah Ghee, "now *thees* is a *pahrrtee,*" as well as Chuck Roastley, Carmela Lechay, Dolly Butterworth and LaQuisha Dzukene who, like a team of EdenFresh® greeters, gave him encouraging little smiles and fluttery finger waves whenever he encountered them. He found it somewhat disconcerting, however, to see Marge, tonight wearing a flouncy egg-white chiffon construction of capitol proportions, her anxious smile appearing and reappearing all about the house like a flattened bicycle tire, at a complete loss what to do with herself in the absence of any culinary chores to perform. At one point he found Marge and Mrs. S'vastapolagniskatzis, even more inutile in this sophisticated realm of haute cuisine, consoling each other in a corner with plates of boiled kielbasa and glasses of homemade potato vodka. Mrs. S'vastapolagniskatzis, it should be noted, had achieved remarkable success with Trey, who, under her supervision had ballooned, swelled, inflated frighteningly, so much so that he wore a constantly bewildered expression on his face. Not to be forgotten, Crocker, the lapel of his coal-black mortician's outfit festooned with a festive pink boutonniere, on his face a grotesque rictal grin. Mrs. Crocker, sorry to say, was unable to attend.

Of course May was the perfect hostess. She refreshed barely touched drinks, she added a dash of wit and pizzazz to faltering conversations, she flirted with the men, complimented the women, all the while *flitting* about the house in a billowing swirl of pink and aquamarine that made her look like an enormous although surprisingly graceful jellyfish propelling itself through the turquoise waters of a tropical sea, Crocker's great black hull usually somewhere in tow.

While May enjoyed herself, he felt wretched. Of course everyone was friendly. They smiled and attempted polite conversation. They offered him drinks and snacks as he wobbled about in his NIBS. But in their voices, in their eyes, in the skeptical glances over martinis and wine glasses, he sensed not only condescension but a certain knowledge that he was not, that he would never be, one of them. On top of that, he hated the constant refrain *Did ya eat yet? Ya did? Well have some more!* He resented having to wear this damned fat suit in his own home. He couldn't wait for everybody to leave so he could take it off. He remembered his mother making similar complaints about her girdle and he felt even greater humiliation at the state he'd been reduced to.

Later that night after the guests had finally left, and the garbage and vacuum bots were cleaning up downstairs, he lay awake staring at the ceiling. The new sleeping pills Doctor Doompling had prescribed, along with the dozen or so other medications he was supposed to take morning and night, as well as his normal regimen of reds, yellows and greenies, he had stealthily placed, as he had been doing for weeks now, in the crayon box in the bottom drawer of his nightstand.

When he heard May's slow, labored breathing, he quietly got out of bed, went to his closet, pulled on a loose-fitting pair of slacks, a shirt, jacket and sneakers, took the crayon box from the nightstand, went downstairs and out the front door.

The car made a yawning sound starting up. *Where we going, Marty?*

"I need something to eat."

It's late, Marty. Everything's closed. Why don't you just have a snack?

"I don't want a snack. I want a Big Bertha's *All-For-One and One-For-All* coconut cream, banana custard and lemon meringue pie. They have them at Abner's All-Nite Deli on the Mainline."

We're going all the way down to the Mainline at this time of night, Marty?

"Look, I gotta have a Big Bertha's, okay?"

If you say so, Marty. I'm glad to see you're getting your appetite back. Hey, by the way, how come you aren't wearing your fat—I mean, your NIBS?

He replied that it was late, they wouldn't encounter many people. Besides, he was starting to get his form back. "Haven't you noticed?" It was true he had put on another pound, maybe two. Not nearly enough, however, to dispense with the fat suit in public, nor to please Mrs. S'vastapolagniskatzis, who followed him around the house with pots of potato soup and plates of fried sausages, encouraging him to "*Eet, Mee*ster *Graw*so! *Eet!*" The car seemed satisfied with this answer, and even grateful when he offered to drive. It only piped up one more time when he stopped at an ATM, but he explained that Abner's was old-fashioned, they offered cash discounts. It wasn't until they crossed Mainline Boulevard, where traffic was still heavy, and began to descend into an ever darker labyrinth of narrow streets and alleys that the car woke up.

Marty, didn't we miss our turn? This is a bad part of town. We shouldn't be here.

By then he was parking at the curb. When he opened his door to get out, he heard real fear in the car's voice.

You're not going to leave me here, Marty? This is a dangerous area. Cars have been completely stripped in less than sixty seconds.

"So I've heard. I hope your insurance is up to date."

Marty, please. Don't do this to me. I don't want to end up on the junk heap.

He slammed the door and walked away.

He didn't know how he had managed to maintain the pretense so long, to act as if he really were one of *them.* Maybe he even believed it for a while, tried to believe it anyway. But all that time a little worm of dissidence lay dormant in his brain, only waiting for a signal, a change of season so to speak, before it revived itself and began to crawl around in his thoughts, gnawing at the tenuous web of security he had created for himself.

He wondered if May would understand immediately, or would she think he was having another *spell,* that he'd come back after he worked out his *issues*. He felt bad about the kids. Ashley'd be all right. Trey, he wasn't so sure. What did Jimmy call it— *cybernation*? Then again, he reconsidered, maybe none of them would even miss him. Maybe they'd all be glad to have him out of their lives. But he had to block that thought from his mind. He had to forget about his former family, life, *home*.

*

Somehow one comes to assume that taking action, *any* action, is preferable to taking no action at all, that what follows will be inherently *better*. The danger is that one is not always correct in one's assumptions.

I don't know what I thought I was going to do. Make a heroic gesture? Stand on the street corner and shout aloud the Upper Echelon's perfidies? Start an underground press and hand out printed pamphlets—a novelty in these bibliophobic times to attract passersby? Who would believe me? Even here in this godforsaken clutter of shabby, soot-blackened tenements uncharted on any city map, a smoky pall of hopelessness and despair hanging over everything like black mourning crepe, suspicion lurking in every darkened window and doorway like an infestation of vermin, even here, among the poor, the minorities, the *Low-Cal consumers*, I found no common kind with whom to share my mission, no ears willing to hear, no voices willing to be raised. Even here I felt like an outcast, pariah. Wherever I went I saw the menacing stares, heard the ugly whispers. In the pathetic little mom and pop corner stores with their nearly empty shelves of over-priced dry goods and bins of rotting produce, someone— Mom? Pop?—would inevitably ask me to leave. The other customers, few as they were, didn't want to think of buying food around someone like me.

I began to confine myself to my room during the day. The solitude I had once desired so fervently soon became its own prison. I sat at the window and stared down into the street, waiting for night to come so I could flee my claustrophobic little cell like a vampire from its tomb and wander the streets to buy a few things to eat, to walk and use my legs. The other tenants seemed to desire privacy as much as I did, for I seldom crossed paths with any of them. The exception was Rolf, the screen junkie, who spent the entire day and most of the night, judging by the lights flickering under his door, staring at his screens. Rolf seemed to live exclusively on a diet of peppermint sticks and SodaRifics® he paid the skulking teenaged son of the lady down the hall to retrieve for him. Sometimes when I came in from one of my nocturnal peregrinations, Rolf's door opened and he scrabbled forward in his armor of flashing screens and stared at me through his screen specs, his eyes swimming in catastrophic images of explosions, buildings in flames, people screaming. *Everything okay out there?* he'd ask, his voice anxious, agitated, then give me the thumbs up and scrabble back into his room like a strange beetle, his back a gleaming carapace of screens.

The last time I saw Rolf, he opened his door part way, gave me a thumbs down and closed the door again. The next morning the door was ajar, his room empty, the only trace of his presence the lighter patches on the walls and ceiling where his screens had been.

Rolf's pessimism proved prophetic. Within days of his exit from the scene, existing energy reserves plummeted and the economy took a dive. One night I watched in awe from the rooftop of an abandoned parking garage as, all over Catábolus, the VRBLs collapsed upon themselves like huge illuminated water fountains and disappeared. Chaos ensued. Riots broke out in stores. Angry crowds mobbed tank trucks as they pulled into gas stations. The pogrom against skinnies worsened. The *food pods* blamed *us* for this disaster. We constantly faced attacks from vigilantes, gangs of thugs, the police were implicated, I heard rumors of resettlement camps. Abreast of current events, the apartment manager demanded more rent. Blackmail would be more accurate. Which placed me in a dilemma of competing exigencies. Pay the food pod bastard the extortion he demanded. Or use what money I had left to eat. If I gave up the room, I'd be just another face in the growing hordes wandering the streets.

I hadn't eaten in days. An old friend, or perhaps I should say enemy, gnawed at my stomach. Hunger. I sat on the bed and stared around the room, searching for something to distract me, a spider on the wall, a new crack in the ceiling, the glass finials on the bare curtain rods I'd only now noticed. The room was just as barren as the day I moved in, the only exception a framed photograph on the small nightstand next to the bed. I don't know if I kept it for sentimental value, or as a reminder of the horror I had escaped. Two young food pods, a boy and a girl, seated on a sofa. Standing behind them, a woman, their mother, also a pod. Next to her, a man. Me. Not that anyone would connect the monster in the photograph with the gaunt, hollow-eyed face reflected now in the glass of the picture frame.

I took the yellow crayon box from under the mattress, examined its contents. Hundreds of pills, reds, yellows, blues, greenies, red and yellow checkers, neon pinks—I didn't even know what most of them did anymore. I took them to keep going, to ease the hunger, to dull the voices that had begun to argue back and forth in my brain. I dumped a couple in my hand. A bluish-yellow gleam caught my eye. Some kind of jewel. I couldn't remember what it was or why I had it. Maybe I could pawn it. I put it in my pocket, swallowed the pills and went down to the street.

I had only gone a few blocks when I felt a strange, vibrating sensation in my body. My thoughts seemed fuzzy, disconnected. I stared at the row of screens flickering in the shop window next to me, trying to understand what it was I saw. The same gaunt face appeared in every screen. Mine. Beneath it in neon red: WANTED.

Someone called out, Hey, Marty! Over here!

A vending machine. It was talking to me.

Hey, Marty! Long time no see! How about a little snack to keep the old motor running?

I increased my stride.

You're making a big mistake, Marty!

I started to run but suddenly the vibrating sensation returned, worse than before. My brain felt like it was trying to rip itself out of my skull. I staggered up an alley, expecting to hear sirens, cop cars screeching to a halt, voices shouting *Hey you, stop!*

For a long time there was nothing, no sound, no smell, no light or darkness, no sense of myself asleep or awake.

Then, violent flashes of indigo and ivory, like thunderstorms erupting out of the black nighttime of unconsciousness. Repeated images of men swinging clubs. A distant *thud, thud, thud.*

I don't know how long I lay in the alley, my head and body a battlefield of exploding aches and pains. I finally recovered my senses enough to stumble out to the street where I was startled to see columns of food pods trudging past like a migration of prehistoric creatures driven by a cataclysmic event. One stopped and stared at me. In his eyes I saw shock, horror, a glimmer of recognition. I staggered back into the shadows, expecting him to cry out in alarm.

Dazed, as if in a dream, I wandered through a shadowy labyrinth of streets and alleys. I felt sick, exhausted. I felt like falling to the ground and never getting up. And yet something, an ancient impulse for survival, an ancestral voice calling out to me from among the howling of beasts, urged me not to succumb. I only moved at night, staying in the shadows as much as possible. I ate half-rotten food from dumpsters, garbage cans. When I was too fatigued to continue, I plunged into two or three hours of oblivion in doorways, stairwells.

I was terrified when I first suspected I was being followed. I kept glancing over my shoulder, expecting to see men with clubs, guns. Then I began to see an occasional flash of pink, like a wisp of silk, a scarf perhaps, appropriated from its owner by a gust of wind. Once I caught a glimpse of a pale, almost ethereal face— female, I thought, her eyes a brief menthol blue gleam in the darkness. The next time I was certain. It was a young woman, a girl actually, not more than fifteen or sixteen. She wore a pink dress that looked something like the loose-fitting tunics women wore in ancient times. It was faded and threadbare in places, but it was clean. The fact that she had managed to keep it that way, to keep it at all, attested to her skills as a survivor. Maybe that explained the odd sense I had that, rather than her following me, I had inadvertently been following her. She never spoke, never made any attempt to communicate with me. She simply appeared on a street corner or next to a soot-blackened building.

One evening we came to a vast concrete wasteland bisected by the incongruous orange canopy of a train tube. The girl led me toward a cluster of rusted metal shipping containers, which, as we drew nearer, I saw were inhabited by gaunt, skeletal-looking people. Old men, women, young mothers with scrawny, mewling babies at their bony chests, children with distended bellies, skull-like faces, some naked. A boy and girl, maybe four-five, picked nits from each other's hair and ate them. Something unidentifiable smoldered over a smoky fire. When this miserable lot saw me they shrank back in fear, but at sight of the girl, their expressions changed to child-like joy and they gathered around her as if she were a fairy godmother. One of them tugged at her arm and pointed toward the train tube. I was horrified to see that an entire section of the canopy had been torn away. A security detail had probably already been dispatched. Oddly, the girl didn't seem concerned, even when the roar of a motor disrupted this unlikely reunion.

Out of the gathering darkness a garbage truck appeared, its lights off. It screeched to a halt and a couple of men in black ski masks jumped down from the back where the gate was now whining open. A putrid stench engulfed me. To my horror, one of the men gestured for us to climb into the stinking black maw. The wretches around me began to whimper and clutch at each other. Only when the girl raised her hands and gave them a faint, reassuring smile did they acquiesce. After she helped a gasping, wheezing old woman into the back of the garbage truck, I started to climb in myself, but the girl shook her head no and directed me to the front.

Climbing up in the cab I had a moment of *déjà vu*, and then again when the girl climbed up after me and slammed the door shut, squeezing me against the driver's corpulent form. The glowing cigar stump clamped between his teeth illuminated a greasy, beard-stubbled face and a name came to my mind. *Elmo*. I felt something hot and oily slide through my gut. It was a trap! Elmo and this *girl* were going to turn me and these other poor creatures over to the authorities. They'd subject us to unspeakable horrors and then throw us down some black hole where we'd never be heard from again.

Another possibility, or rather impossibility, occurred to me.

Elmo must have read my thoughts. "Yeah, yeah, yez had me pegged right, Greaso. I'm a sapper, okay?"

My mind flooded with hope. So it was true. The sappers did exist. "But why didn't you say anything the night I came to you with my family?"

"You wuzn't ready to make the crossin' yet, Greaso. We had to be sure of yer *commitment*. We're people of faith, Greaso. We never toined aside nobody who wuz in need." He put the truck in gear and we drove into the night. No one spoke and the drone of the motor gradually lulled me to sleep.

I jerked awake again when the truck screeched to a halt in a clearing in the woods. Groups of stick-like people huddled around charcoal burners and cooking pots. The girl and I climbed down from the truck and the two men in back opened the gate and the unfortunate passengers stumbled out, blinking and gasping for breath. Human refuse, I thought with no irony intended. Again I noticed the girl assist the old woman, who, though obviously ill, probably wasn't nearly as old as I had thought. I heard the truck engine roar and just before Elmo pulled away, he leaned out the window and growled, *"Don't break a leg, Greaso!"* Wise advice.

I had wandered into the undergrowth to relieve myself when I heard shouting. Another truck had pulled up. Men with guns jumped down and began to overturn cooking pots and club people to the ground. A few tried to flee but they were quickly overtaken. I spotted the girl at the edge of the clearing with the old woman. It was too late to help the others. Why didn't she try to save herself? A bullet zinged past my head and I ran.

I had no idea where I was going, only that I had to get out of the city. I walked for days along a service highway that ran parallel to a line of transmission towers. Every two or three miles I passed an abandoned sentry hut. Once I came across a fire-blackened car with something that looked like a charred body behind the wheel. I chose not to investigate. Another time I watched a convoy of tractor trailers emblazoned with the blue IF logo head in the direction of the city, accompanied by half a dozen military vehicles bristling with troops. Shortly afterward, a convoy of heavily fortified PEWW land barges headed in the opposite direction. Something that might have been a stick-thin human arm waved feebly from a hole in the last barge.

After the convoy passed I continued to walk. On the horizon an oddly stationary mass of red and yellow clouds constantly erupted in thunder and lightning over a small black mountain. As I drew nearer, a horrible wailing came to my ears, like the cries of a million dying souls. Black smoke and ash poured into the sky from gigantic smokestacks. Floodlights illuminated guard towers and chain-link fence topped with razor wire. A refuse conversion plant. I skirted it with the same dread I would a prison or mausoleum.

Soon afterward, the highway crumbled into broken asphalt and finally disappeared altogether in an endless stretch of barren desert. The days were scorching hot, the sun blinding, the nights freezing cold, everything ghostly white from the vast sprawl of stars overhead. One night I noticed an orange glow on the horizon, like the embers of a huge bonfire. Night by night the orange glow grew in size. I began to pass abandoned houses, burned out buildings, then a city limits sign. To my horror it said Catábolus. Had I been going in circles all this time? Even now Catábolus inexorably drawing me back into its vortex like a moth to the flame? For the first time in months, maybe years, I allowed myself to think of May and the kids and I was overcome with remorse. Had I destroyed them as I had destroyed myself? Had they been thrown into the street, homeless and destitute, to face this catastrophe alone? My contrition was short-lived when I remembered the fat suit and the clinic and all the other atrocities I had been subjected to. I clenched my teeth and turned away from the city.

I had eaten nothing in days. I was weak from hunger, thirst. One night I lay on the ground and stared up at the moon glowing in the night sky like a distant streetlamp. Maybe it wasn't even real. What if everything was fake, illusion, even the stars in the sky? And God? What god was that? A useless old god of myth and fairytale? Or was it possible there was another god still, a god no one had imagined yet who would appear on the scene one day with all the right answers?

I saw something moving in the desert. Surely I was imagining this. It was the girl in the pink dress. A band of skeletal wraiths followed behind her. Had they somehow managed to escape? Was she leading them now to salvation? With no other options, I followed them at a close distance.

Staggering, stumbling, I was nearly asleep on my feet when the sky began to lighten, and yet a penumbral shadow of night hovered in the periphery like a black muslin curtain. Tiny lights flashed in my brain like a field of fireflies or a matrix of subatomic particles—a binary conversation between ions and anions engaged in determining the fate of their host. The flashes of light broadened into horizontal and vertical bands of color that further reified into red rocks, a sandy yellow path, a column of black ants, patches of green almost unnatural in their verdancy. It was grass, real grass, the kind of dense green grass I remembered rolling in like a colt when I was a boy.

The grass became a meadow. I had entered a broad green valley. Endless rows of wheat, corn and oats stretched before me. Fruit trees drooped beneath their ripening bounty. I passed ponds and pastures, white board fences, barns and outbuildings. Even more astonishing, real animals, chickens, ducks and geese, cows, pigs, sheep, goats, horses. A new generation of lambs, calves, kids and foals gamboled about. A rustic wooden sign said Green Valley Dairy Farm. I crossed a footbridge over a clear fast stream. On the other side a man stood as if waiting for me. His face was brown and creased like tobacco leaves. He wore a wiry gray goatee. Tight, ash-gray coils of hair sprang like carbonized snakes from beneath his brightly colored cloth cap. I was surprised when he greeted me in a lilting voice that sounded vaguely familiar.

"Course I remember you, *mawn*," he said. "You've lost some *weigh-it*, I see. But *enoff palawver*. I suspect you'd like to rest."

He turned and led me along a gravel path to a large wooden building where a polite young man in a plaid flannel shirt and denim overalls took me upstairs to a large room lined with bunk beds and footlockers. The young man assigned me a bunk and a locker and after he departed I bathed for the first time in weeks, put on the plain white pajamas provided me, consumed the glass of warm milk and plate of oatmeal cookies I found next to my bunk, and gratefully crawled into bed. I woke once to the sound of heavy boots clomping on the floorboards and men talking in low voices, but I only snuggled deeper under my covers and fell back to sleep with the carefree pleasure I used to feel as a boy.

I woke again to birdsong and bright, warm sunlight streaming in the window. I felt as if I had slept for days. I put on the red and black-checked flannel shirt, denim coveralls and brown leather work boots I found in my locker, an outfit I soon noticed most of the men here wore, and went downstairs to the refectory. After a simple but hearty breakfast of *real* bacon and *real* eggs, whole-grained toast with butter and honey, a chunky fruit compote with yoghurt, and a cup of black coffee, I felt like I could chop several cords of firewood, which I more or less ended up doing. A sign on the wall asked for volunteers for a construction project. I had little experience with physical labor but it was an opportunity to earn my keep.

That same day I joined a work crew building terraces on a rocky hillside. I'd never swung a pick or a sledgehammer or hammered a nail in my life. The tools felt heavy and awkward as I hacked ineffectually at the hard ground. My arms felt weak and rubbery. I quickly developed blisters on my hands. The blisters broke and bled, then burned from the sweat running down my arms. While I suffered, the other men laughed and joked as if they were enjoying themselves. The short lunch break we took only made the return to work that much harder. By the time the sun began to go down and we headed back to the bunkhouse, I was exhausted, my body ached all over, my hands were raw and red. I dreaded the next day.

Soon, however, I grew used to this routine. My blisters turned to calluses. The aches and pains in my body were replaced by hard muscle. And the more adept I became at swinging the pick and sledge, the better I understood why the other men laughed and joked so much. It felt good to toil like this, to be outside in the clean air and sunshine, to be part of all this development. Everywhere I went I saw people building barns and houses, planting crops in the fields and tending livestock. And at the end of each day, when I sat at the refectory table laden with good healthy food, I saw the pride everyone took in the products of their labor. This was a good life. These were good people.

One day the entire community ceased work early and gathered at a hillside amphitheater. A tall, thin, older man stood in front of us. His hair was snow white, his eyes pale blue, his skin almost translucent. In a firm, reassuring tone that reminded me of a news commentator from my boyhood, the man talked about the end of one time and the beginning of another. He spoke of the great destruction brought about by greed and ignorance, and he spoke of hope for the new civilization we were creating, which he referred to as the Rebirth Project.

Later I heard people say he had been a scientist, a doctor, a university professor, a priest. Some called him a wise man, some a prophet. Some just referred to him as Uncle Walt, which struck me as funny because I'd had an Uncle Walt. I was surprised when *Uncle Walt* greeted me personally, and even more so at the personal details he seemed to know about me. "Most of those who come to the farm are destitute, driven to poverty by circumstances beyond their control. Many have been persecuted. Some escaped from the camps. But you, Martin, are different. You had a privileged life, yet you left it behind, not out of necessity, but because you saw the lies and hypocrisy of a corrupt system. As you know, Martin, an evil force has been unleashed in the world. It is our hope to stop this force and reverse its course. I believe you have something in your possession that will be extremely beneficial in this endeavor, a certain *memory jewel*."

Uncle Walt had assembled a team that worked in a barn-like structure divided into separate cubes with warm brown burlap fabric on the walls and bales of hay in the corners to muffle sound, and which the team members good-humoredly called *stalls*. Despite this rustic setting, their technology was as good as anything I'd ever seen. I was shocked, however, when Uncle Walt introduced me to the team leader, a young woman named Charlotte. I recognized her immediately. It was the girl in pink. Her eyes had an added weariness around them, but they retained the bright, menthol blue gleam of intelligence I noticed the first time I saw her. Nor did she look as gaunt as I remembered. In fact, she had an almost incandescent glow about her face. It was also obvious that she recognized me. She said nothing, however, and simply went back to work.

Uncle Walt later explained to me that Charlotte had suffered some kind of trauma, that she never spoke to anyone. Despite this disability, he said, she communicated remarkably well with the other team members through a system of signing she had apparently developed on her own. And despite her youth, she was an excellent leader. She projected an aura of confidence that inspired everyone else. She totally understood each team member's individual strengths and weaknesses. She was always solicitous of their needs. More than anything, it was her amazing facility with the screen, her awesome ability to quickly master the most complex systems. It was this gift that helped her discover in the city's worst labyrinths of despair many of the lost souls gathered here. Uncle Walt gave me a significant glance.

While I found this story compelling, I also thought Uncle Walt's adulation seemed a bit overboard, especially his word choice. *Totally? Amazing? Awesome?* Nevertheless, Charlotte certainly deserved the respect he gave her. She seemed to function in another dimension. I observed her once in her stall, staring trance-like at her screen. Suddenly she launched into a furious arpeggio on the keyboard, as if she were simply transcribing masses of data she had retrieved from deep space. Just as suddenly, she stopped and peered up at me. There was something in her eyes, a not quite human look. More like that of an extremely intelligent machine. She reminded me of Ashley—if Ashley weren't a food pod.

Under Charlotte's stewardship, we soon unlocked the memory jewel and began to map out the Vortex's development on the Grid. We had identified a mutant element we designated the *greed gene*, which, like some kind of cancerous growth, slowly metastasized until it consumed its host's entire corpus. The crucial issue? How to come up with an *antidote* not only to stop but reverse this process.

I sat for hours in front of the screen, I worked late into the night. The Grid no longer appeared as the labyrinth of oppressive shadows and doubts it had become toward the end of my tenure at EAT. On the contrary, at times it almost seemed to blossom like the petals of a flower.

One night I fell asleep at my screen and into a curious dream. I was suspended in a warm beam of light. It had a strange tonal quality that seemed to vibrate inside me. I could actually see the light pass through me, and as it did so, it fractured into a rainbow of colors, as if I were a prism.

I woke from this dream full of joy and hope. I thought it must mean we were close to a solution. I wanted to tell someone but everyone else had gone home or dozed off in front of their screens. Then I heard a sound coming from Charlotte's stall. She sat at her screen, humming to herself. I had never heard her make a sound before. I recognized the melody of an old children's song. I didn't remember all the words, just the part that went ... *something, something ... we all fall down!* Suddenly Charlotte turned and stared directly at me, her eyes fierce, her face drawn. Then she relaxed and gave me a faint, weary smile. She must be exhausted, I thought, like everyone else.

To reignite our spirits, Charlotte organized a team-building session in which we were encouraged to let out all our negative thoughts. Everyone seemed perfectly at ease confessing their peccadilloes. The SodaRific® root beer Arthur constantly daydreamed of—good old Arthur, always fumbling in his coveralls for something he never seemed able to find, but plug him into the screen and he was a young man again surfing the waves of cutting edge technology. Or secretly playing video games at his workstation—the sulky, black clad teenager who, when on task, was unparalleled in systems analysis. Or, in moments of pique, poking people with her knitting needles—the brittle-looking Mrs. Whittlesworth, whose intuition seldom failed her. When my turn came I didn't know what to say. I tried to speak but all that came out was … I … I … I … I …

Do you hear what I hear, people? Charlotte signed to the rest of the group with exaggerated frustration.

They all nodded solemnly.

That's right, Charlotte signed—"*I.*"

Later that night, while pushing myself even harder at the screen, and tormented by Charlotte's singling me out like that, I fell asleep into another, more disturbing dream that I faintly remembered having once before. I was on the train and it was moving much faster than normal. There was a blinding flash and the train crashed through the canopy and hurtled into space. But instead of the terrible pain I expected when the train smashed into a nearby hospital or apartment building, there was another blinding flash and I was back in my seat, staring out the window as if nothing had happened. Only then did I notice the reflection of the passenger sitting behind me, a girl in a pink dress.

The next morning I pondered this dream at my screen. I thought it must have something to do with control issues. Letting go. Submitting my will to Charlotte and the team. To redeem myself, I decided to relate this dream to her. I typed in everything I remembered, except for the part about the girl in the pink dress.

I quickly received a reply.

"There was someone else on the train. A girl in a pink dress."

"How did you know?" I typed back.

"Don't you *know?*" Charlotte responded. "I'm a *superhero*. I know *everything*." And then, following a dramatic pause, "You saw me on the train once in the city. I was with a friend. Obviously you only now remembered and incorporated it into your dream. It's simple psychology."

This explanation sounded plausible enough, although something about the superhero stuff, not just a playfulness, but a kind of snottiness, made me think again of Ashley. As if to counter this negative impression, later that day Charlotte set a dish of fresh strawberries and cream in front of me, stepped back and smiled encouragingly. I had never seen her smile like that. For a moment she even looked like a carefree girl, although I was fairly certain she had never had the opportunity to be a carefree girl. I wondered if she wasn't projecting onto me the role of a surrogate father. Or was it I who was searching for a daughter?

The project was going well again, the team's energy levels high, everyone in positive spirits. We no longer struggled forward. Now we leapt ahead, all these fingers furiously hammering at the keys, all these minds at work in some nebulous dimension that existed beyond our screens. I felt it drawing me in and enveloping me as if it were speaking to me alone, this powerful intellect, challenging me to work harder, think harder, *you can do it, Martin, you can find a solution, don't inhibit yourself.* I'd never felt such exhilaration in my life. I felt like I could work all day and night.

Break time!

A message came up on the screen, announcing that Mrs. Whittlesworth had just taken a broccoli quiche out of the oven and Arthur would be doing the honors tonight. And then it all collapsed. The excitement and rush crumbled into large gaps of silence interwoven with rambling swatches of text, people starting to talk again, but more relaxed now, just idle chitchat while we waited for Arthur at our workstations. When Arthur came to my stall, he said in a quavering but mischievous voice, "This broccoli quiche is *killer*, Marty," then stuck his hand under his armpit and made a farting sound. I pretended to guffaw, satisfactorily enough to send him on his way. When I turned back to my screen, a message had come up. Charlotte had mentioned a friend, someone like me—my *age,* that is. Would I care to meet her? I was amused by Charlotte's acting as matchmaker, but also intrigued. The friend's name was Cassandra. After a brief chat, she asked if I would like to join her for dinner at the new Cyber City Café tonight. Of course I said yes.

The café scene was quite pleasant. Potted plants. Rustic wooden tables. A man and woman in folksy outfits played acoustic guitar on a small stage. I found Cassandra at a table in the corner. She must have been beautiful once. She was still attractive but her face looked coarse, careworn, there was a weariness about her eyes, which were an almost iridescent green. Streaks of white showed in her dirty blond hair.

We had a wonderful meal. For the entrée Cassandra had the grilled brook trout, asparagus tips, roasted new potatoes and a glass of chardonnay. I had the range-fed beef sirloin with jalapeño cornbread and a garden salad and a glass of cabernet. As we ate, we continued to chat, awkwardly at first. Cassandra said she thought Charlotte made an *awesome* team leader. She's very nice, I replied, slightly put off by the *awesome.*

Thanks to a second glass of wine, the conversation soon flowed more easily. Cassandra's voice sounded full and throaty as she pronounced the trout excellent, sweet and succulent, and the asparagus tips perfect, juicy and firm. Just the thought of her lips and tongue forming those words filled me with a hunger I hadn't felt in ages. I devoured every word, every morsel, every phrase as if it were the rarest delicacy. We had barely finished our first course and the waiter was bringing another. There was barbecued pork ribs in a spicy red sauce, roast mutton with sprigs of fresh mint, a bucket of steamed clams, a crock of foie gras, plates of cheese and olives, pickles, and relishes. And more wine—of course more wine!

I was half way through some sort of pie when I stopped. Why was I eating like this? And Cassandra—she was gobbling her food like a total glutton. She dispatched dish after dish in a flurry of knife and fork that rivaled the finesse of a sushi chef. And by the way, who turned up the music? What happened to the acoustic guitars? When did these heavy metal dudes come on stage? There were smoke machines, strobe lights. Crowds of people laughed and shouted and danced wildly. I felt drunk, my head was light, my vision blurry. Cassandra's face looked shapeless, her features distorted. I told her I didn't feel well. In a voice that sounded slow and slightly out of synch with her mouth, she suggested we go to her place nearby.

My memory isn't clear after that. I saw myself staggering down a hallway. I felt not just drunk but drugged. And why was I wearing this stupid flannel shirt and coveralls? I felt like a hayseed going courting for the first time in his life. Cassandra unlocked the door and shuffled aside to let me in. I remember she asked if I'd like something to eat or drink. I must have been feeling better because I said a scotch and soda would be fine. And yes, some chips and dip would be nice. And why not a bowl of ice cream and some chocolate fudge brownies?

Then I remember we were sitting on the couch and Cassandra said something like, "It's all right, Marty. It's okay. You don't have to worry about anything now. You don't have to worry about anything ever again because I'll always be with you if you just remember this moment." I remembered my mother had said that, but before I could comment on this coincidence Cassandra said, "There's something I want you to do for me, Marty. Please, don't laugh when you see it. Just humor me. Wait, don't put it on now. Wait until morning. Tonight I just want to be together like this. It's kind of—*kinky*."

Now I understood. In the morning I'd wake up and swallow my latest regimen of pills. After my shower I'd put on my NIBS and on top of that my uniform for the day and go downstairs to eat a hearty breakfast in front of the screen. Then I'd go out the door and back into the horror.

Δ

She was the queen of Sheba, of Mars, of all the galaxies and the universe. She was the queen of the screen. She was the mean teen screen queen. She was Queen Martyr-D, defender of the weak, destroyer of evil. She could do anything she wanted. She could make things *happen*. She could be good. She could be bad. She could throw childish tantrums that were terrifyingly un-childlike in their consequences. She could hurl trains into space, knock down buildings, destroy armies. She could set unstoppable processes in motion—unstoppable even by herself.

Her brother had believed in love instead of hate, forgiveness instead of retribution. He thought he could fix things, return them to their former state. But he was a total naïf, an innocent. For the love of humankind, he stepped out of the screen into mortality, and for that he paid with his life.

Her mother too. She was a broken-winged wreck of her former immortal self, at times half-crazed, shrieking and wailing, at others sunk into a deep and nearly catatonic depression. And for what? She had sacrificed her immortality for the love of a man, but he misunderstood completely. He didn't realize he was undoing all her years of hard work to create the appearance of *normalcy* in their lives, that even at the end she was still trying to protect him.

Poor *Daddy*. He was totally dysfunctional. Not just that he was such an incredible nerd. He knew about systems, but he didn't know how to interpret them correctly. His imagination was limited to the linear, the straight and narrow, to rational explanations, to things that *made sense*.

She felt her old anger rise up again. Why was he so *dense?* She had given him so many chances but he continued in his folly. That *idiot*, that incompetent public servant who called himself her father, the man who had ostensibly participated in her creation, and who was responsible for the wellbeing of his family, had instead destroyed it with his insistence on discovering the *truth*.

Even she didn't really understand. Whether there was some higher power still, whether it was god or alien, whether she too was merely a pawn. And the whole thing simply a whim, a maggot, a game that continued to play itself long after the old gods who created it had departed the scene?

$$\Delta$$

a•aft•alit•aloft•alto•an•ani•anion•anil•ant•anti•
at•fa•fail•fain•faint•fan•fanion•fat•fiat•fila•fin•
final•finial•fit•flan•flat•flint•flit•float•flota•foal•
foil•font•if•in•infant•INFLATION•inn•into•ion•
iota•it•lain•lift•lint•lion•lit•loaf•loft•loin•lot•
oaf•oat•oft•oil•olio•on•naïf•nail•nation•nil•
nit•noil•not•tail•talon•tan•tin•toil•ton•tonal•

UNBABBLING

*

A Novel

In the tour de force called America, one of the tired, the poor, the huddled masses struggles upward to the penthouse of God, discovering too late he's taken the elevator marked down. Resurrected from the rubble of dreams as a messiah and accidental revolutionary, his cry for freedom echoes like a broken record as they lower him into the ground. Like a hopelessly lost coal miner, he digs on, deflating the gloom with slapstick, pensive as a clown, gathering strength for the next round.

Available Now

MARGARITO AND THE SNOWMAN